MURDER IN THE LAKE

THE LAKE

A gripping British Crime Mystery

Detective Anna McArthur Book 3

SADIE NORMAN

Sadie Norman

THE
BOOK
FOLKS

The Books Folks
A Joffe Books Company
www.thebookfolks.com

First published in Great Britain in 2025

MURDER IN THE LAKE is the third book in a series of mysteries by Sadie Norman.

Prologue

The winter temperature had never bothered the old man much before, but this year the icy tendrils that swept over the land, seeped right into his bones and held him in an unrelenting grip. It was as if Death itself was waiting patiently in the corner for the last pieces of warmth to finally die out. Although the fire crackled and spat in the hearth, it too was fading as time went on, now little more than a handful of glowing orange flames amongst the piles of ash. Its heat was powerless.

The old man set down the pen on the table, abandoning any well-meaning thoughts he had of using it. He flexed his fingers.

The dog whined from by the fireplace. It was breakfast time and the old man was neglecting the mutt's most important meal of the day. He eyed the stack of dog food on the kitchen counter. Even opening the ring pull of the can felt like climbing a mountain today.

"In a minute, Tig," he warned the canine.

With her black fur and black eyes, it was sometimes hard to tell whether she was even looking at him, but she laid her head back down with another small whine, seemingly content to wait. The intention had been to train her as a gun dog – he'd never been without a loyal companion yet, but the actual training part hadn't materialised. Still, she was a good girl. She did as she was told.

He eyed the pen, wondering if he should make another attempt at writing the letter, before deciding that today wasn't the day. His hands weren't in a working mood. When he did get round to writing it, he'd pass it on to Shonie, the sulky cow who worked at the weighbridge, and she'd post it for him. Although she'd moan about it.

Or maybe he could ask Harry's boy to do it. He'd been looking shifty lately, especially when they had run into each other at the local hospital. The spineless prick would do anything to buy the old man's silence.

He had been trying to write the letter for several weeks now. His handwriting wasn't what it used to be. Shonie, the moody mare, had snootily told him that no one used fucking letters nowadays, it was all internet-this, video-that, but he'd ignored her.

The biggest problem he had was not his useless hands refusing to work anymore, but that his letter didn't have a destination. He didn't know what address to send it to. The letter was his last chance to make amends for a lifetime of missed opportunity, so it needed to be sent to the right place. Perhaps someone at the farmhouse could help him find an address, using that miraculous internet that seemed able to do everything else. Or they could just pay someone to find it. They paid people to do everything else.

He wanted to reach out but so much time had passed. Everyone reminded him of her, even though he had no idea what she looked like anymore. He saw her in women in the village, at the hospital, even in the carer he supposedly needed to have.

He wanted to make amends. Before the cold got too strong a hold on him.

Tig raised her head – she heard things long before her master did – and was up and off, padding her way to the front door. She barked as she neared it, not recognising whoever was on the other side of the rotting wood.

He wasn't expecting anyone.

Just as he got up to follow her, the old man glanced at the shotgun by the back door. He elected not to bring it – it was more bother than anything else. Tig would see off whoever it was.

She barked and barked at the bulky shadow outside, just visible through the small round, black-mould-covered glass in the front door. Then she froze, head cocked to the side as she looked back towards the kitchen. At first, he thought she was watching him, but no. She barked again. She arched her back, hackles raised, and before he could tell her to stop being so daft, she shot back along the hallway, as the back door creaked open on its noisy hinges.

Chapter One

The relentless pacing of restless feet on the shiny paving had worn the icy sheen away, leaving a runway carved into the frost behind the King's Lynn Police Investigation Centre. December's weather was living up to its reputation and the entire world had been covered in a fine white polish for several days now. At first the sparkle was beautiful, but its brightness soon faded. A muddy slush sat at the side of the roads and the sky was filled with dirty, woolly clouds that threatened snow or rain, or something in between.

I hadn't expected to end up outside so I had left my coat hanging over the back of my desk chair. Regretting that decision, I crossed my arms and jammed my hands under my armpits.

"Here you are," I said. I admired the footprints worn into the frost by the pacing man, who paused at my arrival.

"Anna," said DCI Aaron Burns, surprised by my presence. His cheeks and nose were rosy, but apart from that, he appeared too flustered to be bothered by the cold.

"Is your day going that badly?" I asked. "Would you rather catch hypothermia than deal with whatever's going on inside?"

When he gave me a questioning frown, I nodded at the small heap of fresh cigarette ends in a pile on the ground.

Aaron sighed, a growl almost escaping, but his frustrations faded away and he managed a brief smile. Behind the station, where the broken security camera was one of the station's worst-kept secrets, we were out of sight of everyone. It was the perfect place for a cheeky smoke or just to hide away.

Aaron fumbled his hands inside his jacket pockets, where he always kept a pack of cigarettes for emergencies.

"It's fine. This time of the year is just stressful," he said, although the words came out as though under duress.

Gritting my teeth in case they started to chatter, I leaned against the brick wall of the station.

"You can tell me about it, you know."

"It's not your concern," he replied.

"Professionally, no," I said, hiding a shiver. "I'm just a constable, after all. But personally, I'm a great listener. Go on."

Aaron considered this for a moment, before resuming his pacing and opening his mouth.

"Well, the royal visit to Sandringham is taking up a lot more resources than it normally does, which has impacted overtime budgets for the whole station. Everyone is moaning about their rotas. And the Firearms team are having some trouble with a farmer who's not very happy about having their shotgun licence revoked."

"Surely you don't have to fix all those problems?" I asked. "That's a superintendent's job."

"We don't have a superintendent, remember?" said Aaron with a gesture at the building. "These problems snowball until they crash on my desk. And I have to sort them."

He was cut short as two young trainee police officers rounded the corner of the building and came face to face with us. They were easy to tell apart from the regulars as, apart from being unfamiliar faces around the station, they still had crisp uniforms and eager faces. The longer they stayed, the more those things would wane.

They stuttered to a stop in front of us, their own cigarettes already hanging from their mouths as they anticipated lighting up in the cover of the inconspicuous corner.

Too late to save themselves, they babbled an apology as Aaron fixed them with a serious stare.

"Detective Constable McArthur, remind me, is smoking on police property against the law?" he said to me, glaring until the officers put their fags away.

"I'm sure it's illegal, yes," I replied. I didn't really want to get involved with the probationers. Although, if they were informed enough to know where the secret smoking spot was, they probably knew not to get on the wrong side of Detective Chief Inspector Burns.

"Sorry, sir," one of them managed to squeak back and they beat a hasty retreat, careful not to look downwards at the litter of fag ends on the frosty ground. They whispered as they went, repeating the same rumour the rest of the station was twittering over. The rumour about us.

With the officers gone, Aaron looked back at me.

"That was harsh," I said.

"Trust me, if you knew how useless this new bunch of probationers are, you'd be the same," he said with a roll of his eyes.

"Even the best officers started out as clueless newbies," I replied.

"Not this lot. I swear we've been given all the ones who are going to fail their probation. Head office are probably laughing their arses off at giving us the dud batch."

"They wouldn't do that…"

From the way Aaron didn't reply and only gave back a gruff shrug, I guessed they actually would. He pulled out his phone from his pocket and scowled at the device as it made some muffled buzzing noises.

He muted the call and looked up at me. "Are we done, Anna? I need to get back to work."

"You're very snippy," I said.

"I've got a lot on my plate," he retorted.

"But is it just work or is there something else?" I asked.

His irritableness and short temper had been steadily increasing for a few weeks now, building until it wasn't just those who worked closely with him who had felt the ire of the grouchy boss. But DCI Aaron Burns was not one to share his problems – or anything, really – with other people. Whatever the problem was, he was keeping it to himself.

Once again, the phone buzzed in his hand and Aaron frowned at the screen. Before he dismissed the call again, I jumped in.

"Just answer him."

Aaron turned to me, confused, and I offered him a sheepish shrug back. He may have been good at hiding things when they were playing on his mind, but I was getting better at reading him.

"It's your brother," I said, waving at the phone. "Just answer him already, then we can go inside."

"How did you know that?" he asked.

"He called you this morning," I replied, hastily glancing round to make sure we were still alone in the hidden area before adding, "when you were in the shower."

With a disgruntled expression, Aaron reluctantly accepted the call and put the phone to his ear. Despite the elements outside and the persistent wind pushing the clouds along, I heard the voice on the other end of the line attempt a cheerful greeting.

"Too busy to talk to your own family, huh?"

"Actually, I am busy, Callum," Aaron replied. He resumed pacing along the frosty ground and carefully avoided my gaze. "So, what excuse have you got for us this time?"

The voice travelled easily from the phone's speaker. "We're not coming up to visit. Valerie's parents are travelling over from France in a few days and Abigail says Norfolk is boring. You know teenagers."

"And that's what you're sticking with? A rather flimsy excuse, in my opinion."

Down the line, Callum grumbled under his breath before answering. "Don't treat me like some suspect you're interviewing, Aaron."

"If I treated you like a suspect, you'd have given the real reason already. That you're not coming here because *you* don't want to, not your family."

"All right, less of the smart-ass detective," said Callum, irritation slipping in.

"That's Detective Chief Inspector, thank you," replied Aaron.

"Well, Detective Chief Inspector," his brother mocked, "who are you referring to? You said 'what excuse have you got for us', not 'what excuse have you got for me'. Who are you with?"

Aaron glanced my way. His knuckles tightened around the phone. "No one. It's just an expression."

"Oh. Then you hadn't invited us over for any particular reason?"

"No."

"Then who was the young lady I spoke to on the phone this morning?"

Aaron scuffed a step and almost skidded on a slick patch of ice. Holding in several expletives, he righted himself and threw me a glare. Then he popped the phone on speaker mode and held it out, saying nothing else.

It looked like it was up to me to introduce myself.

"Hi," I called out, raising my hand to wave although there was absolutely no point in the gesture. "I'm Anna. I'm…"

What was I? I didn't really know. The word 'girlfriend' was the most appropriate fit but we were keen to take things slow and labels hadn't been discussed. All we had agreed on was to keep our relationship to ourselves, especially from the gossipmongers at work. Although from the whispers and rumours floating around the station, maybe we hadn't been all that successful.

"Ah," said Callum when my sentence died off in mid-air. "Hello, Anna. I'm Callum, Aaron's brother. I've heard nothing about you."

"I've heard nothing about you either," I replied and we shared a snigger, earning me another slight glare from Aaron.

"Okay, lovely family reunion as usual, Callum," Aaron said. "Send my best to Valerie and Abigail. We'll try again next time." And with that, and a jab at a button on the screen, he ended the call.

I let a silence fill the air, knowing it was applying more pressure to Aaron than it was to me. Discarding the phone into his coat pocket, he turned to me, an exasperated huff escaping with a puff of hazy air. He fished out and lit up another cigarette, but said no more.

"So that was what you were stressing over," I said. "Why were you avoiding your brother?"

Aaron paused, as if considering whether to continue with his openness. "Every time I invite him over, he says he'll come and then he comes up with some excuse not to. It's practically a running joke at this point." He waved his hand, the lit end of the cigarette leaving a trail in the cold air.

"Why were you avoiding him if you were the one who invited him to stay?"

"He's family," he said with a hollow laugh and a shrug. "He's all I've got left. We do these things because we have to, not because we want to." Aaron looked me up and down, blinking as though it was the first time he'd seen me all day. "Let's get inside, before we develop frostbite."

I allowed Aaron to lead the way from the freezing secluded spot, heading round the side of the building and towards the entrance of the police station. The modern structure, all angles and wide metal-framed windows, was lit up like a beacon shining against the restless sky. The tall chimney of the nearby power station spat out white clouds of steam. The sun was noticeably absent and I couldn't remember the last time it had been out long enough to thaw the deep freeze that had gripped the land.

Aaron took a deep breath before crossing the threshold at the entrance to the station, as if steeling himself. In terms of how busy the station usually was, today felt oddly subdued.

"Are Chris and Jay back yet?" he asked, mind already back on the job.

"Not yet," I replied. "At least it's a quiet day."

My mobile phone rang in my back pocket.

I pulled it out with numb fingers, fumbling on the screen. The caller ID made my heart sink.

DI Chris Hamill

"What are you doing?" the detective inspector demanded, forgoing a greeting when I answered.

"Working very hard, I assure you," I replied.

The team leader scoffed back, as usual not believing me, but moved on. "Get moving, we've got a call-out. A body. Jay is texting you the details now. We'll meet you there."

Just like how he'd started the call, Chris abruptly ended it. Aaron looked back at me with a wry smile and a roll of his eyes.

"Serves you right for using the Q-word. Nothing is ever quiet around here," he said.

Chapter Two

As I pulled my car off the tarmac road and down a beaten-up gravel track, I heard the old banger give a worrying clang. My destination was just up ahead; I could already see two brightly marked police cars disturbing the frosty wilderness. *Come on*, I willed the car, just a few hundred yards.

Pepperwell Farm was truly in the arse-end of nowhere, somewhere west-ish of the small village of Wormegay. Around me, a mixture of pine copses and sandy trenches lined the lane, alternating across the furrowed fields as far as the eye could see – which wasn't very far given how flat the landscape was. I passed a sign directing traffic to the left with a picture of an aggregate lorry. My guess was that the quarry carried on further down the track and that was why the lane was in such a poor state; the lorries tore up the ground as they shifted the heavy loads of sand and stone away.

I made it to my destination and stopped next to a patrol car outside a pair of grey-bricked semi-detached cottages. Only a couple of trainee officers were around, walking across the front of the property without much hurry. That didn't bode well for what I was about to find.

When I got out of the car, another officer appeared from a thicket of trees beside the house. I was greeted by PC Harris, an ageing copper who didn't look too thrilled with the predicament we were in.

"McArthur," he said, pausing a few steps in front of me. "Why is it always you on duty when the day turns to shit?"

"Someone asked for an officer from Serious Crimes, Harris, so here I am," I replied. I had learnt my lesson and wrapped up warmer upon leaving the station, but somehow, these eerie cottages felt several degrees colder still.

"I heard you've got a body," I said, gesturing to the surrounding area. "Lead the way."

To my surprise, Harris started to take me away from the cottages and down an overgrown path through the trees. The muddy ground was frozen solid, creating soft thumps as we walked.

"The cottage back there," Harris said, pointing a stubby finger back the way we'd come, "is home to Barney King. We were asked to do a welfare check after he'd missed two hospital appointments last week. He's eighty-five, mostly deaf, lived alone – obviously, we assumed the worst. Only he wasn't in."

"Then where is he?" I asked.

"Through here."

Harris pushed his way through a particularly stubborn bramble patch and we emerged on a wide, oval-shaped pond. Surrounded by leafless trees and overgrown shrubbery, the unnaturally dark waters lapped at the edge of the vegetation as if the body of water itself was restless. Just ahead, I saw another officer, Pres, standing at the edge and scratching his chin. And floating on the surface, like a cloud through a clear sky, was the unmistakeable shape of a body.

Starfished and bloated, it was clear the person was long dead.

"I've been lumbered with one of the probationers today," said Harris as he pulled in a stiff breath, making his moustache wiggle. "Thought a bread-and-butter call like this would ease her in. When we checked the property, we found the house unlocked. It was empty, apart from the dog. It took off through the woods and we followed it here to the old man."

"Where's the dog now?" I asked.

Harris threw his arm out. "Somewhere out here, we lost him. It was a black Labrador in case it turns up again. We were a bit distracted by the deceased."

I looked around. There were no signs of any animal life, let alone a dog. "Fair enough. Is this Barney King then?"

"Well, he's a bit too far out to tell for sure. Sergeant Preston and I were discussing how to pull the body closer to the edge."

I glanced around the pond. It was too big to reach across or throw a line, too overgrown and boggy for any sort of crane. Getting the body out of the water and maintaining the scene was going to be a challenge.

"One of us could swim out," I suggested.

Harris wrinkled his nose. "You are joking, right?"

"I guess so," I replied. "We'll need to call in the specialist diving team to help with recovery."

Harris rubbed his hands together. "They'll moan it's too cold to get in the water."

"They'll moan about it being too wet, but we haven't got much choice. It doesn't look like there's a boat nearby and we need to preserve the scene as much as possible."

My companion huffed, his breath escaping as a white mist around us. "Well, there's no rush. Looks like he's been out there a while."

As Harris moved away, trying to find a good enough signal amongst the trees to request specialist help for the retrieval, Pres started setting up a scene cordon around the water and I made my way back towards the cottages. Barney King's cottage was one of two, so I wondered why his adjoining neighbours hadn't noticed his unfortunate demise. When I reached the grey-bricked buildings, looming at the edge of the lane like a guard house, I realised why no well-meaning neighbours had noticed King's passing. Only one of the properties was habitable; the other was derelict, held up by ivy and prayers by the looks of it.

An old Morris Minor sat in an overgrown driveway beside King's cottage. From the thick layer of frost sitting on it and lack of tyre tracks on the surrounding grass, it appeared the vehicle hadn't moved in several days.

Since the two probationers dithered around without much of an idea of where to start, I sent them inside the house, gloved-up, to check for any obvious clues before the Scene of Crime team arrived. The death of an elderly man like King wasn't immediately considered foul play, but to find him floating on the lake like that was unusual. It was December, far too cold for a swim or any fishing. What had he been doing out near the water?

As I stared at the conjoined cottages, I considered my next steps. I needed to wait for my colleagues, Detective Inspector Chris Hamill and Detective Sergeant Jay Fitzgerald, to arrive before I got too ahead of myself. I was the junior of the team, still not yet trusted enough to work alone unless it was in the confines of the office.

I had a reputation, after all.

Luckily, a sensible family sedan rolled into view. Jay climbed out of the passenger's side of Chris's car and strode over to me, barely taking in the scene. He gave an irritated huff and pushed a strand of his usually perfectly coifed black hair from his face.

"We can't even leave you for one morning!" he said, throwing his hands in the air. "The second we leave you in charge of the office, a body turns up."

"What's got your knickers in a twist this morning?" I asked him.

Jay grumbled back, the noise akin to a bad-tempered dog growl, before eventually settling on, "We were making progress this morning. This case has come at the worst time."

Progressing at a much slower pace over the frosty ground, our team leader Chris joined us. He buried his hands deep into his coat pockets. His wrinkled face was permanently fixed in a deep scowl, although compared to Jay, Chris looked oddly relaxed.

"You've been in a miserable mood all morning. A new case isn't going to change that," he said to Jay gruffly. Chris looked at me. "What have we got?"

"The body is through the trees," I replied, with a nod of my head in the general direction. "We believe it's the occupant of the house, an elderly gentleman called Barney King. Pres and Harris are working on recovery."

"Is that it?" said Jay. "Is this even a Serious Crimes case?"

"Stop whining; you're worse than my kids," replied Chris. "You and Anna go look over the house, I'll check out the scene. Then we'll update the boss and he can decide if this is a case for us."

Jay stalked off towards the cottage, still griping to himself. The pressure hanging over us had been making him malcontent for days now, although he was showing it more than anyone else. The unsolved murder of Ali Burgess was still sitting on the Serious Crimes team's caseload, under the close scrutiny of the chief constable, and at some point, soon, we needed to make some progress or risk the repercussions.

I cleared my throat, gaining Chris's attention before he too strode away.

"You might want to hold off informing Aaron," I said carefully. "He's rather stressed."

Chris mulled this over for a moment and gave a grunt of affirmation in response. Although he knew the true nature of our relationship, he rarely chose to comment on it to me.

As I turned to follow Jay, someone caught my attention from the house. They waved from the front door, beckoning us over.

The trainee officer, a bright-eyed probationer with an excited grin, waited for Jay and I to don gloves and shoe covers and ushered us through the house. It was a rustic cottage, with dank walls and yellow ceilings from decades of smoke. The kitchen was at the back of the cottage, full to the top with clutter. The oven was covered in years of grease and a stack of baked beans cans was piled high in the corner of the worktop.

"Everything all right, Constable…" I let the sentence die off. I didn't know her name and not many of the trainees would stick around long enough to make it worth learning. Those that did would soon become part of the family.

"Er, PC Falini, ma'am," she replied, clicking her heels together. "Or rather, sir. Ma'am. No, sir. Sorry… I'm new."

"That's alright, Falini," I said. "We're not so formal around here. I'm Detective Constable McArthur, but you can call me Anna."

"Crazy McArthur," Jay muttered as he scouted around the kitchen.

"Um, sorry," said Falini, looking between the two of us. "Crazy?"

"You'll reach a point where we either use first names or nicknames," I replied. "No prizes were given out for imagination to whoever came up with my nickname, though."

Jay mumbled some uninspired curses under his breath. Poor Falini looked a little taken aback by our unprofessionalism but she said no more and shuffled over, taking care not to knock the beans. She pointed to a scrap of paper lying on top of a mountain of letters and books on the solid-pine dining table against the wall. It had been laid delicately on top of the pile, as if waiting to be seen. Using the weak natural light from the window, I worked on reading the loose, spider-like handwriting, written with a pen that hardly worked or by a person who barely pressed the ballpoint to the page.

No point in lying any longer. I did it, I killed her. I deserve this for what I did all those years ago. Don't try to stop me. Do not resuscitate.

Jay read the note over my shoulder. I heard his sharp intake of breath. He held it in his lungs for several seconds before releasing it in a drawn-out sigh.

"Maybe this is a Serious Crimes case after all," I said.

Chapter Three

Jay and I joined Chris at the edge of the lake as he observed the newly arrived diving team discussing how best to extract the body from the water. It didn't take them long to have a plan in place and soon two fully clad scuba divers were wading their way into the gently rippling water. It acted like a black hole, swallowing their bodies as soon as they submerged themselves beneath its surface.

"The deceased is most likely Barney King," I told Chris, using the information we had pulled together from the numerous hospital correspondences found on his dining table. "He was eighty-five, with plenty of health problems. It looks like he lived alone in the cottage, no sign of any family, so we'll have to check back at the office for next of kin."

Chris gave a nod of approval. "I can do that. The diving team reckon this is a straightforward recovery, shouldn't take too long."

"There is one other thing." I showed him a photograph of the handwritten note we'd found in the kitchen. The Scene of Crime team had taken over the property and were bagging any evidence they found interesting.

Chris squinted as he read the note, his lips moving with the words. When finished, he blinked and looked at Jay.

"*Killed her*? There haven't been any major investigations around here. At least, I don't remember any, do you?"

Jay scoffed back at him. "I'm not as old as you are, old man. We were hoping you'd remember something from back in the day."

Chris shook his head. "Maybe it was from before even my time. I'll get on the databases and find out. You two should head over to the quarry and see what they know about Barney King."

"We're on it," I replied. I was pleased at the prospect of heading somewhere warmer.

Jay dragged his feet behind me, his bad mood following along too. He restarted his muttering when he realised that we would have to make the journey in my rusty old car.

Half a mile further down the potholed lane, we emerged from the trees on Pepperwell Quarry. An orange sign directed aggregate lorries to keep left on arrival and I parked up next to a metal cabin just inside the entrance.

When I stopped the car, the groaning machinery digging away and the rumble of lorry engines idling next to the weighbridge filled the quiet. Despite the cold, it was all steam ahead for the quarry.

Jay and I walked over to the green cabin, where another orange sign fixed on the door announced *Pepperwell Quarry Office – PPE essential.*

Jay blew into his hands to warm them up and rapped on the door, making the whole cabin shake. An outraged voice shouted from inside, telling us to come in. Opening the creaking door, a swathe of heat escaped the cabin and disappeared into the misty air.

Inside, we were greeted by a portly woman, nestled into a corner of the cabin at an overstuffed desk, piled high with long reems of receipts. She scowled at us, shivering like a dog on Bonfire Night, until I closed the door behind me.

She blustered at the intrusion. "What do you want?"

I held out my warrant card. "I'm DC Anna McArthur, from King's Lynn police. This is my colleague, DS

Fitzgerald. We'd like to speak to someone regarding Barney King."

"Ah, the old bastard. What's he complaining about now?" the woman said, moving some of the papers around in an attempt to look busy. The same paper ticket traded places three times. "You'll have to talk Garrett. He's at the farmhouse."

"Who, sorry?" Jay asked.

"Garrett Hythe, the owner." She waved her hand over her head, motioning to everything around us. "He's the only one who can put up with the miserable bastard."

I stepped forward. "Sounds like you don't like Barney King, Miss, er…"

"Shonie Butler," the woman replied stiffly. "I wouldn't say I don't like him; he's just a pain in my side. He always mumbles and smells like dead fish. Keeps ranting about the trucks being overweight and ruining the track. The trucks are never overweight, I make sure of that." And as if to prove her point, she picked up a receipt ticket and waved it in the air.

"And when was the last time you saw Barney King?" asked Jay.

It was at that moment that Shonie appeared to realise that we weren't there just to disturb her day. She looked between Jay and I, her head moving back and forth like the pendulum of a clock until she found the right words.

"Has something happened?"

Jay looked at me, knowing I would have a better way of phrasing the always hard to say words that needed to be said at that moment.

"I'm afraid Mr King was found deceased this morning," I replied. "We're just looking into the circumstances."

"Oh." Shonie's response wasn't one of grief or shock. It was just a brief moment of deflation and sadness. Just as soon as it came, it went.

She picked up another ticket and continued. "Well, if I can help, I will. I made a point of avoiding him, though, so I might not be any use."

"Anything you do know could be useful," I replied. "Has Mr King lived in the area long?"

"Ages," said Shonie. "He used to be foreman here at the yard, long before I started. He's worked for the Hythe family his whole life, rented the cottage from them. Him and Harry always got on all right. They know Barney much better than I do, you'd be better off asking them. I only saw Barney when he wanted to have a moan or wanted me to post his letters with our franking machine."

She pointed to a small blue machine in the corner of the office. We had a similar device in the police station, although it was so temperamental most officers were forbidden from touching it.

"And Harry is?" Jay asked.

"Garrett's dad," replied Shonie. "You'll find them all at the farmhouse, although I hear Harry isn't doing too well. He had a heart attack; it was touch and go whether he'd pull through enough to get home. Which is a shame. He knows what's what around here."

Pursing her lips together, Shonie shifted some more receipts around the desk, although she angled her head away to keep her expression hidden. I wondered if she was actually upset by the news but then she picked up a receipt and muttered, "Fuck's sake, that's only half a load." And carried on working.

"What do you quarry here?" I asked curiously.

"Sand mostly. There's an empty cell on the west side. The council want to use it for landfill but Garrett is a friend of the earth, he won't let that happen."

From the look Jay gave me out the corner of his eye, I guessed he wasn't entirely sure what Shonie Butler was talking about, and nor did he care enough to ask for more details. A great whoosh of air stole the heat from the cabin again as he opened up the door once more.

"Thanks for your help." I smiled at Shonie. "We'll be back if we need anything else from you."

"I'll be here," said Shonie as she waved me away, eager for us to get out and close the door again. "Always here, all day, every day, for my sins."

* * *

Back outside, the December chill hit us with a vengeance, as if it was angry we had dared to go into the warm cabin at all. I pulled my coat around myself as Jay strode on ahead, turning his head in all directions.

He spotted the farmhouse first through a gap in the trees, smoke rising from its chimney and merging into the grey sky above. It was only a short distance away, but the machinery and vehicles in the quarry yard were busy working away and any attempt to walk through would surely breach some health and safety laws. So, we both clambered back into my old car and I bumped it back along the track, towards the farmhouse.

We were greeted at the door of the red-stone farmhouse by a lithe young woman, with glowing skin and straight black hair down to her waist. She was so stunning that I felt my insides coil; from lust or jealousy, I wasn't sure. Either way, Jay jumped right in, opening his mouth with a friendly smile, his bad mood magically vanishing.

"I'm Detective Sergeant Jay Fitzgerald," he said, flashing his warrant card at the bewildered young woman. "Can we speak to Garrett or Harry Hythe?"

"Ah, *sí*. Come in." She ushered us into the house, where I could hear a crackling fire and the unmistakeable voice of the local radio DJ floating from the kitchen. Led along the flagstone floors, we emerged in a cosy kitchen, where blackened beams stretched overhead and a large inglenook fireplace took up one wall of the room. Beside it, in an enclosing mossy-green-coloured armchair, sat an elderly man, bundled under layers of blankets, which felt like overkill given how hot it was with the roaring fire. A middle-aged man sat beside him, with short mousey-brown hair and round eyes. He rose as we entered.

The young woman waved her hands at us. "Police," she said in a thick Mediterranean accent. "You speak to them, I'll make tea."

At the sound of tea, Jay relaxed slightly and I flexed my cold fingers in anticipation.

"Mr Hythe?" I asked the man as he strode to us.

He took each of our warrant cards as we held them out and studied them carefully.

"Please, call me Garrett," he said. He held tension in his broad shoulders, as he glanced at the old man by the fire. "Is everything okay?"

"We are here about Barney King," Jay replied. "A body was found this morning near his property and we believe it may be him."

"Oh goodness," Garrett exclaimed, although he was the only one who really reacted to the news. The old man by the fire hadn't opened his eyes. The young woman had her back to the rest of the kitchen, although her shoulders rose a little higher, as if she was clenching her muscles.

"Can we ask you some questions about him?" Jay continued. "From what we understand, your family has known Mr King for many years."

"Of course. Please, sit." Garrett motioned to a solid wooden dining table in the middle of the room and we all sat, the chairs squealing in protest against the stone floor.

The young woman brought over a tea tray and set it down, barely making a sound. If she was affected by the news, she was hiding it expertly. Jay flashed her a broad smile as she handed him a cup first.

"Thank you," he said, the words a fraction deeper than his normal speaking voice.

"This is Luisa, by the way," said Garrett. "And that's my dad over there, by the fire. Garrett senior, but everyone calls him Harry. Luisa is Dad's live-in carer."

"We heard your father had a heart attack recently," I said.

Garrett junior nodded with a saddened smile. "About four weeks ago. The doctors want to start him on palliative care but... I don't think hospice is the right place for Dad. He's lived here his whole life. He'll want to be here until the end."

I glanced over at the bundle of blankets. The old man looked asleep. So still, in fact, I wondered if it was already too late for hospice.

"He just sleeps most of the time now," Garret continued. "It was Dad who hired Barney King, many years ago, to work at the quarry. He rented out one of the old cottages to him. Barney has lived there for as long as I can remember."

"What did Barney King do for your father?" I asked and I pulled my notebook from my pocket. My fingers were stiff from the cold but they soon warmed up as a steaming cup of tea was passed my way.

Garrett junior added four helpings of sugar to his cup. "He was the site foreman until he retired. That was about fifteen years ago, when I started taking over from Dad. Barney wasn't happy about retiring at first, he still helped out, but old age took its toll the last few years. We only really saw him out and about when he was poaching."

"Did he ever display any suicidal tendencies?" asked Jay. "Did he struggle with his mental health or give any indication of his frame of mind?"

Garrett grimaced. "He was a grumpy old man; he never had a nice word to say. But I wouldn't say he was troubled like that..."

As Garrett spoke, Luisa took one of the steaming cups of tea over to the old man by the fire, setting it down on the mantel. The man stirred as she neared, waking up enough to give her a suspicious look. She responded with a kind smile. Then she retreated and silently took the seat at the table next to Garrett, who flinched as her long hair caressed the side of his face.

"But then, who really knows. I can't say what goes on in his mind," concluded Garrett. He looked at Luisa expectantly; however, she avoided meeting his gaze, her attention still on the elderly man on the other side of the room.

"Did you know Mr King well?" I asked her.

"Me?" She blinked, as though she thought she had been invisible this whole time. "No, not really. King?"

"She means Barney," said Garrett. "You know, the old man, sometimes brings pheasants and rabbits round."

"Oh, sí. Him. No, I did not talk to him. Paula did."

"Paula?"

"My wife," said Garrett. "She's a GP, works over Fakenham way. She loves rabbit pie." Once again, I caught him look over to Luisa. She didn't return the glance.

Jay took a sip of his tea and immediately wrinkled his nose at the temperature. The steam floated up to the ceiling, like it was desperate to escape the thick, uncomfortable air that had descended on the house with the topic of Barney King's death.

"Can you tell us anything else about Barney King?" he asked. "Does he have any family?"

Garrett considered this for a moment. "Not that I'm aware of. I've known him my whole life and he's always been alone."

"When was the last time you saw him?" I asked.

Garrett scratched his neck, creating ripples with his skin under his chin. "Friday week, I think. He went out poaching; don't know what though, it was too cold for the pheasants to be out. He always calls in to the office to let us know if he's going out with the shotgun, I was there with Shonie."

I looked at Luisa. "And you?"

She shrugged as she replied, "Weeks ago. I've been looking after Harry."

"And your wife?" Jay asked Garrett.

"I doubt she's seen Barney at all these last few weeks. She works full-time and has picked up a few overtime shifts at the out-of-hours service at the hospital these last few weekends."

That left one more person to ask about. Both Jay and I turned towards Harry Hythe, wondering if it was unreasonable of us to expect an answer from him. The elderly man hadn't moved, not even reaching out to take his tea. His head was turned towards the fire, shielding his expression and making it impossible to tell if he was asleep again or not.

Garrett Hythe took pity on us. "He won't be much use, I'm afraid," he said with heavy words. "He can barely remember his own name most days, and when he is lucid, he thinks it's the late seventies. If you catch him at the right time, you might be able to get him to talk about the good old days, but I doubt it will help you with Barney's death now."

Our conversation continued awkwardly until Jay abandoned his half-drank cup of tea and declared that we would be in touch for further information. Garrett Hythe jotted down a list of contact numbers for me in my notebook, including one for his wife Paula. He showed us to the front door and we shook hands in farewell.

"Anything we can do to help, please call."

The wicked weather pulled the heat from the house as we opened the door. A thin sheen of ice lay over my car's windscreen again. As Jay and I crossed the threshold, Luisa appeared at Garrett's side, the two of them filling the doorway.

"How did he die?" she asked.

We paused, glancing at each other before turning back. We'd been purposely vague on any details because there was little that we could say for certain at such an early stage. And the note found in King's house confused matters all the more.

"He was found in the water," Jay replied carefully. "We're still establishing the circumstances."

"But you asked about suicide," Luisa pushed. "Are going to investigate him? You think he killed himself?"

She watched Jay with inquisitive eyes.

"Is there anything we need to know?" he asked.

"No," Luisa replied deftly. She remained silent as Jay pulled a contact card from his coat pocket and handed it over to her.

"Well, be in touch if you do think of anything. My number is on there."

By the time we reached the car, the front door was closed and Garrett and Luisa were gone from sight. I started the car, turned the heaters on full, and waited for the layer of frost to clear. Jay remained pensive until we were back on the road, bumping along the rugged track.

"The carer, Luisa – did you get the impression she was a bit... stand-offish?" he asked.

"Maybe," I replied as I flashed him a smirk. "Although, she made your bad mood disappear fairly quickly."

Chapter Four

From the rosiness of his cheeks and the streaming of his eyes, it seemed like Chris hadn't been out of the cold for long when Jay and I returned to the police station. The heater in the Serious Crimes office was churning out dry air, which was sucked into the stairwell every time someone opened the door. It made the office feel like a sauna without actually penetrating the ice that had gripped deep inside our bodies.

"Well," Chris said, sitting up expectantly, "our gentleman is now heading off to the morgue. I've asked for a rush on the post-mortem. What did you find out?"

Jay flopped into his desk chair with an exaggerated groan as I gave Chris a rundown of who we had spoken to over at the quarry and farmhouse, and what they had to say about Barney King.

"Right, then," said Chris, taking a moment to chew over what we'd found. "Next steps. We need to establish that the body pulled from the water is in fact Mr King and inform his next of kin."

"None of that is a Serious Crimes team job," replied Jay. His bad mood had returned between leaving the Hythe household and arriving back at the station.

"Which is why we will sort that bit out in a minute," said Chris curtly. "SOCOs are going over the house. What we're interested in is the confession. Run a search of the address and see what comes up. I've never heard of Pepperwell Farm. I certainly don't remember any murders around that area that the note could have been alluding to."

Taking my cue, I fired up my computer and waited for it to catch up so I could start the necessary searches. If there was something linked to that address or to Barney King, it would be straightforward to find.

"There'll be loads of records for that area," Jay said knowingly. "All around those sand quarries are deathtraps. Drownings, accidental deaths. There's usually one a year."

"Why?" I asked.

Chris hummed, the noise perfected to make him sound wise and all-knowing. "They quarry for sand, gravel and carrstone around that way, from Shouldham up to Bawsey. Once done with, the old quarry pits are used for landfill or filled with water and rubble. It's very easy to drown in them. The water is unbelievably deep and cold. Years ago, we used to give talks to the kids at the local high schools about swimming in them."

Jay nodded along. "Yeah, doesn't stop people from swimming in them, though. Especially in the summer. As I said, there's going to be a lot of records."

"You're right, there is," said Chris. "So, get on and help Anna, rather than just sitting there."

Jay continued to grumble and gripe to himself as we set to work. Beyond the office, the station felt oddly deserted, missing the usual hubbub that filtered through the walls. It had been that way for a few days since patrols had been stepped up in the area for the impending royal visit, and the freezing weather had turned every road into an ice rink. So, it was impossible to miss the sound of footsteps as they came up the metal staircase and made their way to our office door.

Without a knock, Aaron let himself in. "Wow, you're all here?"

"Unfortunately," came Jay's sour reply.

Aaron closed the door quickly, before the heat was stolen by the draft from downstairs.

"Suspicious death?" he asked.

"Not entirely a suspicious death." Chris shook his head. "Looks likely it's a suicide. But there are suspicious circumstances."

"Like what? Come on, fill me in." Aaron leaned against the back of the door, crossing his arms against his chest. His frustrations from earlier had lessened, but I got the feeling he was trying to distract himself by focusing on our case.

"Our victim is Barney King, of Pepperwell Farm Cottages, outside Wormegay," I replied. "His body was discovered in a nearby pit by officers who were performing a welfare check this morning. A note was found in his house."

"A suicide note?" Aaron asked.

Jay tutted to himself. "Just bloody selfish, committing suicide when we're so busy."

As the computer started to load the results from the records search, I pulled out my phone and passed it over to Chris, who handed it to Aaron. He scanned the photograph of the scrawled note I had taken in Barney

King's kitchen, his eyes darting from side to side as he read it over and over.

After a worryingly long minute of silence, Aaron swallowed hard and handed the phone back to Chris. "Pepperwell Farm, you say?"

"Yeah, why?" asked Chris.

"I know that place," he said. "I know that man."

My colleagues stared. Jay sat up in his seat. "You do? How?"

"It's a long story," said Aaron, much quieter than before. "We might need to call Price about this one."

"Price?" Jay exclaimed. "He's the last person we should be calling."

"I know, but this time we might have to. I don't think we can take on this case."

"Why not?" asked Chris.

"It's not important."

"Well, it clearly is," said Jay.

Chief Constable Ian Price was not a man any of us enjoyed working for. However, the deadline he had given the team to solve the outstanding murder of Ali Burgess was almost up and we knew that soon the chief constable would be back, breathing down our necks. But that didn't mean we wanted to invite him in any sooner than was necessary.

Just as Jay had predicted, records regarding the area surrounding Pepperwell Farm and Quarry were surprisingly numerous. Whilst the guys argued with Aaron in a pretty futile attempt to convince him otherwise, I tried a new search for any cases naming Barney King as a person of interest. The computer dinged as it returned a result.

"What is it?" Jay asked.

I glanced over the screen, reading the results aloud. "Barney King was a person of interest in an archived investigation. Forty years ago. The disappearance of a woman called–"

"All right!" Aaron cut in. The forcefulness of his voice stopped me in my tracks. "We don't need to go through this right now. We can't handle this case as it would be a conflict of interest for me. I knew Barney King."

"How?" asked Jay.

"Because of the cold case."

"From forty years ago?" Chris tapped his fingers on his desk, his expression clear that he was growing impatient with Aaron.

"Yes."

"You were a child."

"I was still involved," said Aaron. "In fact, I was two years old."

"How about you cut the bullshit out now and tell us? Because you better have a bloody good reason for wanting to drag Chief Constable Price back into our office."

"I don't need to tell you my bloody good reason. I'm DCI, I say what cases you can take on."

"Aaron," I said gently. My voice succeeded in snapping them all out of their sniping. Aaron avoided meeting my eye. I couldn't tell what was going through his mind but there was something there, just beneath the surface, threatening to spill out After a moment, his frustration waned and defeat crossed his face.

"Fine. Barney King was the main suspect in the disappearance of my mother."

A hollow silence fell over the room as my colleagues and I digested Aaron's words. I spied Jay glance at me, trying to see if I knew more. I knew nothing. Aaron had led me to believe his parents were both dead.

As the guys grappled for something to say, I returned to my computer screen, unable to watch Aaron any longer. His discomfort was clear. I scanned the cold case in front of me, the information merging into a blur of familiar names and shocking news.

"Clara Burns disappeared from her home on the night of September 17th, after putting her children to bed," I read from the notes. "She had a husband, James, and two sons, Callum, age ten and... Aaron, age two. They lived at 1 Pepperwell Farm Cottages, Wormegay. Next door to Barney King."

When I looked up, Aaron was nodding. The movement was slow and contained. "As I said, I knew Barney King."

"What happened?" asked Jay.

Aaron rolled his shoulders and his cheeks flushed. "I don't know. I don't remember it. Apparently, she put us to bed, my dad was down the local having a few pints like he did every night. When he got home, my brother and I were asleep, but she was gone."

"And they suspected Barney King was involved?"

"The old man lived next door, alone," said Aaron. "Prime suspect for quite a while, but nothing was ever pinned on him, there was no evidence. No one ever found out what happened to her."

"Until Barney King left that suicide note," finished Jay. He shared a look with Chris and me, and I was sure his expression matched my own; we were now overwhelmed with guilt for even showing Aaron the note, let alone telling him about the death.

"I guess you're right," Chris concluded, although he sounded far from happy. "We should call the chief constable. Even if King's death is just an open-and-shut case of suicide, the cold case will have to be re-examined too. We can't have you dragged into that."

With a sudden spark of energy, Aaron straightened up and strode to the door. "The last thing we need is to give Price more ammunition against us. I'll call him now."

The door closed behind him, leaving in its wake a stifled air, thick with unspoken words. Jay and Chris exchanged a glance, experts at speaking to one another without using words. I was getting better at reading their looks, but this time, I couldn't decipher it. I racked my brain for every piece of knowledge I had about Aaron, hoping for a clue to show me what to do to make it all better.

How could I make everything better when we were already forty years too late?

Chris turned to me. "You should probably talk to him."

I was already halfway out of my seat. "On it."

* * *

Unnerving and heavy, the silence followed me as I let myself into Aaron's office without knocking. It was at the end of the corridor, where a wall of windows looked out onto the fields beyond the station. Sharp, white sheens clung to the furrows and ditches, creating a wintry wonderland that looked beautiful, but had a nasty bite.

Aaron set his desk phone back into its receiver and let out a heavy sigh. He rubbed his chin thoughtfully, eyeing me as I slunk in and perched myself on a seat opposite his desk.

"Are you okay?" I asked.

"Yeah," he said, unconvincingly.

"You never told me about your mum."

"Don't take it personally," he said with a half-hearted smile that was quick to fade. "I don't think I've ever told anyone. As I said, I don't remember it. I don't remember her."

I felt a desperate sadness at his words; I couldn't imagine not having a mother. Or growing up knowing that you had one, but something terrible had happened to her and you couldn't even remember her. My mum was a pain in the neck sometimes – or often – but I loved her unconditionally. Aaron didn't have that.

"Anna," he said, sitting up in his chair. "I mean it, don't pity me for this. I don't remember it."

"But you still lived through the aftermath," I replied.

My heart ached furtively as Aaron gave a small nod. Was this why he pushed away anyone who ever got close to him? Maybe he didn't want anyone finding out his dark family secret, maybe he wanted to leave a space in his heart

31

for his mother. This grown man in front of me was still deep down that child wondering where his mum went.

"That note might not mean Clara Burns," I said, but my own voice was only a whisper, as if it was afraid to come out. "Barney King might not have killed her; he could have been referring to someone else."

"Well, we'll never know now."

"We might do. Even cold cases get solved sometimes when new evidence comes to light."

"Cold cases get reopened, but they rarely get solved," he said bitterly. "The only person who knows the truth is dead now. I don't see how reopening the case will help."

"You never know. Don't lose hope, Aaron. We'll look into Barney King; we'll tear his life apart until we get to the truth."

"I don't have any hope to lose, Anna."

There was an edge to his voice, an undertone of frustration that I knew wasn't aimed at me specifically, but I was the closest target.

"You don't understand," he said. "I've lived with this mystery almost my whole life. I will never know what happened to her, and to be honest, I don't want to. It won't change anything. It won't bring her back. It won't replace the childhood I had without her. So, what does it matter if Barney King was involved? Reopening this cold case won't help anyone anymore."

As Aaron sank back into his seat, defeat finally threatening to crumble him, a ray of sunlight escaped the dense clouds in the sky and shone through the wide windows of his office. Pale yellow light bounced around the room and highlighted the frustration in his brow. Aaron didn't want the past dragged up. Unfortunately for us both, it wasn't his decision.

"What did Chief Constable Price say?" I asked. Breaking the silence felt painful.

"Apart from chastising me for calling him in the first place? He says he's sending someone over." Aaron gritted his teeth together as he spoke. "They'll be here this afternoon. I said the case just needs handing over to a different team."

"Do you think that's best?"

"It's a conflict of interest," said Aaron. "I can't oversee Serious Crimes if you're looking into the death of my mother. Best to get it taken off our hands altogether."

The ray of sunlight vanished, leaving shadows behind that weren't there before. As dazzling as everything outside was, it had a way of stealing the light and leaving a perpetual, unnatural darkness inside.

"I know," I said, choosing my words carefully. "I was just thinking; if we're the ones to look into the cold case, then we can at least ensure sensitivity. Privacy. You know what things are like around here – people grasp for the latest piece of gossip. Didn't you hear those probationers whispering about us this morning?"

Aaron rolled his eyes a little. "You don't need to protect me from gossip, Anna."

"Well, I need to do something," I confessed. "I can't sit here twiddling my thumbs until the bigwigs get here. What can I do?"

"Go back to the office and work," he said simply. "We'll carry on. I don't really know what else we can do."

Chapter Five

"Come on then," Jay said, tapping his fingers impatiently on the steering wheel of his car. He'd insisted on driving the short distance from the station to the secure storage facility on the outskirts of town where archived investigations and evidence were kept. In the short time I had been speaking to Aaron, Chris and Jay had located the cold case files for Clara Burns and now we were on our way to pick them up.

"Come on, what?" I asked.

"What did he say? Was he upset?"

"No," I replied. "Aaron doesn't get emotional. He's just keen to get this case handed over."

"Well, I'm not," Jay said flatly. "I don't want those stuck-up bastards from head office taking cases off us."

"We've got our own cases to worry about, like Ali Burgess," I said. Aaron's resolution to hand over the case had worn off on me. Stuck between a rock and a hard place, I wanted to get to the bottom of Barney King's death and his involvement in the disappearance of Clara Burns. But I also wanted to support Aaron and his wishes.

Jay grumbled under his breath, his foul mood apparently still clinging on.

After signing out two boxes of evidence and files from the storage facility and going through what felt like as many checks as at airport security, we were back on the road. My phone beeped as a message came through from Chris.

"The SOCOs have reported in from King's house," I read out. "They've found a few partial footprints around the lake but it's not clear how recent they are. And we need to swing by the morgue."

Jay wrinkled his nose. "We don't have to view the body, do we?"

"Isn't that generally why we have to go to the morgue?"

With a huff, Jay clicked on the car's indicator and swung the car around the next roundabout.

* * *

The morgue was located in the depths of the local hospital and a cool blast of air hit us as Jay and I entered. It was probably the only part of the hospital not currently cooking as the heating system battled to keep the cold outside. Pete Kerry, the pathologist's assistant, didn't appear bothered by the coolness of the room as he hunched over a desk, tapping slowly on the keyboard and singing along with the radio under his breath. He had the collar of his lab coat pulled up around his ears, making him look like a shorter, rounder version of Elvis. The song *Hound Dog* was coming from the radio.

"Morning, Pete," Jay said, before checking the time on his phone. "I mean, afternoon. What a day it's been already."

"So, I heard," Pete replied. He smoothed down his collar, hoping we hadn't noticed his impersonation attempt. "I was just finishing up prepping your gentleman. Want to go and have a look?"

He pointed a thumb towards the steel table.

"Sure," I replied, before Jay cut in.

"No, I do not," he said. "Unless we have to."

Pete looked a little taken aback. "Well, you don't have to. But I thought it might help with your investigation."

"Ignore him," I replied to Pete. "He's been in a bad mood all day. Please, talk us through what you've found."

As was standard, Pete whipped on a pair of surgical gloves and mask before heading over to the steel table and removing the stark white sheet that lay on top. What was underneath probably once could have been called a body. All clothes were removed, but the lifeless shape had lost its definition since coming out of the water. The skin was yellowed and unnaturally textured, with a waxy sheen. The face was so swollen, it was hard to recognise it as human at all.

I noticed Jay stand further back than normal. I knew from past experiences he disliked scenes with large amounts of blood, but I guessed his queasiness extended to bloated bodies as well.

"When the body was brought in, PC Harris told me that this is believed to be Barney King," said Pete. "I can confirm that. He had a pacemaker and a quick check of the serial number showed this was Mr King indeed."

Behind me, Jay craned his neck to get a look at the chest area, where a tidy incision ran from neck to hips.

"Good work," he said to Pete. "What about the rest of the post-mortem?"

"We'll get it done and dusted by the end of the day and we'll send you the report in the morning," Pete assured him. "In the meantime, I can tell you Mr King was in the water for around a week. Look at his fingers."

I followed Pete's gesture to the balloon-like left hand. Jay glanced but quickly looked away.

"It takes around a week for the skin to start to come away on the digits," said Pete. "The body has lost a couple of nails already. I estimated he was in the water for around six or seven days, no more. It's been cold lately, which slows decomposition down."

"Well, which is it?" said Jay. "Six or seven?"

Pete blinked, but continued on. "I'm leaning towards seven days. I'd say he died sometime last Tuesday."

"Did he have a wedding ring?" I asked.

"Not one on him," replied Pete. "No jewellery at all. He was a traditional chap; he had on a shirt, corduroy trousers and a fleece. No shoes though."

"And he drowned?" I asked. It was the jackpot question.

Pete gave a stiff nod. "I believe so. Lab tests on his blood will confirm if there were any substances involved, but there was water in the lungs. Given his age, the location and the weather for the last couple of weeks, I should think cold water shock took effect. It would have been minutes."

I looked at Jay. "Do people normally take their shoes off if they're going to drown themselves?"

"I don't know," he said with a shrug. "I've heard of people dressing up or wearing their nicest clothes, but can't say I've heard of removing shoes before doing it. I guess you never really know what goes on in someone's mind."

"Well, that's a mystery for you to figure out," said Pete. "I can only tell you what the body tells me. The only other thing of note is quite hard to see given the state of him, but he has a few wounds. A couple of broken fingers, broken wrist, quite a lot of bruising of the forearms."

"Signs of a struggle?" I asked.

Pete shook his head. "It's possible but I can't say for certain. Could just be clumsiness and old age. The chief coroner will make a more educated guess and put it in their report for you."

"I'll look forward to it," mumbled Jay, without an ounce of honesty in his voice. He took the chance to turn away from the steel table, heading for the exit with purposeful strides. "Thanks, Pete. We'll see you next time someone dies in suspicious and disgusting circumstances."

Pete re-covered the body of Barney King with the sheet, the material falling softly over the misshapen contours of the remains. The door rattled as it closed behind Jay, leaving a void behind. Only the smooth voice of Elvis filtered through, now singing the all-time classic *Love Me Tender*.

"See you later, Pete," I said.

The pathologist's assistant flicked up the collar of his lab coat again and gave me a grin. "Later, Anna." He nodded in the direction Jay had gone. "And good luck with him."

* * *

Keen to get a head start, Jay and Chris launched themselves into the old files from the investigation into Clara Burns' disappearance as soon as we returned to the office. That left me with the task of collating all the information we had on Barney King. Routine searches failed to produce any details of next of kin, so I sent off requests to King's bank and his doctor's surgery, hoping one of them might have someone on file.

The scene-of-crime officers had found a batch of medical letters in the kitchen of the house. I worked on logging each one, growing increasingly surprised each time a new diagnosis appeared. Barney King was under the care of almost every department at the hospital; ENT, nutritionist, cardiology, diabetes and, most recently, neurology. But there was nothing about mental ill-health that would explain his suicide.

Despite my best efforts not to appear overly keen on investigating, I found my interest piqued as Chris and Jay swapped reports from the forty-year-old cold case.

"We should go back to this system," Jay remarked. He had paperwork covering every inch of his desk which was starting to spill over onto mine. "Good old-fashioned reports, written by hand. None of these poorly typed case files and bad spelling."

"You wouldn't be saying that if you had to handwrite all your reports," Chris replied. "What have you got so far?"

Jay cleared his throat and held up a piece of paper like a newsreader. "The lead investigator was Detective Inspector Larry Daley. He was trying hard to build a case against Barney King, but couldn't gather enough evidence in the end. There are some statements on file from Clara's family; her husband's is a bit woolly. He describes how he was out drinking, came home to find the children in bed and no sign of her. He started looking for her the following morning, checked with relatives and friends nearby. He finally reported her missing that evening."

"Unusual that it took him so long, but not entirely suspicious," replied Chris. "Some people like to deal with problems themselves before involving the police."

"Daley notes that friends and family corroborated what he said," said Jay. "They couldn't rule him out completely but they focused more on King after that."

"Any searches in the local area?" I asked.

Both of the guys looked up at me, as if surprised I was paying attention to them. I shrugged back self-consciously, feeling a heat rise to my cheeks. As much as I wanted to respect Aaron's wishes and not reopen his mother's case, I couldn't stop the investigator in me from wanting to find out more.

Chris took a moment and cleared his throat before fixing me with a firm look. "It goes without saying, both of you, that we need to mind what we say to people about this case. Not just to Aaron. Rumours travel faster than the wind around here and it'll soon get out what this death has led to."

"We'll keep the gritty details to ourselves, won't we, Anna?" replied Jay with a wave of his hand.

Chris's glare was still on me, as if he expected me to crack at any moment. I gave him a furtive nod back, as much to reassure myself as it was to reassure him.

"Of course," I replied. "Whatever develops, we will keep it between just us."

"Although," said Jay and he tapped his chin, "Maddie is back on duty tomorrow and she'll be like a dog with a bone if she hears about this one."

PC Maddie Greene, a good friend and trusted colleague, was also the spearhead of most gossip around the police station.

Chris rolled his eyes but returned to the decades-old paperwork in front of him.

"In answer to the question, yes; searches of the area were conducted, including the quarry. There weren't as many pits back then; they were quarrying closer to the cottages than they are now, judging by these maps. But the lake where we found King was there. The searches didn't bring up anything."

"I feel sorry for DI Daley," Jay said. "Sounds like there wasn't much to go on. Clara Burns just vanished into thin air."

Chris picked up another piece of paper and gave it a cursory glance. "He was thorough. He even interviewed her son."

"What, he interviewed a two-year-old?" Jay asked.

"Not Aaron. The older son, Callum. He was ten at the time. Just goes to show that even being as thorough as Daley was, sometimes investigations just don't get solved."

That thought stung me. I hated the feelings that having to shelve a case brought; the unending wonderings, reminders of failure, the unfairness of hard work not paying off. Although it was a fact of life that investigations stalled and cases remained unsolved, I could guarantee that every detective I knew felt the same way. Everyone wanted answers; they wanted justice. Sometimes, it just didn't happen.

The shrill ring of Chris's desk phone snapped us all out of our contemplative daze. Chris scowled at the handset, as if hoping his glare might shut it up, before picking it up and barking a greeting down the line. A couple of seconds later, he put the receiver down again.

"Come on," he said, simultaneously inhaling deeply and stretching, as if preparing for a fight. "The important twats from head office are here. Let's go and see what they have to say."

Chapter Six

Yowls like a wounded animal's floated through the building from the custody suite as we trudged downstairs; clearly my use of the Q-word earlier that morning had jinxed the entire station. Whatever was going on in the cells sounded more inviting than what we were about to face.

King's Lynn Police Station had a large meeting room at the opposite end of the building to the custody cells. Most of the time, it was commandeered by other teams for task forces, special ops or top-secret meetings. Or the occasional nap. But today was one of those rare days when the room was not only free, but also the biggest meeting space available for us to talk in private. The message was that everyone involved in the case of Barney King had to be there, so that meant calling in PCs Harris and Falini, as those first on scene, as well as Aaron, Chris, Jay and me.

Chris led the way to the meeting room and he faltered at the threshold, then approached the table with caution, warily eyeing the woman sat on the opposite side.

"Detective Inspector Hamill," she said, her unnaturally smooth face trying to smile but not doing so convincingly. "Please, take a seat."

Chris did as he was told, sitting down next to Aaron. Harris and Falini were already seated and Jay and I took the last spots. A quick glance around the table showed me a range of emotions; Jay and Harris looked as confused as I felt, whilst the newest PC was frozen like she was trapped under a spotlight. Aaron and Chris were forcibly suppressing looks of annoyance.

As we sat, the door to the room swung closed, but not before another howl of protest from one of the guests in the cells echoed through the corridor outside. The woman raised one perfectly manicured eyebrow and looked at Aaron.

"Busy little station you have here, DCI Burns," she said.

"Indeed," he replied, any friendliness absent from his words. "Which is why I'd appreciate moving this matter on, Superintendent Goodwin. As I explained to the chief constable, this case just needs to be handed over to another team. I didn't realise he would send you."

"Chief Constable Price is a busy man, Burns," the woman replied sharply. She pushed a strand of greying hair behind her ear, as if offended it dared to move out of place. "You can't expect him to drop everything for whatever little piece of drama you have over here. And…" She paused, turning her narrowed gaze on each of us in turn. "It's Chief Superintendent Goodwin now."

"Of course," Aaron mumbled back, with just a hint of sarcasm.

Goodwin ignored him. "So, it seems we have an unusual conflict of interest here. Bring me up to speed and I'll decide whether this is an investigation that can be removed from your caseload or not."

Harris gave a rundown of the initial call-out and discovery of the body that morning, whilst the rest of us listened patiently. When it came to PC Falini's turn to talk about discovering the suicide note, she only managed a quiet babble, so I took over and filled in the remainder of the story and how far into the investigation we'd gotten. Whilst Goodwin gave Harris and Falini barely a look, absently writing notes, she paid me far more attention. Her green eyes bore into me, hardly flitting over the case notes I handed her as I spoke.

"Right," she said when we finished up, "so the victim appears to have killed himself and left a note to that effect. Has that been confirmed?"

Sat on the other side of Aaron, Chris spoke. "We are waiting for the full post-mortem to confirm it, but that is the indication at this time."

Goodwin gave an indifferent hum. "And what are your other impressions?"

"Other impressions?" Jay asked.

"Yes," replied Goodwin. "You've had all day to look over Barney King's death."

Jay glanced around the table with uncertainty. "Well, nothing at this moment. But there are still some questions surrounding his death. He had no family; no one checked in on him."

Goodwin nodded along with an expectant look on her face. "Go on. What else?"

"Well," Jay continued, "there are several questions around his method. King was eighty-five years old and in poor health. Drowning seems a bit of an effort for someone that age."

"Maybe an effort, but it's not impossible," replied Aaron.

Across the table, Goodwin's thin lips pursed, almost becoming a smirk.

"But if you were eighty-five and wanted to kill yourself, wouldn't you pick an easier way?" said Jay.

"I thought that too," Harris chipped in. "On our initial search of his house, we found a shotgun and pellets by the back door. I figured the bloke was a poacher. Why not use that?"

Harris's observation rang a bell with me and I flipped through the pile of paperwork from the case file. "According to the owners of the quarry further down the lane, King did keep the local pheasant population down. I didn't find a valid firearms licence for him, but he may have had one in the past."

"Exactly," said Jay. "Drowning, no matter how quick due to cold water shock, is not a pleasant way to go. Why would King put himself through that?"

"And what about his admission of guilt in the suicide note? Do you believe he was referring to Clara Burns?" Goodwin asked.

"Possibly. DI Daley was thorough, but he had a strong suspicion that King was involved in Clara's disappearance at the time," said Chris. "We would need more time to find out what led him to that conclusion and how that fits in to King's death now."

"So, what you're saying," Goodwin said, pronouncing each word slowly as though she was savouring them, "is that even after reviewing the cold case and the circumstances of King's death, you can't be certain who or what his suicide note is referring to?"

"It's too early to say," replied Chris simply.

"If we investigate King's death then we will need to reopen the cold case too," Jay added. "The two are linked and we won't be able to definitively say who King's suicide note is referring to without reviewing his involvement with Clara Burns."

"We don't need to do anything," Aaron cut in. "This case isn't staying with this team."

Everyone around the table turned to Goodwin, expecting some sort of wisdom or ruling. She leaned back in her chair with a thoughtful grin, bordering on amusement. Her silence seeded a niggling of doubt within me; had she purposely set us off speculating, knowing it would annoy Aaron?

After an uncomfortably long time, Chief Superintendent Goodwin finally cleared her throat. "I agree; it, at least, warrants further investigation. But potentially opening a decades-old unsolved case is not something done lightly, so it needs leading by a senior officer who can be trusted. You three" – she pointed to Chris, Jay and me in turn – "will need oversight from someone with experience in the sensitivity of cold cases. And you" – she turned to Aaron – "can't be that senior officer for obvious reasons. We have an SO back at head office who can be spared for the duration. DCI Matthew Chase. I'll send him over first thing in the morning."

Goodwin once again looked at us, taking time to measure each of our reactions. She lingered a little longer on me, as if I had something to hide from her and if she stared long enough, I might reveal it.

Goodwin's gaze fell on Aaron last. "Any other requests, DCI Burns?"

Aaron slowly shook his head. "I'd rather the case was handed over entirely. Serious Crimes already have a full caseload."

She smirked back. "I think it sounds like your team are keen to get investigating, actually. And if by full caseload you are referring to the unsolved murder of Ali Burgess, well, we all know you've had plenty of time to close that one."

Just as Aaron opened his mouth to reply, Goodwin snapped her gaze away. "How is the Burgess case going, by the way? The chief constable will be pleased to get an update."

Aaron thought for a moment, gritting his teeth, before he answered. "No substantial progress."

"Well, that's not the update the chief constable will be hoping for," Goodwin replied curtly. "I suggest you use these next few weeks to change that, as well as getting to the bottom of this suicide and cold case. After all, DCI Burns, you have assured Chief Constable Price that your Serious Crimes team are capable professionals."

"They are," Aaron replied.

"Then there shouldn't be any problems. The conflict of interest is easy to work around and shouldn't impact on any working capacities. Get these matters closed quickly and without drama, and there won't be any need for me to return. Isn't that right, Detective Constable McArthur?"

I felt a sharp heat rise in my cheeks as all eyes turned to me.

"Yes, ma'am," I said quickly, before my burning red face gave me away. "There'll be no problems at all."

"Good to hear," she said, giving a stiff smile. "Your reputation precedes you, McArthur. You have a knack for using unconventional methods. With such a personal case at stake, now would be the time to say if any of you are not able to work on this investigation."

Her eyes didn't leave me. My face seared until I had to look away. I resisted the urge to look at Aaron, to seek out whatever small amount of emotion he was hiding in his expression. Instead, I focused on the table. I couldn't excuse myself from the investigation. I had already outrightly lied to Chief Constable Price previously and told him there was nothing going on between Aaron and me, so now I had to stick to my guns.

If Goodwin was disappointed from my lack of reply, she didn't acknowledge it. Her stern gaze fell away from me and refocused on the rest of the group.

"Although DCI Chase will be the senior investigating officer on this one, he will be keeping me abreast of the developments. I trust you will all make him welcome."

A murmur of agreement ran around the room.

"Good. Now, let's get going. With any luck, we'll have these cases closed swiftly and painlessly."

And with an affirming nod, she rose from the table, straightening up to an imposing height. She exited the room, and only when her footsteps were lost to the bustle of the station, did the tension start to ease. I released the breath I'd held frozen in my lungs.

"Jeez," said Harris, rising to his feet as Falini and him also turned to leave, "she's a ball ache."

"You can say that again," Aaron muttered back. "Georgia Goodwin. She has always worked closely alongside Chief Constable Price. Do you know what they call her at head office? 'She-Hulk'."

Falini snorted a laugh, then looked horrified with herself for her slip in professionalism.

Harris apparently didn't get it.

Aaron dismissed the two officers, waving them off with a thanks and once they were gone, he turned to Chris.

"Have you heard of this DCI Chase?" he asked.

"No," Chris replied. "Have you?"

I gathered up the case notes, trying to tell if any of them were worried about a new addition to our team. Chris's expression was settled into his usual resting-frown. Jay wasn't going to be pleased whatever the outcome was, given his already cantankerous mood. Only Aaron looked apathetic to the new development.

"No," said Aaron, "but I'll ask around, see if anyone has worked with him."

"It's been a long time since I've seen the She-Hulk," Chris remarked, eyes falling on the meeting room door. "Last I heard, she was head of the Internal Investigations team."

"She still is, I think," Aaron replied. "That was why I was surprised she was sent over. Her whole job is to look into complaints and scrutinise officer's integrity. Just how closely is she going to be watching us?"

"Well, it sounds like she's already got the measure on Anna," said Jay.

As I stuffed the last of the evidence logs into the manilla folder of case notes, I felt a burning on the back of my neck that came with someone watching me. When I looked up, Aaron, Chris and Jay had all fixed me with a stern stare.

"What?" I asked. "Way are you looking at me?"

"We don't need any of your Crazy McArthur stunts whilst on this case," said Jay.

"I don't do this Crazy McArthur stuff on purpose, you know," I replied. "It just sort of… happens."

"Of course you don't," said Jay with an exaggerated roll of his eyes.

"I don't!"

"All right, that's enough," Chris chimed in. His flat tone and serious nature smoothed down any unrest before our tempers flared. We were all on edge; we all felt the heaviness of knowing that we were just getting started.

"This will be a difficult case, for some more than others," Chris continued, glancing Aaron's way. "But we are a good team. We look after each other. We can do this."

"Fucking hell," Jay mumbled under his breath, before taking the case file from my hands and heading for the door. "Hell must be about to freeze over if Chris Hamill is giving the pep talks."

Chapter Seven

Overnight, the weather conditions didn't improve, and the next day brought a fresh round of frost-covered trees, icy roads and slippery paths. Beautiful but deadly. I was first in the Serious Crimes office, beating both Jay and Chris, but I knew they wouldn't be far behind. We were all eager to get a head start on the case of Barney King and wrap this investigation up as soon as possible.

I was only alone in the office for seconds, as almost immediately, there was a soft knock at the door and someone let themselves in.

"Hello?" a man called into the space. A wide grin spilled across his face, making his eyes crinkle at the corners as he met my gaze. He strode in with a confident air, comfortable already with the unfamiliar surroundings.

"You must be DC McArthur," he said as he reached over the corner of Jay's desk to offer me his hand. He shook it vigorously.

"DCI Chase, I assume," I replied.

He seemed young for a DCI; he couldn't have been much older than Jay, probably late thirties but with the carefreeness of someone ten years younger. Although he wore a stiff suit and long overcoat, his dark-blonde hair was a fluffed-up mess and his face sported several days of uneven stubble.

"Yeah. You can call me Matt if you like, although no one does. Everyone calls me Chase. Even my father-in-law, which is weird. But then I married his daughter and he scares the shit out of me, so I'm not about to tell the man otherwise."

He beamed at me, still shaking my hand. His overly positive expression felt at odds with the circumstances of his presence and I wondered if I needed to point it out to him. He was only here because of a sensitive case, personal to one of our own. He didn't need to look so happy about it.

"Call me Anna," I said.

Like an excitable dog, he dropped my hand and spun around the room, taking it all in. His eyes fell on the whiteboard behind Jay's desk, where I had pinned up the details of our case the day before. A photo of Barney King stared out at us, the gruff old man scowling as though he didn't trust the camera not to steal his soul.

"Interesting case," Chase said, his eyes darting side to side as he scanned the information. "A suicide but also a confession. It's amazing how common deathbed confessions are. Guilty conscience eats away at you, I suppose."

"I suppose," I said in agreement. I wasn't even sure if I was meant to be agreeing with the guy. He was talking away like I wasn't even in the room.

"There must be more to this than meets the eye, apart from the obvious connection to the disappearance of Clara Burns."

Chase scoured the board but there was no information relating to Clara Burns up there. Not yet anyway. None of us felt comfortable with putting her up on the whiteboard. Instead, I handed him a frail and tattered folder from my desk, with a summary of the cold case inside.

"Why now?" Chase said as he took the file and leafed through it. "Why would the old man kill himself now, after keeping this secret for all these years? It doesn't make sense."

As he mumbled to himself and read, footsteps approached the office. Chris and Jay entered, pausing a fraction as they saw the stranger in the room. They tensed and, after a round of awkward introductions, they settled at their desks, both holding onto stiff postures and distrusting gazes.

"Now that the gang's all here," said Chase, clapping his hands together, "let's have a catch-up and see where we are. I've already been filled in on the connection between Barney King and Clara Burns. So, what did you manage to find out about his death so far?"

Jay and Chris only looked at each other, still unsure of the outsider in our midst.

"The body was recovered yesterday," Chris eventually replied. "The post-mortem report should be through this morning. Drowning is looking likely."

Chase nodded for him to continue. "King's house?"

"Searched thoroughly yesterday by the forensics team," I replied. "Anything of note was taken to the lab including the suicide note, but it doesn't look like Barney King had a mobile phone or any sort of technology really. Just an old TV, and an even older radio. We found lots of letters in his home; most were from the hospital for appointments for various ailments. It was his doctor's surgery that requested the welfare check after the hospital contacted them about his missed appointments."

"Well, the man was eighty-five." Chase grimaced. "Good job they did ask for a check, or who knows how long it could have been before he was found. Any family or next of kin?"

"We haven't tracked down any yet. There was none on file."

"Any sign of the dog?"

The three of us shook our heads. One of PC Harris's main grumbles, after the pain of figuring out how to recover the body, was that the dog had vanished into thin air.

"There definitely was a dog," I replied. "Plenty of dog food in the house. But no sign of it."

Chase rubbed his thumb over his chin with a thoughtful hum. "Strange, something must have spooked it. Dogs sometime wander but they often seek out people eventually. Were the quarry company contacted?"

"Jay and I visited yesterday and spoke with the owner," I replied.

"And what about Barney's last steps?"

There was a pause as the three of us exchanged looks. DCI Chase didn't notice, his attention still taken by the whiteboard of progress.

"Last steps?" Chris asked tentatively.

"Yeah. You know," said Chase. "Retracing the last steps of the deceased, figuring out the how, the where, the why. It's something I like to do; I start from where the body was found and go backwards through their day, looking for clues."

He spun around on his heels and faced us. Another smile, this one a little more restrained, crossed his face.

"We'll start there," he said. "Hamill, Fitzgerald, get stuck into the cold case and find out exactly what drew suspicion to Barney King in the first place. It's been forty years, most of the main players will be dead or retired. Find out who we can contact and how."

Straightening his back like a bolt of lightning had struck him, Chase stretched and headed for the door. "Come on, McArthur."

"Where are we going?" I asked.

"Last steps!" Chase said simply, as if it all made perfect sense.

I glanced at Chris and Jay, and noted their tight grimaces. Usually, they were the champions of keeping their thoughts between themselves, but today, I could read their expressions as clear as day. They weren't impressed and I got the distinct feeling there was little DCI Chase could do or say that would change that.

Grabbing my coat, I made for the exit of the office too, but Chase paused in the doorway.

"Oh, and one more thing," he said, lowering his voice. His eyes fell on Chris and Jay in turn, before finally settling on me. "This case needs the utmost confidentiality. DCI

Burns cannot be informed, not even a benign comment, about our findings. Understood?"

I nodded and swallowed hard. I had no intention of doing that anyway, but under Chase's searching gaze, I knew I had no wriggle room. He was going to be watching us keenly.

Accepting my nod, Chase beamed again. "Great. Let's go."

* * *

"Usually, I like to visit the crime scene when things are still fresh," DCI Chase said as we bumped my trusty old car along the track, heading for the dilapidated cottages outside of Wormegay village. He hadn't stopped talking from the moment we left the station car park. "You know, really get in the mind of the victim, understand how they were feeling. That usually leads on to the killer and gives an insight into their motives. Bit trickier to do that with this one."

I nodded, just as the car hit a particularly cavernous hole and the bumper scraped on the road. A quick check in the rear-view mirror showed we hadn't accidentally left it behind.

Chase snorted. "Thank God we took your car. No way I'm driving my Audi down here. She's only used to smooth, city streets."

"Ah," I said under my breath. "You're an Audi driver."

As I pulled the car onto the grass verge in front of the cottages, Chase was already climbing out. He ignored the patrol vehicle parked beside the cottage, his long legs taking the front garden in a handful of strides and, before I could unclip my seat belt, he was waiting at the front door, flicking the police tape with impatience.

The officer manning the crime scene jumped out of the police car and ran across the frost-covered grass to intercept.

"Sir, you can't go in there!"

I recognised the rosy-faced officer as PC Falini, who flapped her arms until Chase turned to her, stopping her in her tracks with his overly confused expression.

"If you're meant to be acting as scene guard, Constable, you're doing a poor job. Any old Tom, Dick or Harry could've got in by now," he said.

PC Falini floundered and babbled an apology, until I got out of the car and joined them. She relaxed at the sight of a slightly friendlier face.

"Chop, chop, McArthur," said Chase, not waiting for an explanation from Falini as he motioned at the cottage entrance.

As I unlocked the front door of the cottage, a cloud of dank air hit us, rustling Chase's hair. It was like the house was breathing, finally free from being stuffed up for so long. Although the house had been opened and aired yesterday when the SOCOs were working, it still smelled like it held decades of smoke and dust in its lungs.

Chase turned to PC Falini before he entered. "You, erm… stay here. Eyes peeled. Don't let anyone else in."

"Yes, sir!" she said, snapping her heels together but stopping herself just short of giving a salute.

"Top marks for showing the appropriate respect to a senior officer, though," Chase replied with a nod of approval and a pointed look at me. Then, he disappeared inside.

Left on the doorstep, I shared a glance with the newbie.

"I don't think I've met him yet," Falini said, barely above a whisper as if she was scared DCI Chase might hear. I remembered the pain of being a new officer. Finding your feet was hard work in the police when you were thrown in at the deep end, but then, it wasn't exactly a job you could learn without seeing whether you would sink or swim first.

"That's DCI Chase," I replied and I gave her a reassuring smile. "Don't worry, he's only here temporarily. At least, I hope so."

After donning shoe covers and gloves, I followed Chase inside.

"You take upstairs," he called from down the hallway, in the kitchen. "I'll take down. Shout if you discover anything useful."

"I thought we were, I don't know," I replied, "retracing King's last steps, or however you put it."

"We are." Chase's head appeared around the doorway to the kitchen, his smile far too wide considering the circumstances. "Pretend you're starting your day, Barney King-style."

His head disappeared back into the kitchen without further explanation. I decided to humour him, happy for a few minutes alone, and I climbed up the creaking staircase.

There was a bedroom at the back of the house, a small one filled with junk, clothes and thick layers of dust. It seemed a lot of the boxes contained pieces of lawnmowers, although how and why they were up here was a mystery to me. This room was far too small for any sort of workshop.

Since the SOCOs had already removed anything relevant to the old man's death, I left that one and wandered into the master bedroom, trying to get a sense of Barney King, as Chase wanted. A fireplace stood opposite the end of the bed, sullen and dark. A wardrobe spilled out clothes, and the bed was nothing more than a collection of blankets and sheets in a tight bundle. A pair of work boots sat neatly by the foot of the bed. Something about the room pushed against me, as though the house was trying to throw me out.

Rather than climb into the bed and pretend I was Barney King waking up for the day and deciding to kill myself, I edged into the room, making the dust particles swirl around me. A loose floorboard by the fireplace creaked as I stepped on it. It rattled noisily compared to the silence of the rest of the house. I jumped off it before a thought struck me. I tested it again with the tip of my shoe. It clanged at the intrusion.

Dropping to my knees, I found the purchase to wiggle my gloved fingertips under the board and it lifted with ease. It wasn't just loose, it was entirely unsecured, left there on purpose. There was a tiny space underneath and floating dust particles disturbed by my actions landed on a red tin box.

A few minutes later, Chase found me on my knees on the bedroom floor surrounded by the contents of the rusty box. There were love letters – both to and from – and a host of old school reports. Two aged photographs were hidden at the bottom; one of a couple on their wedding day and another of a baby in a christening gown, crying in their mother's arms. Both photos had the same woman.

"What have you got there?" Chase asked as he dropped down next to me.

"SOCOs must have missed this," I replied. "It was under the floorboard."

Chase took a moment to glance over the array of items before he plucked the school report from my hand. "Good find. Special keepsakes? We all have a box of memories hidden somewhere, right?"

"We do?"

"You don't?" He scowled but his attention was taken by the report as he scanned it. "No first-date cinema tickets or love letters?"

"Not any that I wanted to keep," I mumbled back. "What does it say? I had only just deciphered the date."

"It says our boy Barney was an average student. Unremarkable in almost every way. Bit harsh. Any more of them?"

From the widening of Chase's eyes, I knew he had spotted the two photographs. He studied them carefully for a few moments, holding them inches from his face.

"Is this King in the wedding photo?" he asked.

"I think so," I replied. "A much younger King. He must have been, what, twenty? There's a date written on the back."

Without a reply, Chase glanced at the back before setting aside the two photographs. He clicked his fingers and I handed him a few more school reports to look at whilst I scanned the love letters. They were a back and forth between two dreamy young lovers named Barney and Mary. They fantasised about finishing school, finding jobs and starting a life together. Mary's letters were wistful, covered in doodles and small hearts in between her tight handwriting. Barney's letters were more uniform, his writing looped and curled in the same cursive style I struggled to read on the school reports. I was thankful that style had all but died out now, it took me far too long to figure out if a flourish was a *J* or a *T*. And that was before I got started on *S*.

"Oh, here's something nice," Chase remarked. "'King's handwriting has improved over the year. I would say he now has the best in the class. If only he applied himself with this much dedication to his mathematics.'"

"Bit of a back-hander."

"That's about as good as it gets from old school headmasters in those days."

"It was quite nice handwriting," I said and handed Chase one of the love letters from Barney.

He scanned it with interest. "Wait a minute." Chase's face fell and he clicked his fingers at me. "Have you got the suicide note?"

I didn't, given that it was already logged into evidence, but I did have the photo of it on my phone.

Chase scanned the photograph of the note, his eyes darting back and forth between that and the letter. Over and over. For a full two minutes, he didn't speak, leaving me with no option but to listen to his quickening breaths and the creaks and groans of the house.

Then he turned both the letter and the image to me. "What do you make of this handwriting?"

I scanned the spidery suicide note, the pen alternating between thick inky lines and thin raspy ones. It was a stark contrast to the love letters from King's youth, with their even, undeviating loops.

"That's not the same handwriting."

"That's not the same handwriting," Chase repeated, nodding slowly. "Our boy Barney didn't write that suicide note."

Chapter Eight

"I thought you said you'd looked into King's next of kin," DCI Chase said as he swept into the Serious Crimes office like a tornado. He held the red tin box under his arm inside an evidence bag, the letters and photographs safely inside. I followed behind, keeping a comfortable distance between us.

"We tried yesterday," replied Chris, giving the new DCI a wary look. "Why?"

"Because Barney King had a wife and child." Chase pulled the two photographs out and thrust them at Chris, who gazed over them with his usual scowl before handing them to Jay.

"We ran a cursory check," said Chris. "No next of kin with his bank, none on his medical records, council tax. No will in place. We didn't trawl through the marriage records from sixty years ago yet."

"In fact, that would've been Anna's job today if you hadn't pulled her away," Jay said. A satisfied smile slid onto his face. It took the wind out of Chase's sails and I found it hard to keep the grin from reaching me too.

"Well, so far you've managed to miss a hidden box of treasures and a family we didn't even know about," said Chase. "But what's even more interesting is this." He handed over one of the love letters, sealed neatly in its own evidence bag to Chris. "Get that over to the lab for analysis. It looks nothing like the writing on King's suicide note."

"The handwriting's different?" Jay asked, as he leaned across to get a look at the letter. "Are you saying you don't think King wrote that suicide note?"

Chase clicked his fingers together, as if tapping out a jazz rhythm. "Bingo! Ten points. Which also means he might not have killed himself. Is the post-mortem report back?"

"Not yet," Chris replied.

"Chase it," said Chase. "Seriously, call them, now. I want answers. And get that letter off to the lab."

He spun on his heels, his long coat flapping around his knees, and strode to the door.

"I'll get this box and the contents logged into evidence," he declared, before pausing at the door and turning back to the room. "And McArthur... Get the kettle on."

"But—" I began. I was ready to get stuck in and help Chris and Jay find the elusive next of kin. Just because I was the junior on the team, didn't mean I was the tea lady.

"But nothing," the DCI replied. "Listen to your senior officers. Most important part of the job, making the tea."

And with that, he left and the door swung closed behind him.

I felt my body relax as I heard his footsteps disappear down the corridor. Tension had gripped my shoulders ever since I found that memory box hidden in King's floor and I realised there was a family somewhere. Why hadn't we found them yesterday? Had we missed something?

With Chase gone, Jay groaned dramatically and sunk into his chair. Chris had a look on his face that told me without words his exact thoughts on Detective Chief Inspector Chase. His mouth moved as though he was testing out swear words, before he eventually settled on one.

"What a twat."

I flopped into my seat. There was an extra chair beside mine, which I guessed would be for the new DCI, however, our office was barely big enough for us currently. I already shared my desk with the office printer.

"Is that your word of the day?" Jay asked Chris. "So far, you've called everyone a twat this morning. Even me. To my face."

Chris shrugged his shoulders, looking unusually self-conscious.

"The little one is starting to talk," he explained, "so Alicia says I need to stop swearing so much. 'Twat' is allowed, though."

"Why is 'twat' allowed?" I asked.

"Because Alicia appreciates that in our line of work, we encounter a fair few twats." Chris glanced at the office door, as if he was expecting Chase to be listening on the other side. "And I think we've been saddled with another one."

* * *

After an hour of digging, we hit the jackpot. The date on the back of the wedding photograph led us to a marriage certificate for Barney and Mary. Then we managed to find a birth certificate for a Margaret King, which listed Barney King as her father and Mary King as her mother. Although the daughter had married since and changed her name, it appeared that she still lived locally, in the nearby town of Wisbech, so DCI Chase insisted we visited right away. He also insisted on driving.

It didn't surprise me at all that Chase's car was a large, luxurious sedan, its ride impossibly smooth even on the bumpier stretches of road. We sailed west along the A47, traffic building as we got closer to town and soon, we were stuck in a crawling tailback, trying to get to the roundabout ahead.

"So how long have you been on the team? And do you want a coffee?" Chase asked as he turned into the drive-thru for a coffee chain store just off the roundabout.

Just the sight of it made my mouth water and I nodded enthusiastically. As we joined the queue, Chase shuffled in his seat, his keen gaze falling on me now that he didn't have to watch the road.

"You only get a coffee if you answer both of my questions. How long?" he asked.

I chewed on my tongue for a moment. If this was some way of breaking the ice and getting to know each other better, his attempt was a little too late.

"I've been on this team for six months now," I replied. "It's been a busy six months."

"So, the rumours say," he said, a knowing glint in his eyes. "You're the same officer who got stabbed last year, right?"

My shoulder twinged, as if it was a guard dog preparing for an order. I pushed the thought of it away. The old wound hadn't bothered me in months, I wasn't about to let it start again.

"That's me," I replied with a grimace.

"What was it like?"

I blinked, not sure if I'd heard him right. He asked the question as though he was asking how a recent holiday abroad had been, not enquiring on a near-death experience.

"It hurts."

"I bet," he said. "I broke my leg once, when I was eighteen, playing football. That fucking hurt. The bone had slipped, so they had to reposition it and I thought I was dying. Is it worse than that?"

"Um. I don't know. I've never broken my leg."

"I bet yours was worse," he said.

Chase rolled down his window as we approached the order point. He ordered two flat whites with more sugar than I thought the poor attendant would allow and we drifted across to the next window. Chase handed the cups over to me and then we were back on the road, moving at a quicker pace now as the traffic flowed.

"Is that how you got the nickname? Crazy McArthur?"

"No," I said, sipping on the hot brew which filled the car with steam. "I had the nickname long before that. But that incident during the Ali Burgess case kind of… cemented it, I guess."

"And what do your colleagues think of your knack for trouble?"

The stab wound twinged again, along with a prickle of embarrassment at the personal questions.

"I don't know."

"Oh come on. I doubt they keep their opinions to themselves that well."

"You'll have to ask them," I replied.

As much as I wanted to work well together and hurry these cases along, I couldn't just ignore the alarm bells in my mind telling me to be careful. Was DCI Chase just trying to be friendly or was he here for another reason? He was fishing for information of some kind.

Soon we were turning off the main road into Wisbech, the sign at the edge of the town welcoming us into the *Capital of the Fens*. Wisbech was a small market town, almost as unexciting as my home town of Downham Market, but its reputation in the local area set it aside from most places. I'd been called over to assist Cambridgeshire Constabulary more times than I could count over my career. Locals had plenty of unaffectionate nicknames for the town, most of which were not politically correct.

I directed Chase to the centre of town, entering a small estate of tightly packed semis. It was the only time I'd spoken since leaving the coffee drive-thru and when we pulled up outside a house labelled 65, with broken wheelie bins out front and overgrown grass weighed down with frost, Chase turned off the engine. He made no other move.

"Do you want some advice?" he asked, but it wasn't really a question. I was about to get some, whether I wanted it or not. "I know none of you want me here."

"What do you mean?"

"This team, this station. You've got this strange, close-knit dynamic going on and outsiders like me aren't welcome. But that's tough. We're here to look into a suspicious death and hopefully close a cold case. And both of those things will happen quicker if you trust me."

He allowed a moment for that to sink in, before he tapped on the steering wheel, waiting for a reply.

"All right," I decided, now more confused than ever.

And with a nod of satisfaction, Chase opened his car door. "See, that wasn't so hard, was it? Now if we could just teach you a bit of respect for your senior officers, you'd be the perfect constable."

And with that, he hopped out of the car and strode up the garden path to the front door of the house.

When I joined him, Chase rapped impatiently on the front door of number 65, but the commotion from inside was enough to drown out even his hardest knock. He glanced at me. Loud shouts and disgruntled retorts reverberated off the mouldy glass pane.

"Shall we try round the back?" he asked.

"Lead the way, *sir*," I replied, emphasising the last word.

Chase squinted at me. "No need to be sarcastic."

I followed him around the side of the property, where a broken gate let us into the back garden. Even with the obscured sun failing to burn away the dense clouds, the back door to the house was open and the argument we could hear grew louder and clearer.

"You ungrateful little turd. If I find out you've been hanging around with that lot again, I'll string you up myself. And don't you dare even think about skipping school again."

"It was just history this afternoon, Nan, it doesn't bloody matter."

"It matters to your mum, so get your arse in gear."

Chase and I peered into the open door, spotting a heavyset teenage girl sat at a dining table, with a school blazer and tie thrown at her feet. A hunched-over older lady stood on the opposite side of the table, wagging her finger at the youngster. The pair both stopped dead as they spotted us, glares turning feral at the intrusion.

"Excuse me?" the woman demanded, wobbling over to the door. Her hair was unnaturally red and spiky on top of her head but her face gave away her many years. Her walk was one of someone with a dodgy hip, cumbersome and slow.

"Who the fuck are you? What do you want?"

Chase waved his warrant card in her face. "We knocked but you didn't hear. I'm DCI Matthew Chase; this is DC Anna McArthur. We're looking for Margaret Bowen."

Behind the older lady, the teenage girl sniggered. "Margaret."

The woman turned back to the girl, slapping her hand on her thigh. "Shut up, you." She turned her furious glare back to us. "I'm Margaret, although no one calls me that. Call me Mags."

"Mags?" Chase repeated.

"Maggie if you must. What do you want?"

"Can we come in?" I asked. The coffee from the journey had warmed my insides but the weather outside was quickly stamping the sensation out.

Mags scrutinised us for a moment, before stepping aside.

"All right," she said before turning back to the girl. "Lucy, lunchtime is over. Get back to school."

"I told you; I don't want to go."

"And I told you, if your mum gets one more call from that school that you've bunked off, I'll go down there myself. You want that?"

At the threat, the girl's smirk vanished, replaced with a brief look of terror. It seemed like a threat from Nan was enough to get her moving and she stood up, picking up her blazer and tie from the floor. She paused at the back door, stooping to plant a kiss on her grandmother's cheek before pushing past Chase and me with a mutter under her breath. "Bloody fuzz."

When she disappeared from view, Mags stepped aside and ushered us into the kitchen, shutting the door firmly behind us. She limped over to the worktop and flicked on the kettle.

"So, what do you want then? If it's that bloody girl again, I'll kill her. Her mum is asleep though, she just got off a night shift and I'd rather not wake her. She needs her sleep now she's in the family way. She's a carer and works bloody hard."

"You live here with your daughter and granddaughter?" Chase asked.

Mags plonked three mismatched mugs down on the counter, not bothering to ask if we wanted a brew.

"No, they live here with me, it's my house. They've been here ever since Kelly left that useless boyfriend of hers, Patrick, the cheating prick. You know all this, though; you've been here enough times recently when he's turned up at the door, drunk off his arse."

"I don't think we have," said Chase, slowly. "We're from Norfolk police. Not Cambs."

"Oh." Mags threw teabags in the cups and sloshed water in. "What's Norfolk want?"

"It's about your father."

The kettle landed back in its cradle with a clang and a hiss as some water escaped the open lid. For a moment, Mags stayed still, her back to us, as she digested the information. Then, without a word, she resumed making the tea and set down two mugs in front of us before joining us at the table.

"I don't have a father."

"Well, you do. Everyone does," said Chase, lacking even the smallest amount of sympathy. "Yours was Barney King, who lived outside of Wormegay."

"So, what of it?" Mags demanded. "I haven't seen the old bastard since I was a girl. I thought he died years ago."

"He didn't. He died last week."

Mags licked her lips, her gaze shifting away from Chase and scrutinising the cup in her hand.

"How?" she asked, before changing course. "Never mind, I don't care. Good riddance. Shame you had to waste a journey out here to tell me. Bet there wasn't anything left, was there? No money, no inheritance."

Chase shrugged his shoulders. "Probably not. We're looking into his death, there are suspicious circumstances. We were hoping you could tell us a bit about your father."

"Well, I can't," said Mags. "As I said, I haven't seen the bastard since I was about five. Mum got me out of there as soon as she was able."

"Got you out of there?"

With a deep breath, Mags abandoned her tea and glowered at Chase. She didn't like him, that much was obvious. This was a woman who probably didn't trust police much in general, and now here we were, trying to pry information from her about a man she had relegated to the recesses of her mind for decades. To her, her father was long dead and she wasn't going to thank us for telling her she was wrong.

Reaching into the case file Chase had brought along, I found the two photographs hidden in King's house. I held them in my hand. We had to earn her trust first.

"Your mother left your father?" I asked, letting calm and kindness into my voice, and she nodded to confirm.

"Yeah. She left him in the middle of the night, when he was down the pub, and brought us over here to live with her sister. Haven't heard or spoke to him ever since. Not even a birthday card."

"When was that?"

"Almost sixty years ago. Fifty-five. I dunno. I was a child. Mum never spoke of him again. So, if you want me to be sad about his death or arrange his funeral, you're shit out of luck. I want nothing to do with it."

"That's okay, we understand," I said. "As DCI Chase said, we're just looking into his death and his connection to Clara Burns."

"Who?" Mags asked.

"Her and her family were neighbours to Barney. They lived in the cottage next door."

"Name doesn't ring a bell," said Mags. "When I lived there, we lived next to Mr and Mrs Herbert. They were elderly though. They certainly won't be around now."

"What do you remember about your dad?" asked Chase.

Mags took a moment to think on that question and her gaze drifted back to her drink. When she finally looked up, she looked at me and not Chase.

"He worked at the quarry. And he had this gun dog, a daft old Lab called Puck. At the weekend he'd go out for pheasants in the morning and take them down to the village to sell. He never had a nice word to say to anyone. I was sad about leaving the dog, I loved Puck. Should think he's long gone now." A slight frown crossed her face and she bit her lip.

"And you really never heard from him again?" Chase pressed.

"I already said, no." The woman glared at Chase. "Why are you really here? I've had nothing to do with the old man all my life and I want nothing to do with him in death. I can't help you."

"As we said, we're just trying to find out more about Mr King," I replied, cutting in before Chase could.

"Anything about his life might help us. Do you have any other memories?"

Mags shook her head. "None. He didn't exactly leave a good impression behind."

"Why's that?" Chase said quickly.

"He was a bad-tempered bastard, made my mum's life a misery. She was happy when we left."

"Is this her?" I asked and I slid the two photographs over to her.

Mags took one, the wedding photo first, and held it close to her face, squinting at the image. In an instant, her contention was gone. She lightly touched the photograph, fingertips trailing over the beaming bride.

"She was so beautiful," she said with a slight crack in her voice. "Where did you find this?"

"In your father's house," I replied.

My heart wrenched at her expression; her entire demeanour changed in a moment. Tears were threatening to fall and ruin her matriarchal authority. Not a fierce grandmother and mother anymore. She was a child, a daughter, with her family torn apart.

"Where?" she whispered.

"In a box of keepsakes. There were love letters too, old school reports. We have them all at the station, they're evidence for now, but once this is cleared up, we can arrange for them to be returned to you. They would be yours now."

She nodded, a cry held back in her throat. "My old mum was a beauty. Everyone said so. And he didn't scrub up too bad, I suppose."

Mags handed the photograph back to me, almost thrusting it away like a bad omen. Her eyes lingered on her mother, one final look, before she returned to her tea.

"Did your mother ever mention your father again?"

She shook her head. "She never spoke of him. Never spoke to him either."

"Why did she leave?"

"I don't know." Mags rolled her shoulders, one looser than the other. "I think she'd just finally had enough. She changed her name, avoided crossing over into Norfolk whenever she could. And never mentioned him again."

"Can we speak to her?"

Mags flinched, turning the movement into a slow shake of the head.

"She died a long time ago. Cancer."

"And you're certain you never spoke to your father again?" Chase asked one last time.

Mags shook her head again, this time assured and defiant, and with very little patience. "Never. As far as I'm concerned, the old man died when I was a child. I had no father after that."

Chapter Nine

"This handwriting thing is bothering me," said Chase as we climbed the metal stairs at the police station, heading for the Serious Crimes office. The truth was that he hadn't stopped talking the whole way back from Wisbech and I had tuned him out somewhere around the village of Walton Highway. His thoughts were all case-related, but he had a habit of using ten times as many words than was needed.

"If Barney King didn't write that suicide note, then who did?" Chase continued. "Who wanted him to confess, or look like he was confessing, to a terrible crime? All the major players from the disappearance of Clara Burns are either dead or so old they're eating mushy pear for breakfast, lunch and dinner. His daughter and wife had left long before Clara and her family moved in next door."

Before I could interject, Chase burst through the door to the office. His gaze flickered between Chris and Jay, sat at their respective desks, before settling on Chris.

"DI Hamill, when did Clara Burns and her family move into the cottage next to King's?"

"Three years before she disappeared," he answered, as if expecting the random question.

"So, Mags was right. Her and her mother were long gone before the Burnses moved in." Chase stroked his chin thoughtfully as he headed across the room and took a seat in the empty chair that had appeared in the office next to my desk. In order to get to my own chair, I had to squeeze past him.

"What if the note is not alluding to Clara?" I floated the idea, although to be honest, I didn't know where I was going with it. "We've just assumed King's suicide note meant Clara."

"We've no evidence of any other crimes in the area, or missing people, or whatever. Clara Burns is the biggest mystery, a forty-year-old case that has never been solved. The note must have been referring to her murder," concluded Chase.

As I discarded my coat and settled at my desk, I pulled out my mobile phone. Apart from a couple of texts from my mother, annoyed that I wasn't responding right away, I had no other messages. Nothing from Aaron. I wondered if he was okay.

"We need some confirmations before we can move forwards," said Chase. "We need the handwriting analysis to know for certain if Barney King could have written that note. And we need to know his cause of death."

"I can help with one of those," said Jay, producing a piece of paper. He handed it over to Chase with a flourish. "Post-mortem has confirmed death was due to drowning. King also had a large amount of alcohol in his system."

"So, did he enter the water voluntarily or not?" asked Chase. He looked over the document too fast to actually take any of it in, before handing it over to me.

"It's impossible to say," replied Jay with a grimace. "King had quite a few bruises on him, so there could have been force used against him. But given that he'd been in the water for a week before he was found, we don't know exactly how he got there."

"That's not helpful," Chase snapped. "We have an elderly man, who may or may not have killed someone, before maybe killing himself, or maybe not." He sat up straight and looked over the computer monitors to Chris. "Tell me you've dug up something useful from the investigation into Clara's disappearance."

"I've found the old interview transcripts from when they had Barney King in for questioning," Chris replied, holding the files out for Chase.

"That sounds more promising." Chase gave Jay a pointed look, as if the disappointing post-mortem report was his fault. "Is the lead investigator still around?"

"He is, actually," said Jay. "Detective Inspector Larry Daley. His address is a nursing home in Dersingham. I've tried calling them but they're not answering."

"Daley." I hummed. They'd said the name yesterday but this time, a bell rang in my mind. "Not related to Inspector Matilda Daley?"

Jay nodded back. "Her father, I think."

"Maybe we should go and ask her," I suggested.

Jay shrugged, looking at Chris. "It would be easier, I suppose." He picked up the phone, calling through to the station's control room and asking for Inspector Daley's duty roster. "We're in luck, she's on duty today."

"I'll go with you," I offered as Jay rose to his feet. "Daley loves me."

"Why do I not believe that?"

He looked at Chase, who had slipped down in his seat to a slouched position and was scrolling through his phone with a slight frown. The transcript files sat on his lap. Chase glanced up and waved his hand at us. "Go for it. When you get back, we'll look into Mags Bowen and her mother a bit more."

"Thanks, *sir*," I said, once again emphasising the last word and we filed out of the room.

As I left, I caught a sneer cross Chase's face.

"Now you're just taking the piss."

* * *

Inspector Matilda Daley – Matilda, never Tilly – was a formidable officer, with sparkling grey hair tied into a tight bun and small, keen eyes. She'd been a sergeant when I was in uniform, often having the same shifts as me, which she always called a curse. And when I said she loved me, I was exaggerating.

"No," she said, spotting me approach her desk as Jay and I made our way across the bullpen. Only a few uniformed officers milled about in here today, grumbling about their paperwork. My guess was most of them were out on patrol. The icy weather tended to bring plenty of call-outs.

"No, no. She's a detective now, she's your problem, not mine anymore," Daley said to Jay, who glanced around us as though he expected her to be speaking to someone behind him. There was no one there.

Daley rolled her eyes and huffed at his confused expression. "I've done more than my fair share of looking after Crazy McArthur. You're not bringing her back."

"I'm not coming back," I said to Daley. Jay hid a snort behind his hand, making it look like he was scratching his nose. "We want to ask you some questions about your dad."

She looked at me like I was growing a second head. "My dad?"

"He was a detective inspector, right?"

"Yes."

"We're looking into an old case of his."

"Oh." The pieces of the puzzle fell into place and the woman physically relaxed in her chair. "Oh, right, the disappearance of that woman, right? It must be that one, it's the only case of his that didn't get closed. It's his greatest regret."

"Can we speak to him about it?" Jay asked.

"He'd love that. It would save him trying to talk to me about it." Daley whipped a page off her notebook on the desk and scribbled down an address. "He's at Maple Court House, here's the address. Although you'll have to visit him tomorrow, he's at a hospital appointment today."

I handed the scrap of paper to Jay, who mumbled his thanks to Daley as he left. As I turned to leave, she coughed for my attention and fixed me with a dissecting stare. "Is that all you want, McArthur? Nothing else?"

I spun back around slowly, looking pensive. "You know, I do miss being on patrol. The excitement, never knowing what the day would bring. I've been thinking of coming back."

"Like fuck you have," Daley said, jumping to her feet. She practically pushed me to the door. "You're a good detective, so someone reckons. Stick with that."

And the door slammed in my face.

I caught up with Jay a few strides further along the corridor. He scoffed at me, unimpressed by my sniggering.

"Daley loves you then, huh?"

"Well, maybe I misremembered that part," I said, smiling to myself. "I loved winding her up though."

* * *

When Jay and I returned to the office, DCI Chase had disappeared. I quickly took my place at my desk before he returned and wanted the space.

"Where's he gone?" Jay asked.

Chris gave a shrug. "Said something about keeping head office up to date. I assume he's speaking with the She-Hulk."

I had an email waiting for me on the computer, from the records office.

"That's strange," I remarked as I read it.

Jay raised his head in curiosity. "What is?"

"Well, Mags Bowen said her mother was dead, but the records office don't have a death certificate on file for Mary King. Only a birth certificate and the marriage certificate."

"Death certificates can get lost," he said.

"It's not just lost, it's non-existent," I replied. "Isn't that strange?"

Jay shrugged back, losing interest fast. I looked at Chris, hoping he would back me up, but as usual, no such luck.

"It's not unusual," he replied gruffly, before shutting his mouth as the clinking sound of footsteps climbing up the stairs reached our office.

For a fraction of a second, all three of us held our breath, expecting Chase to burst back into the room. But we were wrong.

There was a light knock on the door and PC Maddie Greene let herself in. She looked frozen, her teeth chattering and her nose rosy-red from too much time outside. This was despite her wearing every piece of police uniform possible to combat the cold. She smiled as the heat of the office hit her, blasting out from the radiator by Chris's desk.

"Oh good, you're all here." She slipped into the room, holding the door closed. "How are you getting on with the spy?"

"Spy?" I asked.

Maddie nodded enthusiastically. "Of course. Detective Chief Inspector Chase."

"How do you know?" I frowned.

Maddie tapped the side of her red nose. "Everyone knows by now. We've all heard about this super-secret case Aaron isn't allowed to oversee. The bosses have the perfect opportunity to put a spy in our midst and report back on the goings-on around here. So, what's he like?"

"Chase? He's..." Jay replied. He looked over to me, as though I had a better grasp of the English language.

"Odd," I finished. "Seems keen to get to work, though. I suppose that's a good thing."

Jay shuffled in his seat, growing excited. "You have perfect timing as always, Maddie. We could use your superpower."

"My superpower?"

"The gossip queen. Nothing happens around this station that you don't know about. Think you can extend that to Norwich and find out the gossip on Chase? What he's really doing here. What exactly is he spying on?"

A ripple of amusement ran over Maddie's face, growing steadily until she was laughing outright, a sound rarely heard. She bit her lip to stop herself, earning a glare from Chris for her outburst.

"You guys are a step behind the rest of us," she said, revelling in our confusion. "Aaron has already asked me to look into him. Word on the street is that Chase was sent here to check on your progress with the Ali Burgess case for the chief constable and perhaps dig up some other dirt."

"Stop this spying nonsense," snapped Chris. "The man's a detective; he's here for the investigation. He's not here to catch us out."

"Not you, maybe," said Maddie and her gaze fell on me. "Face it, we all know Price suspects something is going on over here with Aaron and Anna. And he sent Chase over in the hope that one of us might let our guard down."

"I'm with Maddie on this one," said Jay, "the timing is just too good. It was the perfect opportunity to get some dirt on us that he can use in the future."

"For Christ's sake, we're talking about the chief constable of the police force, not a Russian KGB agent," Chris replied, his tone sharp enough to end the conversation there and then. "You're all looking too much into this. Chase is here to lead on a difficult job and it's in our best interests to work with him, not against him. The sooner we do that and close this one, the sooner we can get him out of here and back to Norwich. Understood?"

Although their faces fell, Maddie and Jay both nodded, crestfallen that their scheming was put to an end so quickly, but neither of them could deny that Chris was right. If we just worked with Chase rather than against him, we'd get the answers we wanted and get rid of him faster.

Chris fixed his stern gaze on me and I shrank back, feeling the pressure on top of my shoulders. I nodded too, if only to get his eyes off me.

Chapter Ten

I miss you.

Nope. Too sappy.

How are you?

No, too nonchalant.

I was still agonising over the best way to phrase a text to Aaron when I set off for work the next morning. I hadn't spoken to him since the beginning of the case and now I was growing worried about his silence. He was facing a difficult time but also one that those closest to him weren't allowed to discuss.

Dawn hadn't yet broken over the vast Norfolk sky, leaving the station in a misty shadow. A sharp frost covered every surface yet again, making the roads gleam and the leafless trees sparkle. I was glad to get inside, where the heating was on and the scent of strong coffee shocked me awake. I was even more glad to find that I was the first one to arrive to the office. This meant I had a few minutes spare.

I decided to head down the corridor, and let myself into the large office at the end of the hall.

"Morning."

Aaron's face lit up briefly when he saw me. I closed the office door behind me, keeping out the rest of the station. For a short while, it could be just us.

"How are you?" I winced to myself the moment the words left my mouth. Even if there was some perfect combination of words to say to someone in his situation, nothing could be said that would make any of this better.

"Fine," he answered curtly. An obvious lie.

I waited, hoping for more. Nothing came.

"So, will you be coming over tonight?" I asked. It came out a little more suggestively than I had intended but that wasn't necessarily a bad thing.

Aaron stood up, straightening his suit jacket as though he was about to leave, but I was by the door. Exit blocked, he grimaced.

"No. I have work to do. In fact, I'm swamped trying to sort out these arrangements with the royal estate, and–"

"You're avoiding me."

"I'm not," he said, visibly hurt by the accusation, but he dropped his gaze.

"Yeah, you are," I replied. "It's okay. I understand. With DCI Chase here, it makes sense we don't see each other."

"It's not that, it's not that I don't want to see you."

"Then what is it?"

I waited as Aaron contemplated the answer. In three strides he was in front of me, glancing at the door behind me and the quiet corridor beyond. We were still alone but it wouldn't stay that way for long.

"I'm not avoiding you. But, I guess, I have been avoiding having this conversation with you," he said.

"What about?" I asked. My stomach dropped as I caught a glimpse of his nervousness, just peeking out.

He opened his mouth but no words came. A heavy pressure descended over us. I reached out for the door handle behind me, hoping that holding onto something would ground me for whatever was about to come. There was something important, something unnerving, that he needed to tell me.

"I've just been trying to work out the best way to say this without sounding like a selfish prick," Aaron said, babbling now that the words were finally there, "but I want some time to myself. This stuff with the cold case has brought up a lot of memories. I've always dealt with things on my own and although I'm grateful to know that you're there for me, Anna, I really am, I just…"

As the words died out, I released my grip from the office door and lunged forward to him. I wrapped my arms around his neck and kissed him. He wasn't expecting it and staggered back but caught me quick enough for us to stay upright. After a moment, he kissed me back with just as much longing, and after another moment, we broke apart.

"You can't do that here," he stuttered, regaining his composure.

"There's no one around," I said, but I put some distance between us. "I understand. I will give you all the space you need. Just don't expect me to pass up an opportunity to steal a kiss."

"You're playing with fire, Anna," Aaron warned, although the smile left behind by the kiss still lingered on his lips.

I gave an innocent shrug as I opened the office door. "You know me, always attracting trouble."

However, as I watched him, Aaron's face fell.

"I mean it, Anna. This... This will take time."

I paused at the threshold. Beyond was work; the usual bustle of the station, the burden of the investigation, long hours, sleepless nights. We usually got through it all together, as a team. This time would be different.

I gave him a resolute nod as left the office.

* * *

Although he was the last one to make it to the office, DCI Chase entered with the energy of a rock star taking centre stage. He even caught the edge of the stack of paperwork on Chris's desk and sent the top few sheets flying into the air. They scattered across the floor.

Chris waited a beat to see if Chase had realised what he'd done, before muttering "Twat" under his breath and bending down to pick them up.

"Morning!" Chase declared as he settled into the extra seat in between my desk and Jay's and pulled out his laptop. "This is what I like to see. Nose to the grindstone first thing. What have we got?"

Jay bit the bullet and went first. "King's financial records have been sent over. It'll take me a while to go over them, but he didn't have millions squirreled away."

"Medical records are here too," I said. "Same story though. He wasn't a healthy man; it'll probably be easier to list what ailments he didn't have."

"What are the highlights?" Chase asked.

I scanned the record. "Well, King had a pacemaker fitted about eight years ago. It looks like most appointments were annual reviews except for the neurology clinic. He was having lots of appointments with them in the last two months before his death."

"What for?" Chris asked, interest piqued.

"Decline in fine motor skills and memory loss," I read out.

"None of those things are going to help answer any questions about Clara Burns," replied Chase. He clicked his fingers, as though a brilliant idea had struck him out of the blue. "DI Daley. He's free today, isn't he? Let's get over and visit him."

He propelled himself from his seat and was striding for the door before any of us could blink. We only moved as we heard him call "McArthur, come on!" as he left the office.

I scrambled to put my coat on and grabbed the address Inspector Daley had given me the day before.

Chase insisted on driving again, so I directed him up the A149 coast road towards the large village of Dersingham. It lay just north of the Sandringham Estate. Most roads in Dersingham had a royal theme to them; Balmoral Close, Mountbatten Road. The nondescript care home where Larry Daley lived was down a quiet cul-de-sac whose name made Chase snort a laugh.

"Duck Decoy Close," he said as he pulled the car to a stop and turned off the engine. I couldn't deny his luxurious vehicle had made that morning's icy ride look easy.

Before getting out of the car, Chase pulled his phone from his pocket and glanced at the screen.

"Waiting for something?" I asked him. He hastily put it away again.

"Yeah, got a hot date tonight," he replied with a waggle of his eyebrows. "I'm joking, of course. Don't tell my wife. No, I made a complaint to the hotel this morning. The heating in my room stopped working."

"Hotel?" I asked before I could stop myself. If Chase was embarrassed by this, he didn't let on. He just unbuckled his seat belt and removed the keys from the ignition.

"I know, I shouldn't expect the Ritz on police expenses," he said. "But I can't stay at home and getting a hotel over here just seemed easier if I was going to be working this way."

And he got out of the car, before there was a gap in the conversation for me to ask any more.

Just like the Hythe household, the heating inside Maple Court House was working on overdrive to combat the frosty weather outside. The swathe of hot air hit us, making my eyes water and Chase's fluffy hair sag. After seeking direction from an irritable young woman in a green tabard, who didn't look old enough to have left school let alone work there, we found our way to the residents' lounge.

An elderly man was sitting at a table in the corner of the room, with a chessboard set up before him. His heavy gaze was looking out of the window, as if mesmerised by the whiteness outside. He gave a slow blink and a tut as Chase took the seat opposite him.

"Larry Daley?" the DCI asked.

There were no other chairs apart from saggy-looking recliners in the room, so I remained standing. The old man was the only one around; through a set of scuffed double doors, a gentle commotion floated through, of muffled talking and cutlery scraping on plates.

The man gave a curt nod. His eyes flittered over Chase, then over me, full of suspicion. I gave him a small smile and pulled my warrant card from my back pocket. DI Daley relaxed at the sight of it.

"I don't recognise you two," he said, but he didn't wait for an answer. "Oh, I guess I wouldn't, would I? I probably retired before you were even born."

His skin was mottled and drooping, as if hanging off his face. He gave a grimace. Or maybe it was a smile. It was hard to tell.

"Detective Chief Inspector Matthew Chase," said Chase with a gesture. "And this is DC McArthur."

"Do you have time to talk?" I asked.

"I suppose," replied the old man. "I'm only waiting for breakfast to finish up so I can give Myrtle a game of chess. She's got her grandkids visiting later, so she'll want to finish quick. And that's when she makes mistakes, you see. I might finally get a game go in my favour."

"Well, we shouldn't be long. We're looking into the disappearance of Clara Burns," I said.

"Mmm, I heard," said Daley. "Matilda told me something had happened over at Pepperwell Farm. A body recovered from the water, wasn't it?"

"Do you remember Barney King?" I asked.

Daley nodded, the movement slow, as though his joints were a grinding machine about to seize up.

"Of course I do. Never had a stronger gut feeling than I did when I met him. I always knew he'd played a part in that poor woman's disappearance. Just wish I could have proved it at the time."

Chase bristled slightly at this. His fingers danced over the white chess pieces in front of him, pausing over a pawn.

"Policeman's nose, eh?" he said. "Did you suspect King from the start? Surely, strange disappearances like this one usually warrant looking into the family. What about the husband? What were your thoughts on him?"

"Well, he wasn't going to be winning any awards for chivalry," replied Daley, "but James Burns cooperated with the investigation at every step. Once we'd established his alibi and spoken with friends and family, we had no reason to suspect him. He was quite a closed book, that man. He didn't give much away."

"Then what convinced you he wasn't involved?" asked Chase. Tentatively, he moved a pawn forward a square.

Daley watched the action, his eyes narrowing as though it was a highly tactical move.

"I know it isn't the done thing to say, but I just never believed it was him," he said. "He drank, yes. They probably argued, like all married couples do. But James

Burns loved his wife and he was broken when she disappeared. I think it took him a long time to accept that she was really gone."

"All right," said Chase. With a nod, he motioned to the board.

Daley gave a slight frown before catching his meaning and after a moment to consider, he moved a black pawn forward two places.

"What can you tell us about the Hythe family then?" Chase continued. Now his hand hovered over the white rook. "Both Barney King and the Burns family rented their cottages from Harry Hythe, isn't that correct?"

"Oh, he was easy to rule out," said Daley. When Chase moved another white piece, Daley moved another black pawn. "He had an alibi for the night. His wife was out of town, staying with her sister, and he was at the Freemasons gathering. Nothing to indicate he'd even been near Clara Burns."

"So, that just left King," said Chase.

Chess pieces continued to move across the board, one at a time. DCI Chase was making moves with confidence and haste. DI Daley was choosing his turns with more care and consideration.

"What did you know about King's family?" I asked Daley.

The old man shrugged, focus on the board. "There wasn't one. I noted that he'd had a wife and child, but they'd left years before. Couldn't find any trace of them. James Burns confirmed he'd never known King to have any family around. It didn't seem pertinent to find them if they weren't involved."

"Did you retrace Clara's last steps?" asked Chase. He moved a bishop with a flourish. "Who was the last person to see her?"

"Well, her husband saw her before he left to go to the pub that night. And her eldest son when she put him to bed. He was only a boy though; we didn't push him too hard. Both the boys were confused about what was going on."

"You remember her sons?" I asked.

Chase glanced at me, only briefly, as if my question had been more than an innocent slip. I wanted Daley to tell me everything he knew about the Burns family, to find out more about Aaron's childhood than he had ever told me, but that wasn't right. This investigation was bound to be intrusive, but I had to balance that with my own curiosity of the man I knew.

Daley nodded and moved a rook. "Yep, of course. Poor mites. I just hope they did all right for themselves."

I opened my mouth, about to alleviate Daley's worry, when Chase jumped a rook sideways with excitement, knocking over several other pieces on the board.

"Check!" he declared.

Daley took a moment to look over the board, squinting at the checkered pattern. Then he sat back in his chair and let out a long, raspy sigh.

"What are your thoughts on the case?" he asked, looking at Chase. "What do you think happened to Clara Burns?"

Chase shrugged with ease, as if he had already lined up an answer. "I don't know yet. It's too early to say. I think Barney King is the key to it all, but I need to figure out how…"

DI Daley looked at me. "And you?"

"Do I think a mother would willingly leave her children? No," I said simply. "Someone did something to make her disappear."

"But, of course, we have nothing to back that up," Chase pointed out. "Only your investigative work and our gut feelings forty years later."

"Ah," said Daley, tapping the side of his nose, "but that's the greatest tool we have. We can find evidence; we can search and interview. But none of that matters if we don't have a gut feeling of where to start. Always trust your gut. The copper who follows his instincts gets the result. Not the one sat on his arse waiting for the answer to fall into his lap."

Chase made a non-committal noise, something akin to agreement.

Daley looked back at the chessboard. He scrutinised the game, as if the pieces were alien to him and the black and white squares were dancing and swaying. He licked his lips and raised a trembling, liver-spotted hand to his forehead.

"Tell me, DCI Chase," he said. Chase bristled upright as Daley motioned to the board. "Have you ever played chess before?"

A broad smile broke out on Chase's face.

"Is it that obvious?"

"That you haven't a bloody clue how to play?" replied Daley. "Yes. It's obvious."

Chapter Eleven

Back on the road again, Chase tapped the steering wheel and hummed a tuneless melody to himself that was completely at odds with the techno song that was coming from the radio. Traffic was crawling along the slippery road, a snaking line of rear lights creeping ahead as vehicles headed up Knights Hill, towards King's Lynn.

Whilst Chase was happy humming his own theme song, I knew one of us would have to break the silence soon.

I thought back on DI Daley. Whilst his body was failing him, he wasn't missing an ounce of his mind. His words about gut feelings resonated with me, but then my whole reputation was based upon the fact that I frequently went with my gut rather than my head.

"What did you think of Daley?" asked Chase, but before I could answer, he jumped in. "Sounds like the type of copper I would've liked to work with. Experienced. Methodical. We'd be wise to listen to him. He had a bad feeling about Barney King forty years ago but he couldn't find the evidence to back that up. Maybe we can now."

"And how are we going to do that?" I asked.

Just as Chase opened his mouth again, my mobile phone rang. The screen told me it was Jay.

"Fancy checking out somewhere since you're out and about?" he asked after we greeted each other.

Chase turned the radio down so he could listen in on the conversation.

"Where?" I asked.

"The self-storage place on the Hardwick Narrows, Lynnstore. Barney King was renting a unit there; the last payment came out of his account just last week. I've spoken to the manager, he's happy to let us have a look in the unit. Furthermore, he said the last time King visited was a week ago. Right before he died."

"We'll stop there on our way back to the office," I replied. I ended the call and looked at Chase. He had stopped humming now and was excitedly drumming his fingers on the steering wheel.

"This sound promising," he said.

"You saw the amount of junk King had in his house," I replied. "Can you imagine what we're going to find in that unit? I don't think it'll be hidden gold."

"Oh, don't be so pessimistic, McArthur," said Chase. He flicked the indicator on the car as we approached the Knights Hill Roundabout. "You'll have to give me directions, though. Where is it?"

"The Hardwick Narrows Industrial Estate. It's off the Hardwick Roundabout."

Chase threw his head back and let out half-hearted groan. "Not that roundabout."

"What's wrong with the roundabout?" I asked. The Hardwick Roundabout was the biggest roundabout in the area, right outside of King's Lynn. It joined the A47 with the A10, A149 and the main thoroughfare into the town.

"It's a crap roundabout," he replied. "No one knows what lane they need to be in. It's like taking your life into your own hands, every time you want to go anywhere. I don't know how you locals put up with it."

"It's not that bad," I said and to my surprise, a small laugh escaped. "Although that is quite a strong opinion for just a roundabout."

"I have plenty of strong opinions about this area."

"Go on then. Let's hear them," I urged.

"Ah well," he said, before taking a big breath as if he was about to launch into a long list. "For a start, the phone signal around here is shit. How do you live like this? I can't even get a signal in my hotel room. Oh, and don't get me started on the tractors on the roads. There are hundreds of them."

I laughed, feeling my lungs contract from the effort to not let loose too much. Laughing at such a time felt wrong; I shouldn't be laughing in the middle of a case. Not a case like this one, with trauma so close to home. But there was something about Chase's delivery that told me that as much as he tried to be serious and authoritative, this was more natural to him.

I regained my faculties as fast as I could and looked out of the window. If I avoided Chase's expression, I wouldn't crack up again.

"I'm a city boy," he continued. "I was raised in East London, although I managed to avoid the worst of the accent. Moved this way to be with my wife. Even Norwich is a bit too tame for me."

"It's not that bad around here," I replied.

"All right, then where are you from?" he asked. "That's not much of a Norfolk accent you have."

"A bit of everywhere," I said. "My dad was in the RAF, so we moved every few years to different corners of the country."

Chase made a noise, halfway between an expression of interest and one of disbelief that I had actually answered him. I was beginning to let my guard down with him, although I couldn't yet be sure if that was a good thing or a bad thing.

Twenty minutes later, after navigating traffic, poorly thawed roads and Chase's irrational dislike of the Hardwick Roundabout, we arrived at the self-storage site. A bright-yellow sign larger than a single-deck bus sat at the apex of the metal unit, like a beacon to the surrounding area, beckoning people in. A group of seagulls sat on top of it, huddling together. They gave a squawk and watched warily as Chase and I left the car.

At the large bay doors, a keypad and doorbell prevented us from entering, but once we neared, something buzzed and the door began to open. It rolled up to reveal a long tunnel lined with metal doors either side. Poor lighting prevented us from seeing to the very end.

A portly man with a shaved head appeared on the other side of the bay door. He gave Chase a confused look, then me, before it finally occurred to him who we were.

"Police?" he asked.

We nodded and presented our warrant cards.

"I believe you spoke to a colleague of mine about a unit here that was rented by Barney King," I replied. "What's your name?"

"Rob," he replied and with a jerk of his head, the man started off down the long tunnel, leaving us to follow.

"Your colleague said King was dead," Rob called over his shoulder. He shoved his hands deep into the pockets of his worn black fleece. Inside the building was just as cold as outside was.

"He is," replied Chase, using his long legs to stride ahead until he was level with the bloke. "What can you tell us about him? Did you see him much?"

"Not much," Rob said back gruffly. "He's rented a unit here longer than I've worked here, probably since this place was built. Visits once in a blue moon but always pays on time. Well, he does now. There was a point where he got a bit forgetful, so I persuaded him to set up one of those, you know, direct payments."

"Direct debits?" I offered.

Rob nodded. "That's it. Never had a problem since."

He stopped outside one of the metal doors, secured by a heavy-looking padlock. The number *42* was stencilled on the door frame. The man produced a ring of keys from his pocket and after minute of searching, he unlocked the padlock.

He hesitated before opening the door.

"Shouldn't you have like a, you know, warrant or something? Paperwork?"

"Oh yes," said Chase. He rocked back on his heels with impatience. "We should. And we don't. But we can go back to the station and get one sorted. Just to warn you though, it's quite a long process. Lots of forms for you to fill out. Then you'll have to file it all, maybe get in touch with the company's solicitors, properly make sure you've crossed all the *t*'s and dotted all the *i*'s. You know, do things the proper way, because when investigating a suspicious death, we have to do things properly."

Rob blinked at Chase, and for a moment I wasn't sure if all the DCI's ramblings had sunk in. Just as a question formed on Rob's lips, Chase carried on.

"Or, of course, you could let me have a quick peek inside whilst you chat with my colleague here, and we'll be out of your hair in no time." Chase's gaze flickered to the man's bald head. "Figuratively speaking."

Rob weighed up these options for a moment, giving Chase a wary look, before letting go of the padlock and stepping away from the door.

"Knock yourself out," he said, although his cautious expression didn't ease as he watched Chase undo the door.

Inside was nothing more than a dark, lumpy mass until with a click, a light came on. Chase pulled a pair of gloves from his pocket and stood in the doorway, taking a studious look at the contents of the unit.

It was just as I expected. Much like King's house, the unit was rammed floor to ceiling with junk. Boxes and boxes of it.

Leaving Chase to it, I pulled my notebook out and flexed my cold hands, ready to write.

"You told my colleague that King visited here last week. What day was that?" I asked Rob.

"Monday," he replied. "About midday. He was on his way to the hospital for an appointment, he said. I helped put a few boxes away from his car."

"What was in the boxes?" Chase asked. He hadn't yet ventured into the unit, but was peering in a plastic crate full of old tools.

"It's those ones, down there," said Rob, pointing to a pile of old milk crates. Boxes of old rags and newspapers by the looks of it.

"How did he seem?" I asked. I tried to phrase the question as innocently as possible.

"All right," Rob said with a shrug. "As all right as he ever is. Moaned about the cold. Said he was going to stop and get some more de-icer for the car before the frost hit. Oh, and some kindling."

That piqued my interest. "Did he? Did he say anything else?"

"Nah. Not really."

"McArthur!" Chase snapped, but when I turned to look, he was nowhere to be seen. His voice came from within the piles of crap in the unit. "Get in here and see this!"

I gave Rob an apologetic look. "Thanks. If we need any more, we'll find you."

With a grumble and a shuffle, Rob wandered off, back to where presumably his office was near the main entrance. I pulled on a pair of gloves too, and with a sigh at the mountain in front of me, clambered my way into the overstuffed unit.

Chase was near the back, somehow over a solid-pine side table that had stacks of old farming magazines balanced on top. Rather than vault the furniture, I peered over the top, craning to get a look.

"What is it?" I asked.

Chase stood up straight. His height made it easy for him to see me over the junk. "Look."

He held up a pale, yellow dress. Small. Child's size, in fact.

"There's a whole wardrobe back here, full of girls' clothes. And another full of ladies'."

"Maybe his wife's and daughter's," I said.

An unsettled frown fell over DCI Chase's face and he scowled at the frilly dress as if it was to blame.

"From the way Mags Bowen told the story, it sounded like her mother planned to leave King. Why wouldn't she pack their clothing? And why would King keep it all these years?" He discarded the dress. "We better get forensics in here, just for a look. Who knows what else he kept in here?"

I was already pulling my phone out of my pocket, ready to call in.

"Rob said something interesting," I said to Chase before dialling the office. "He said he spoke to King about the cold weather coming. Barney told him he was going to get de-icer for the car and kindling for the fire. He was preparing."

Chase's scowl deepened. "Why would he get those if he was planning on killing himself the next day?"

The words came from his mouth before his mind caught up, but a fraction of a second later, the frown was gone.

"Unless he wasn't planning on it!" he said.

Chapter Twelve

"We're letting this cold case distract us!" Chase declared. An irritable mood had overcome him, either through frustration or perhaps hunger. By the time the SOCO team arrived to comb over Barney King's storage unit, lunch had been and gone.

"We don't know exactly how the old man ended up in the water, but we can still retrace his last known steps," said Chase.

We were back in the car, trying to warm up with the heater on full, with Chris and Jay on speakerphone through the dashboard.

"Well, we now know he visited the storage unit the day before he died," I said, in between blowing on my fingers.

"And then he went to a hospital appointment. So far, there's no indications that anyone saw King on the day he died, or that he even left his house apart from, you know, to drown. You minions in the warm office, find out which hospital department he visited," said Chase.

Although it was muffled by the blasting of the heater from the car and the shuffle of papers from the other end of the line, I was certain I heard Chris mutter "Twat" under his breath again.

"Got it," said Jay. "He had an appointment at the neurology clinic. Dr Rasketh."

Chase revved the car engine. "McArthur and I will head there now. You two, head out and conduct some local enquiries. Maybe some people from the village remember seeing King before he died."

If Chase had been hoping for some sort of affirmation or acknowledgement of his order, then he was disappointed as the call back to the office cut without even a goodbye.

With a huff, he put the car into gear and I directed him around the edge of town to the local hospital. It didn't surprise me to see a host of ambulances parked outside the entrance to the A & E department. This time of year, the hospital was always overrun and the icy weather wouldn't be helping that.

A dry blast of hot air hit us as we crossed the threshold of the main entrance. There was a directory on the wall in front of us, with different colours denoting the different areas of the hospital. It wasn't a huge place, but it was the only main hospital for nearly forty miles so it needed to cater for all ailments.

I led the way to neurology, weaving in between exasperated-looking nurses with their squeaky rubber shoes and porters wheeling patients along in beds or wheelchairs.

Chase fell into step beside me. He walked in silence but his gaze lingered warily on the many wooden and metal posts that lined the corridors. They stood floor to ceiling, heading up through gaps in the suspended ceiling tiles and into the blackness beyond.

"Props," I said to him, with a grimace. "The ceiling is falling down. The building is full of them."

Chase was taken aback by this. "You're kidding."

I shook my head. "It's been all over the local news. The hospital was only built to last thirty years. It's well past that now."

"See. Nothing good about living round here," he replied with a tut.

The waiting room of the neurology department was empty when we arrived, only one receptionist sat behind the counter. The young woman looked bored until she spotted me over the top of the tall counter.

"Hi," she said, with a note of confusion. "Can I help? We haven't got any clinics today so if you're here for an appointment, you're in the wrong place."

Her gaze drifted to Chase as he appeared over my shoulders.

"We're looking for Dr Rasketh," I said. "We're with the police. We need to ask him some questions about a patient he's seen recently."

"Oh dear," she replied. "I afraid you can't see him."

Chase took a step forwards, now brushing my shoulder and he leaned over the counter.

"Why not?" he demanded.

"He's gone," the woman babbled. "I mean, not like, gone gone. But gone. Out of the country. He's on holiday."

"Where?" asked Chase.

"I don't know," the receptionist replied with a squeak.

"Then when is he back?" I asked, which seemed a much more pertinent question.

"I don't know," said the receptionist again. "I'm not allowed to speak to the consultants. All I know is that he hasn't got a clinic for the next three weeks."

Without another word, Chase spun on his heels and set off again, heading back the way we'd come. I hurriedly thanked the receptionist and left her a contact card to pass on to Dr Rasketh.

I caught up with Chase back at the directory board. He scanned the departments, but before I could ask him what he was looking for, he strode off again.

I struggled to keep up with his determined strides until we were deep in the bowels of the hospital. The foot traffic was less here, but the lack of people was replaced by more and more wooden props. Chase finally stopped outside a door labelled *Security Office*.

"What are we doing here?" I asked.

Chase pounded on the door with a hefty knock. A policeman's knock. One that told the occupant inside we were here on business.

"If we can't speak to the doctor, we'll have to retrace Barney King's last steps another way," he said, before fixing a wide grin on his face.

A well-built young man opened the door to the office. As tall as Chase, they were eye to eye and the lad flinched a little at the DCI's unnervingly friendly smile. His hair was shaved short but a patchy beard around his chin gave away his young years.

"Yeah?"

Chase held up his warrant card to the lad's face. "Police. Need your help with something. Mind if we come in?"

As soon as we stepped into the security office, I immediately regretted it. The room was fully internal, with no windows to allow natural light or fresh air. Inside was a bank of screens displaying CCTV views of various areas of the hospital. Most prominent were the main entrance and foyer, the A & E waiting area and the outside bay where the ambulances parked.

"Fourth time I've had the police here this month," said the lad as he settled back down into his chair. His only job was to stare at the screens all day long and I got the impression he rarely left otherwise. That was clear from the masses of snack wrappers littering the desk and the stench of sweat and pickled-onion crisps that was unable to escape the room.

He carried on when Chase gave him a quizzical look. "It's usually the Saturday night drunks they want to see," he explained. "They want the tape evidence of the dregs causing a scene or kicking off at the nurses. So, what can I do for you?"

"Something a bit different," said Chase. "We're looking for someone in particular. He had an appointment at the neurology department last Monday at midday."

The lad – Bradley, by the name on the crest of his white short-sleeved shirt – gave an exaggerated sniff.

"Well, I hope you know what he looks like, because hundreds of people visit here every day."

"We do," said Chase. "Can you find it?"

"Gimme a minute," said Bradley, turning to his screens and a confusing-looking console on the desk with several keyboards. "You'll have to sign the log though. Over there. Make sure you leave your badge numbers."

Chase and I found a red lever arch folder open on top of a filing cabinet in the corner of the room. We signed our details down, Chase filling in the box labelled *REASON* with a scrawled answer of *police business*.

"What will this achieve?" I asked him in a whisper. "You want to watch Barney King arriving and leaving his appointment?"

"Yes," he said back. "What better way to get a measure of the man than to see what he was like when he thought no one was watching him? How he held himself, where he went. If he spoke to anyone."

"But what will that tell us?"

Chase folded his arms and glanced at Bradley. "If you were feeling low or were planning to kill yourself, would you bother going to a medical appointment? No. Would you bother putting some junk in your storage locker or stocking up for the cold weather? No. None of King's actions the day before he died lend towards a man who was grappling with a guilty conscience. If suicide doesn't fit, then we need to look into the murder angle. So, what was it that caused someone to kill him and make it look like a suicide? If we retrace his last steps, we might just find out."

Chase was grasping at straws. We couldn't conclusively say either way whether Barney King was murdered or not; there was no forensic evidence of anyone else in his house, no results on his handwritten suicide note. Following this line of thinking could well turn out to be a total waste of time. But we had nothing else to go on.

"Here you go," announced Bradley, motioning to one of the screens. "Neurology waiting room, midday last Monday."

It didn't take us long to spot Barney King. He sat in a high-backed chair along the back wall of the waiting room. He, and every other person in the room, had done the usual thing of leaving an empty seat between them. He spoke to no one, looked at no one and didn't acknowledge anyone until the receptionist called his name and he rose on unsteady legs.

"Go backwards," said Chase. "Let's see him arrive."

Flicking a switch, Bradley made the footage run backwards at double speed. We watched as Barney King sat down, then got up again, shuffled over to the receptionist and finally walked backwards out of the double doors to the room. With some clicks and switches, Bradley was able to swap cameras, following King's reversed course as he limped his way through the hospital corridors, caught the lift, back through the main concourse and across the car park, where we could just see his scratched old Morris Minor parked up in a disabled spot.

"Want me to go forwards again?" Bradley asked.

"Yeah, let's see the rest of his visit," said Chase.

"There's no cameras in the consulting rooms," said the security officer. "But I can find him again when he leaves."

It took a few minutes before Bradley was able to pick up King again, approximately twenty minutes after being called in for his appointment. He left the waiting room, taking the same route back downstairs via the lifts. However, he paused just before the lift bay, coming face to face with a couple coming from another area of the hospital. The couple stopped too, frozen in place with their backs to the camera. Words were exchanged, King looking suspicious. His expression wasn't clear but his body language gave him away. After a brief, tense exchange, King caught the lift to the ground floor and the couple walked away, heading for the stairs.

"Who were they?" asked Chase. He tapped the screen, making it blur with a mirage of colours where pressure was applied.

"Well, I dunno," replied Bradley.

"Can we have a copy of that footage?"

"I'll have to email it."

"Do it," said Chase, before reciting out the email address to our shared team inbox. "Oh, and trace them back. Which department did they come from?"

"Obstetrics," Bradley replied instantly. "That's the main department down that corridor. Also, the newborn ward, NICU and Central Delivery Suite."

"Thanks." Chase clapped Bradley on the shoulder, making the muscular lad flinch in surprise at the unexpected gesture, before he strode for the door with a new vigour. "Come on, McArthur. We've got a couple to track down."

"Hang on," I said.

I didn't expect my words to work now that Chase was onto something and for a moment they didn't. The door to the security office closed behind him and it took almost a full minute before he realised that I wasn't following and returned. He opened the office door and gave me a withering look.

"What?" the DCI demanded.

"We don't need to track them down," I said and I pointed to the screen. "I know who they are."

Chapter Thirteen

The frost crunched beneath my feet as I strode from the car to the front of Pepperwell Farm House, Chase already a few steps ahead. He hammered on the farmhouse door, ignoring the bell, and a few seconds later, a confused-looking Garrett Hythe answered.

"Hello," he said with a nervous glance behind him. "Can I help?

Chase practically shoved his warrant card in the man's face. "DCI Matthew Chase. I'm sure you remember DC McArthur. Mind if we come in?"

"No—"

Whatever Garrett Hythe was about to say was cut off as Chase pushed his way through the door and into the farmhouse, glowing with warmth. Garrett stepped aside to let me in, then hurried to follow Chase. I closed the front door before the December air stole the heat from the house.

"Back so soon? Is this normal for a suicide?" Garrett asked as we made our way to the kitchen.

Chase was bouncing on the balls of his feet, his fluffy hair gracing the beams of the ceiling. Boundless energy had driven him since leaving the hospital and apart from a brief moan about driving his beloved car down the potholed track to Pepperwell Farm, he hadn't stop theorising.

"Some new evidence has come to light," said Chase. "Is your wife at home? It'd be great to talk to her as well."

"No, I'm afraid she's at work," said Garrett. "It's her long day too, so if you want to speak to her, you'll have to call her. She might be holding surgery though, so she might not be available until later. What sort of new evidence?"

"Evidence that suggests Mr King may not have killed himself."

In the warm kitchen, the smell of burning wood was thick as the fire crackled away in the hearth. Harry sat in his usual spot, gazing at the flames. Luisa was there too, her back to us as she fussed around by the sink, the sleeves of her oversized woolly jumper falling down her elbows. It took her a long time to turn around and face the intrusion and when she did, I could see her mouth was set in an unimpressed frown.

"Is this not a good time?" Chase asked, forgoing any tactfulness as he read the room.

Garrett shook his head and waved at Chase and me to take a seat at the table.

"No, no. Do you think someone killed him?" he asked, his voice rising higher until it sounded like the question came from a mouse. He glanced over at Luisa, but her steely gaze was back on the sink, avoiding Garrett.

"We're certainly considering the possibility," said Chase. "But if, theoretically, this wasn't a straightforward case of suicide, do you know of anyone who might have wanted Barney King dead or wished him harm?"

"No," said Garrett with a squeak. "Of course not. He was a crotchety old man but I don't know anyone who wished him dead."

"And what about you?" Chase asked, leaning over to get a better view of the elderly man in the pile of blankets.

Harry groaned back, waving his trembling hand in the air. Chase took this as a no.

"And you?" he asked, turning in his seat to face Luisa at the sink.

She froze on the spot, as if she expected herself to be invisible to us, and slowly turned around. "No."

"No, you don't know who killed him, or no, you didn't wish him dead?" asked Chase.

Luisa replied with a cold glare back.

"Look," Garrett cut in. "Barney wasn't everyone's cup of tea, but he was harmless. He was a product of his generation. He might have said things that were a little politically incorrect, but he meant no harm by it. No one would hurt him for it."

"What does that mean?" Chase spun back in his seat like a weathervane in the breeze.

"I mean he…"

"He called me 'the help'," said Luisa.

"Luisa," Garrett hissed at her. He hastened to smooth the tension that rose in the air, babbling noises until he was able to string the sounds into a sentence. "It was just a joke, I'm sure he didn't mean it. King said things like that all the time."

From Luisa's glowing red face, she didn't believe it was just a joke.

"He's dead," she said to Garrett, ignoring me and Chase. "It doesn't matter what we say now, because he's gone."

"You shouldn't speak ill of the dead." Garrett's face was as almost as rosy as Luisa's, and I got the distinct feeling that we had interrupted an argument that was already taking place. Luisa was holding something back, something on the tip of her tongue. Over from the corner, Harry snorted at Garrett's words; although it could have been a snore, it was hard to tell.

When the pair fell quiet, still glowering at each other, Chase caught my eye. He looked intrigued but unsure of which one of them to focus on.

"You know," he said, with the smallest hint of a conceited smile, "that rule about speaking ill of the dead doesn't apply to police stations. Perhaps you'll feel more comfortable to speak freely there."

"Speak about what?" Garrett gave a nervous laugh. "We never hurt Barney, why would we want to?"

Chase continued. "Don't worry, we'll call your wife and let her know that you're at the station. Someone will need to look after Harry after all."

Garrett glanced over at his father. He licked his lips, slowing opening his mouth before closing it again.

"I don't understand," he said, stuttering through the words. "What new evidence are you talking about? No one here wanted to hurt Barney, none of us did anything to him."

Chase leaned across the dining table, pointing his index finger into the wood, just in front of Garrett.

"We know you saw King at the hospital last week. As you were leaving the ultrasound suite with a woman who wasn't your wife."

Garrett froze, unable to even blink. Luisa sank down into the chair next to him. She glared his way, before turning to Chase and I and taking a deep, shuddering breath.

"We will tell you the truth," she said.

"Luisa!" Garrett implored, although he hadn't moved an inch from his petrified state.

I took a seat on the other side of Luisa, taking her attention away from Garrett and Chase. She softened as she looked at me, her defences dropping away.

"I can't be dragged to the police station. Paula wouldn't pay me," she said with an ironic snort of laughter.

"Then tell us the truth," I replied kindly. "Did you and Garrett see Barney King at the hospital the day before he died?"

"Yes," she said in a whisper. "But you don't understand. Barney King was *asqueroso*... how do you say, a disgusting man. I didn't like to talk to him; his eyes wandered, his hands..." She demonstrated with a groping motion, a sneer on her face. "You get my point?"

I nodded back; that sort of behaviour was universal, regardless of the language spoken. Every woman I knew had experienced unwanted attention like that.

"And when I told him to stop, then he would call me things, like 'the help', 'foreigner'. Treated me like I was an idiot, even though I am a qualified nurse and speak better English than he did!"

"Does this have anything to do with his death?" Chase asked. "What happened at the hospital?"

Luisa twisted her hands together on the tabletop and lowered her head. "Nothing happened. He just... saw us." She gestured with one finger to Garrett. "We had been for a scan. The first scan of the baby."

As she spoke, Garrett Hythe had turned as red as the berries on the holly tree in his garden.

"You're having an affair?" asked Chase, his bluntness making both Luisa and Garrett wince.

They avoided looking at each other, and at us, instead both shivering as though the stifling heat from the fire wasn't reaching them.

Taking their reaction as a yes, Chase continued. "What did Barney say?"

"His usual disgusting words," Luisa replied, wrinkling her nose. "He said Garrett was finally acting like the lord of the manor, sleeping with the servants. He said he would tell Paula."

"And did he?"

"No," Garrett replied quickly. He looked at Luisa, as though trying to reassure her. "He didn't tell her; she still doesn't know. I figured he wanted something in return for his silence, but he just said that we'd owe him when the time was right."

Luisa dropped her head and her long black hair fell over her face. Guilt washed over Garrett but he made no move to comfort her, too spineless to even do that in front of other people. He shrank back into his seat and tried his best not to look at Chase or me.

Luisa's hands were balled together in a frantic knot, turning her knuckles white. She looked up, tears welling in her eyes. She tried to smile at me but couldn't.

"It's still early," she said, "but he promised to leave Paula before it got too noticeable. Then Barney found out and Garrett wanted to wait, to let it blow over. And now Barney's dead and Garrett still wants to wait… I think he's scared. He's a coward."

Despite speaking about him as though he wasn't in the room, Garrett only clamped his mouth shut, no reply forthcoming.

"So, Barney didn't say any more about the baby?" I asked Luisa, catching her gaze. "Just that you would owe him in the future?"

She nodded. "That was all he said."

"And that was the last time you saw him?"

A tear rolled down her cheek. "Yes."

"And did either of you decide it was best to get him out the way before he told your secret?" Chase cut in, every inch as tactless as I was kind. "Drown him in the lake before he blabbed?"

"No!" Garrett said.

Luisa shook her head furiously. "No, of course not."

Chase tutted to himself and started to fidget in his seat. I could tell what he was thinking; that there was still a little bit more to this story, but we weren't going to get to it with Garrett and Luisa feeling so vulnerable and attacked. There was every possibility that King had told Garrett and Luisa's secret. It was possible Paula Hythe knew of her husband's infidelity. This was a mess best unpacked at the police station rather than in a cosy country kitchen.

"I'm afraid, in light of this, we're going to need you both to come down to the station and give an official statement," said Chase as he rose to his feet. He fished his phone from his pocket, dialling a number and putting it to his ear. "Now, in case that wasn't clear."

"But what about Harry?" Luisa asked. The bundle of blankets hadn't stirred in a while, presumably he was asleep.

"Don't worry, I'll get some colleagues to assist us. Detective Constable McArthur will stay with Harry until you get back."

As Garrett and Luisa steadily rose to their feet and set off to find their coats and shoes in a moody silence, Chase leaned in closer to me, whispering right into my ear.

"Will be a good chance to have a snoop around the house, don't you think? Find some handwriting samples."

"Without a search warrant?" I whispered back and I felt air rush by my ear as Chase snorted.

"I don't think old Harry boy will be telling on you."

Chapter Fourteen

The peppy voice of the local radio DJ floated through from the kitchen of the Hythe household, echoing off the flagstone floors down the hallway to the study. I'd felt sorry for Harry, sat there alone with nothing but the fire to keep him company, so I'd switched on the small DAB radio which sat on the windowsill. The traffic report came on; the ice had caused a few delays and accidents, but things were picking up now.

In the tidy, underutilised study at the front of the farmhouse, I found several notebooks full of accounts which I guessed were from the quarry, most likely written by Garrett. The handwriting was messy, but not scrawling enough to match up to the writing on the suicide note. I also found a birthday card on the desk, addressed *Dear Garrett*, and *with love, Paula*, in a loose cursive script, but again, unlike the suicide note. It was just a generic card with a rainbow cake on the front and a lame birthday greeting inside. There wasn't anything sentimental or loving about it, considering it came from a wife to a husband.

Leaving the study, I made my way upstairs, peeping in on Harry on the way. He was asleep, his chest rising and falling with a great effort. Off the landing there were at least four bedrooms, each with an en suite. In the master, I found more birthday cards lining the windowsill, glints of colour against the grey backdrop outside. One by one I checked inside, until I found one of interest.

Lo mejor está por venir. Luisa x

I couldn't read Spanish so I snapped a photo of it on my phone. I'd find a way to translate it later. I forwarded the handwriting examples over to Jay, to pass along for analysis.

I found one bedroom made up as a guestroom, pristine and perfect. Another housed a large recliner bed, which I guessed was Harry's room, and the last with a flurry of clothing on the floor and a shelf of family photographs. It must have been Luisa's. The photographs revealed plenty of sunny beach scenes, family gatherings, parties. Each looked so joyous that I wondered why Luisa would leave her home. Things were not that warm over here.

Just when I had snooped as much as I dared to without being caught or waking up Harry, my phone rang. It was Jay.

"How's it going?" I asked.

He gave a hefty sigh down the line, his bad mood back again.

"Chase insisted he and Chris could take statements from the Hythe family," he said indignantly, "so I've been relegated back to the office."

"Oh, poor you. So, you didn't get to see the lovely Luisa again?"

"Shut up."

"What's up with you?" I asked. "I've never known you to be this miserable for this long. I mean, you get grumpy but you're usually the positive one compared to Chris."

"You don't have to worry about me," he said, forcing a laugh that was wholly unconvincing. "Nothing that a night of heavy drinking won't fix. You up for drowning your sorrows later after work?"

I considered my options for a moment, but it didn't take long to realise Jay's offer was the best one.

"Sure. I'm up for it. It's that or see my parents."

"What about Aaron?" he asked.

A prickle of heat ran up my neck, flushing my face with self-consciousness.

"He, um… asked for some space. So, I'm up for drinking away my sorrows as much as you are."

"That's the spirit," Jay said with a chuckle, and thankfully, this one sounded a bit more like his usual self. "In the meantime, I've just gotten off the phone with the so-called handwriting expert that the lab contracted. Can you believe handwriting analysis is an actual job? You'd think there would be a computer program that could do that by now."

"I bet they get paid a hell of a lot more than we do," I replied. "What did they say?"

"Well, as frustrating as this is to repeat, he said he couldn't be sure. About King's suicide note, I mean."

I blinked.

"He wasn't sure?"

"Inconclusive," said Jay. "The samples of King's writing contained similarities but not enough to make a judgement. He basically said that given King's age, it's possible he wrote that note. Age causes deterioration of the joints, which causes crappy handwriting. The only useful thing he did say was that he was certain the note wasn't written by anyone from the Hythe household. He took a quick look over the samples you'd sent whilst we were on the phone."

"Well, that doesn't really help," I replied. I wiped my hand over my face and stretched my back, feeling the stress lingering in my shoulders. "It feels like we're going round in circles. We can't be certain of anything in this case."

Jay gave another sigh, deep from in his lungs. "You know what this reminds me of? The Ali Burgess investigation. Not that this is the same, it's completely different, but it feels the same, you know? That no matter what we do, what avenues we explore, we're not getting any closer to the truth."

Despondency curled up inside of me, sitting right in the middle of my chest. I could hear it in Jay's voice too. If we weren't careful, it would set its claws into us and not let go.

"Chin up," I said, more for myself than for Jay. "We've still got every chance of finding out what happened to Barney King and Clara Burns."

I couldn't let this case be the one to haunt me. I would never be able to face Aaron again.

"Eurgh!" Jay shuddered down the line. "Don't you start with the positivity as well. I'm not sure how much peppiness I can take."

* * *

I was eventually rescued from the Hythe household by Maddie, who had been lumbered with another probationer and given the task of ferrying Luisa and Garrett Hythe home again. When we returned to the station, the day had slipped into night, the grey sky gone and replaced with a blanket of nothingness. The street lights didn't penetrate it; the stars didn't pierce through. It was just an ominous cloud of unknown, threatening to smother the land below.

"Pub?" I asked Maddie as we entered the station, about to part ways at the stairs. She would go towards the downstairs office to hand over to the next shift and I needed to go upstairs.

"Always," came her simple reply. And she gave an exhausted wave as she walked away.

When I made it to the Serious Crimes office, I wasn't entirely surprised to find it almost empty. Chris had a healthy habit of knocking off work at a reasonable time whenever he could, to get home to the family. He always took advantage of this when a senior officer was around to man the fort. And with Chris gone, it was likely Jay had already set off for the pub.

Only Chase remained. He was stood behind my desk, striding back and forth, taking only three steps each way before he reached the wall of the office. His phone was held to his ear. A shrill voice screamed down the line.

"I know, I know," he replied. Frustration edged into his voice but he was making sure to keep it under control. "I know what you said, that's why I got a hotel. You said *get out*; I got out!"

The voice on the other end launch into a tirade of insults.

"I did what you wanted, Izzy," Chase hissed back. "You can't blame this on me."

I winced at the noise from the phone. It was relentless. Whoever Chase was speaking to was not happy with him.

"I didn't– Izzy– I didn't steal the car."

And with an abrupt scream from the device, the call ended. Chase paused his pacing, staring at the phone screen in disbelief. When he turned, he saw me by the door. If he was surprised by my presence, he didn't show it, but instead gave me a tight smile and an overexaggerated roll of his eyes.

"Sorry," I said. "I didn't mean to intrude."

"No intrusion," replied Chase, sweeping across the room. "In fact, I've decided we're knocking off for the day. We've covered enough ground. Luisa and Garrett Hythe have given their statements and we don't have anything to hold them on at present, so on we go. Let's get a good rest and come at this with fresh eyes in the morning."

He ushered me back through the door.

"Actually," I said, turning back to him, "I'm off to the pub. Do you fancy coming along?"

Chase's face lit up with amusement. "Well, I am flattered, McArthur, but I'm a married man."

"Not like that," I snapped back. I glanced around, hoping that no one had heard him. I already had enough rumours swirling around about me. "No, I mean, as a team. Kick back after a long day. What do you say?"

"That's the best thing I've ever heard you say, McArthur. I'm in." With a new surge of energy, Chase set off down the stairs. He appeared keen to get away, whether from the case or from the phone call he'd just taken, I couldn't tell. But as always, he walked with purpose, head held high.

I caught up with him at the bottom of the stairs, when he finally paused. "Where is the pub?"

* * *

Chase was staying at a guest house several miles outside of town, along the A10. Whether this was on purpose or it was just the only place in the nearby area that could offer a room on a police-expenses budget, I didn't know. And I didn't want to pry. From the conversation I had overheard in the office, it sounded like there was a lot going on in Chase's personal life and that was not my business.

My car idled in the guest house's car park and I warmed my hands over the heating vent. The weather had taken a nasty turn over the evening. Sheets of icy hale were raining down, almost sideways in the wind. It warped the rear lights of passing cars on the road, making them look like jagged snakes of red winding their way home. It was the type of weather that everyone was warned not to go out in unless necessary, but it didn't take much to convince myself that a trip to the pub was necessary. After all, I had nothing else to do with my evening.

I checked my phone. It had only been that morning when Aaron had asked for space, but part of me still expected something from him. A text, a check in. We rarely went a day without some sort of contact.

The car door opened and Chase landed in the passenger seat, hurriedly shutting out the elements again.

"Thanks for the lift," he said as we set off.

Progress was slow, although the evening traffic had gone, leaving behind only those who were brave enough to risk driving in such conditions.

"I'm surprised you agreed," I admitted. "You made your opinion of my car quite clear."

"It's not just the car," Chase mumbled back and he gripped the handle above the door. "A good driver drives to the road conditions, not the speed limit. Maybe you should try it."

"I can handle a bit of bad weather and a few potholes," I said. "Don't forget, sir, it's a long walk back and you don't know the way."

Chase ignored me, which was probably for the best.

After a few minutes of uneasy silence, I decided to risk addressing the obvious. "I'm sorry for interrupting your phone call in the office."

Chase chuckled to himself as he stared at the road ahead. "I'm sorry to you. You didn't need to hear my marital problems. She's just angry because I've gone away for work and taken all the cutlery in the house with me."

"You've taken all the cutlery?"

"I'm not a complete monster," said Chase, still sniggering. "I left her the knives. I got every bastard spoon in that place, though. Good luck having cereal in the morning, Izzy."

I just couldn't help myself. I laughed too, feeling the twisting in my gut as I relaxed for the first time that day. Chase joined in, giving a genuine cackle that it looked like he sorely needed. We laughed as we travelled through shadowy villages and past darkened fields. The poor visibility was making sure they were hidden from view, only allowing us to see a few feet ahead.

"I didn't steal her car, by the way," said Chase as the laughter died down. "Well, I mean technically, it might be classed as taking without consent, but I drive it more than she does."

"I'm not interested in sticking you for theft," I assured him.

"Good," he said. "And I'm not interested in having you for driving worse than a seventeen-year-old boy in a rusty go-kart."

"Shut up, my driving is fine." But just to please him, I eased off the accelerator.

"This investigation must be so hard for you," said Chase, filling the silence as though he was allergic to it. "You've worked with DCI Burns a long time. It's a small team over here. Everyone must know everyone."

I rolled my shoulders, hoping he wouldn't notice my knuckles grip the steering wheel tighter. "We do. It's an unusual case and it's always harder when there's a personal connection. But I know we can support Aaron through this."

"I like that about here," Chase mused. "It's a small station, a small team. You are close and it shows. Must be great to have that comradery when things get tough."

"Don't you have that with your team over at headquarters?"

He breathed out through his nose. "Not really. Sometimes the senior leadership team oversee us a little too closely. It's a different… atmosphere, shall we say. Can be hard to motivate a team when the brass is breathing down your neck the whole time."

I didn't reply, knowing that Chase wouldn't let the quiet seep in for long, and he soon continued.

"I know you think I've been sent here to spy on you all."

"Huh?"

"Chief Constable Price," he said, with a level of calm that only seemed to exasperate my racing heart. "He's applying an excessive amount of pressure on your team to close the Ali Burgess case with a positive result. You think he has sent me here to check up on your progress. See the dynamics of the team."

"Didn't he?" I replied after a pause.

"Well yeah, but he didn't use those exact words. He wants to be kept in the loop with developments. Not that there's been anything to feed back, you're all just getting on with the investigation. However, Price doesn't like it when he doesn't get the results he wants."

"What does that mean?" I asked. Either the cold or Chase's words sent a shiver down my back. I couldn't be sure which it was. The road sparkled in front of us as the frost settled on the surface.

"It means if you are hiding something, he'll find out eventually. Either from me, or someone else."

Out the corner of my eye, I caught Chase grimace as the street lights from an approaching roundabout illuminated shadows over his face.

He opened his mouth, his focus on the route ahead, and he snapped at me. "For Christ's sake, slow down!"

I pulled my gaze back to the empty roundabout, shiny with thick frost, just as the car's steering wheel jumped under my cold hands. It threw the car too far round the bend. The brake pedal didn't respond. The dark shadows of the roadside loomed around us, ready to swallow us whole. And a sudden, solid object stopped us in our tracks.

Chapter Fifteen

A numbness cocooned me, a blackness keen to stick to every corner of my mind and not relinquish its control. It was protecting me from something, an urgent thought that was trying to fight its way through. What was it? What was so important?

A thick, irritating air filled my lungs, leaving a bitter taste on my tongue. Underneath the numbness, a piercing headache loomed, threatening to incapacitate. Strange voices filtered through the ringing in my ears, distant and fraught. They grew louder.

"Ambulance. No, fire. Goddamn it, I don't know! Send everyone."

The headache grew behind my eyes and squeezed them tightly closed. It was better to block it all out; the noise, the urgency trying to break through. It was peaceful this way. If I let it in, the peace would be shattered.

"Hey." Something creaked to my right, a sound like metallic groaning. Someone touched my shoulder then thought better of themselves. "Hey, you two! Are you all right?"

On my other side, someone moaned with great effort.

"Fuck…"

"Oh good, you're alive," the relieved voice said, intruding still. "What's your name?"

"Matt."

"Right, Matt. Let's get you and your girl out of here. I don't like the look of that smoke."

That explained the thick taste in the air, I realised, remembering the last time I'd inhaled too much smoke. The urgent thought pressed forwards and it peeled my eyes open, forcing me to face reality. I was greeted by dust and a white deflated cloud. An airbag. I was still in my car.

The urgency took a grip and I glanced around. To my right was a woman, with a round face and a manic smile. She was trying her best to stay calm, but panic threatened to overwhelm her.

"Hey, sweetie," she said to me. "Are you hurt? Can you reach your seat belt?"

She looked worried as she glanced at the front of the car. Black smoke drifted around her, rising from my car bonnet which I could see through the fractured window screen. Next to me, Chase groaned again, fighting with his seat belt. His airbag hadn't deployed and blood dripped down his face from his forehead.

He released himself and then released me. I checked myself over, testing each arm and leg. All still attached, all still working. On shaky legs, I manoeuvred out of the car, into the woman's arms. We only made it a few feet before she dropped me to the frozen ground and raced around the car to find Chase. The car, my trusty old steed, rested the wrong way in the centre lane of the roundabout. On the approach, metal railings were warped out of place and a traffic light lay on its side. It was the only thing that had stopped the car from rolling over.

The vehicle looked alien, all crumpled and misshapen. This wasn't a dent my dad could buff out for me.

"Yeah, yeah, I'm here, I'm here." I heard the voice of our rescuer from the other side of the car, followed by grunts as she tugged on the passenger's door. "There's two people inside, both injured. I can't get one out, the door's jammed."

With my brain as thick as the smoke billowing from the mangled bonnet, it took me a moment to realise she was still on the phone, presumably talking to the emergency services. Chase was still in the car. I picked myself up from the damp ground and wobbled over to the passenger's side, my legs barely holding me upright in the slippery, icy grass.

"Chase?" I called. "Pull the door handle, it sticks sometimes. And I'll pull."

From inside, obscured by the smoke, I heard Chase muttering under his breath, something ending with "...piece of shit car." There was a click as he pulled the door handle, and the good Samaritan and I yanked the door opened. Chase spilled out onto the ground.

Still grumbling under his breath, the woman helped Chase to his feet and she ushered me away from the wreckage. Her own car was parked on the side of the roundabout, under the next lamp post; a shiny black roadster with its hazard lights on. No one else had passed by but in the distant stillness of the night, I heard sirens heading our way.

"What happened?" the woman asked, as we reached her car.

Realising there wasn't enough space to sit inside her two-seater, she lowered Chase to the ground and he leaned back, the blood dribbling down his face in streaks. He looked like a red zebra now.

"I don't know," I replied as I sank down next to him. Chase glanced at me, just a quick look, but he didn't say anything. Everything felt fuzzy but his look was clear enough to me; going too fast, I hadn't accounted for the icy roundabout quick enough as we approached the Hardwick. The tyre tracks cut through the shiny surface like black pen on white paper.

"Must have been black ice," said the woman. "You were lucky there were no other cars in the way. I'm Sally, by the way. I was on my way to my work's end-of-year party, if you can call a piss-up in the pub a party. My boss couldn't organise a takeaway, let alone a good works do. Where were you two going?"

"Please, stop talking. Every word is like a dagger." Chase gritted his teeth and held his head. He seemed to be struggling to keep his eyes open but his usual keenness was still there, not missing a beat. His head lolled to one side, the blood starting to soak through his coat.

Sally's manic, panic-driven smile dropped. "All right. Help isn't far out."

She gave me a sympathetic look, mouthing the words 'he'll be okay'. I nodded. The fact he was talking was a good sign in itself.

"Head wounds always bleed a lot," she said reassuringly.

"Enough," Chase growled.

"Is he always this cranky?" Sally asked me.

"Only when my subordinate tries to kill me," he grumbled back.

Taking the hint, Sally retreated from us and stood up to prepare for the sirens as they raced towards us. I shrugged off my coat and jacket underneath, balling it up, and I shuffled over the cold ground to Chase. In the dimness of the street lights, it was hard to see exactly where all the blood was coming from but I held the jacket to his forehead, pressing it against where the worst of the blood was. Chase pressed his hand over mine, wriggling my fingers away. Through heavy eyes, he regarded me.

"I didn't try to kill you," I said quietly. "It must have been black ice."

He inhaled stiffly, as if about to bite back. I had no doubt there were a million words in his mind, ready to come out. But then he sighed, saying nothing and we both turned as an ambulance drew up to the roundabout with a reassuring fanfare that filled the night.

* * *

Dr Leonard Walker pushed controlled breaths through his nose as he appeared in my hospital bay, eyes darting over a paper file in his hands. His usually perfect hair was sticking out at odd angles and his sparkling eyes were tired and sunken. He frowned as he watched me pace the short length of the hospital bed.

"You look well," he said.

"Better than you do," I remarked. My favourite doctor in the Accident and Emergency department of King's Lynn hospital rarely looked so fraught and downtrodden. If it wasn't for the worry about Chase already eating me up inside, I would have had more room to be worried about him.

Dr Walker rolled his eyes. "I'm on my second double shift of this week. But I'd rather be overworked than in a car wreck. How do you feel?"

"I'm fine. There's nothing wrong with me."

"Well, that's for me to determine, not you."

I waved my hand back, something far more pressing on my mind. "How's Chase?"

I was fine, it wasn't a lie. Apart from the recurrent niggling in my shoulder flaring up again, slight tenderness around my nose and cheeks where I'd hit the airbag face first, and what I was sure would be a pretty bruise across my chest from the seat belt, I was intact. Chase had been taken off for a scan half an hour ago and I hadn't seen or heard from him since.

"He'll be okay," Dr Walker assured me, wary of my edginess. "I ordered the CT scan as a precaution. You could have picked a better night to stack your car though; we've had two other RTCs in since you arrived. But with a nasty head wound like that, he's top of my list."

"Okay. Good." The assurance didn't stop me pacing. I couldn't rest until Chase was back and I heard his ill-tempered moaning again. It was my fault he was here. My fault we were in this predicament to begin with.

"Do you want me to call anyone for you?" Dr Walker asked, still eyeing me over. He knew me well enough to know that I would say I was fine even when I wasn't. I'd been a frequent visitor to the A & E department over the years. But really, this time, I was. I was bloody lucky.

I shook my head. I'd already called Aaron, struggling to briefly explain the circumstances. Thankfully, he was happy to act on what little information I gave him and hearing that I was at the hospital was enough to spur him on. That gave me a few minutes at least to work out how I'd explain to him what I was doing out with DCI Chase.

Dr Walker reached into his pocket and pulled out a mobile phone, ringing shrilly now exposed. The screen was cracked from the impact but I recognised it as Chase's and I caught sight of the caller ID, garbled but still legible.

Izzy

"It's been ringing non-stop," Walker said as he handed it over to me. "Is it yours?"

"No, it's…" I clicked my fingers and pointed, but Dr Walker didn't seem to get my meaning. "My passenger's. It's his wife calling. Should I answer it?"

Dr Walker shrugged. "Depends. You know him, I don't. I can answer if you'd like but I saw his wedding ring. I'm not lying for you two."

"We weren't doing anything sneaky. We work together. He's my boss." I scowled at Dr Walker, a little hurt that he'd assume that of me.

"Well, some people like that sort of thing."

"That's not…"

I failed to finish the sentence, but luckily a better way to prove my point came to me. I pressed the phone screen on the little green icon and answered the call. Before I could get a word out, an ear-splitting shriek erupted from the speaker.

"What the hell are you playing at? You think you can bombard me with messages and then just ignore me! You've got some bloody nerve, Matt. If I want to talk, it'll be on my terms, you got that? It'll be when I say, not when you've finished work and finally find the time to pay me attention!"

"This isn't Matt," I said, but I wasn't sure my voice would even break through the tirade. Izzy Chase was rabid.

"Who the hell are you?" she snapped down the line, her tone even more full of venom than when she thought she was talking to Chase.

"I'm Anna, I work with Chase."

"Oh, of course," she hissed. "The moment he's away… He's a coward, having you answer the phone. Whatever my husband has told you, don't listen to him. He could talk his way out of a murder if he wanted. He'll deny it, but you're just the latest in a long line of meaningless women."

"I'm not…" I wasn't even sure where to start, but convincing her that I wasn't some meaningless other woman wasn't the most important thing at this time. "Chase is in hospital. We've just had a car accident."

For a moment, Izzy fell silent. "Is he okay?"

"He's got a nasty head injury. He's now being checked out."

The wrath returned. "If he's crashed that bloody car… it's not even paid off yet. I told him not to take it. Fucking useless man."

"It wasn't him driving, it was me." And it was my beloved car that bit the dust. I felt sorry for the poor baby, spewing smoke and being doused in some sort of foam by the fire department.

"Good," Izzy spat back. "Because as soon as he's back in Norwich, I'm taking my fucking car back. And you can tell Matt that he can fool around with his work colleagues all he wants; as soon as my dad finds out what he's done, he's finished."

And with that, the line cut and Izzy's fury vanished from the air. I glanced over at Dr Walker, whose suspicion had now been replaced with guilt.

"That sounded like a threat," he said, giving a pointed look at the phone.

"I'm sure it's just hot air. Sounds like they're having a disagreement," I said calmly but Izzy's words had left me feeling unsettled.

Dr Walker hummed and settled onto a chair, leaning on the bed to scribble something on the paperwork in his hand. "I think that sounds more like a break-up than a disagreement."

He motioned for me to sit, and after a quick examination, he flourished the paper with a signature and handed it over to me.

"You're good to go, although you can wait around for your colleague if you want. Have you got someone who can pick you both up?"

I nodded a yes.

"Good. I don't want your passenger driving until the stars have gone from his vision. Providing his scan comes back clean, he should be fine in a few days. Although it might be a good idea if someone can stay with him tonight, just to keep an eye."

"I'll sort something out," I said. "Something tells me his wife isn't going to help."

From outside the curtain, there came the scuffle of footsteps and a rustle as the material was pushed aside. On the other side, stood my long-suffering and impossibly tolerant boyfriend, a firmly unimpressed expression on his face. He surveyed me up and down and settled into a mild frown when he saw that I was standing, looking dishevelled but unharmed.

"You will be the early death of me one day," Aaron said. He exchanged a nod with Dr Walker, who gave a half-hearted laugh at Aaron's reaction as he stood to leave.

"She's fine. Her passenger needs a bit of looking after, though."

"Passenger?"

As Walker left the bay, Aaron turned on me. Now I could see the worry edging through. 'It's always you.' The words were right on the edge of his tongue.

"I can explain," I said hastily.

"Go on then."

"We were off to the pub. Chase didn't know where it was, so I offered him a lift. It wasn't anything else, I promise."

I caught a flicker on Aaron's face, measuring how much a promise was really worth from me.

"And your car?" he asked. He pulled out his mobile phone from the deep pockets of his coat and with a flick, unlocked the screen. He turned it to me, showing a photo of my poor vehicle laying in pieces over the tarmac. "Pres was on shift tonight; he's just sent me this. So not only will everyone know that you stacked it, but by morning the whole station will know you were out with DCI Chase tonight. Why didn't you tell me? Why did you even call me if he's here?"

A little taken aback by his anger, I struggled for an answer and shrugged my shoulders. It hadn't crossed my mind to call anyone else, not even my parents. He was Aaron; he was always there when I needed him.

Aaron took a deep breath, releasing his frustration. It wasn't completely gone, but being angry at me wasn't going to solve anything right there and then.

"Right," he said. "So, DCI Chase is here and he's injured. How badly?"

"Head injury, but Dr Walker says he'll be fine. Might need someone to watch over him tonight."

"Hasn't he got any family or anyone who can fetch him?"

I nodded. "He has a wife; I've spoken to her on the phone. However, it's not a pleasant relationship at the moment. I've told her he's at the hospital but she won't help him. She said something along the lines of wait until her dad finds out what he's done."

Aaron considered this. "That's odd. But not the main problem right now."

Before he could say any more, a disgruntled voice filled the air, growing closer to the hospital bay. Aaron reached round to draw back the curtain just as Chase was wheeled into view by an impatient-looking porter. His wheelchair was promptly dumped at the edge of the bay and the porter disappeared, catching a nurse by the arm as he went and mumbling, "He's all yours now."

I took a good look at Chase, relieved to see he looked a bit more like his normal self now. His pale complexion had faded and the blood was cleared from his face. The wound by his hairline was covered over by a large white gauze, a red patch seeping through the white. From the irritation in his voice, he sounded absolutely fine.

"A likely mild concussion isn't a proper diagnosis. Not for someone who just escaped death by the skin of their teeth. I was nearly murdered!" he called after the porter.

When he realised the nurse and porter weren't listening to him anymore, Chase turned his attention round to me. His expression grew confused as he spotted Aaron.

"DCI Burns. What are you doing here?"

Aaron's gaze flicked over to me, but I was blank. Whatever story I needed to explain this strange turn of events was completely evading me.

Aaron filled the silence, sinking his hands into his coat pockets and shrugging nonchalantly. "One of the joys of having a name that begins with a double-A is always being the top of everyone's contact list. You'd be surprised how often this happens. Anyway, I'm here now, so let's get you both home. You look like you need a lie-down, Detective Chief Inspector."

"I need a fucking drink," Chase replied and on unsteady feet, he straightened himself upright. With a hard blink, he managed to stop himself swaying and waved me away as I stepped forwards to help. "You can stay away from me. I don't want to give you any other opportunities to kill me."

"I was only trying to help," I said in defence. I held out his phone to him and he took it tentatively. "Your wife called. I told her where you are."

"That must have been thrilling. Let me guess, she's not coming to help me?"

"No. She wasn't very sympathetic."

"She was probably the one who told you to bump me off," he muttered and he pocketed the phone.

Without another look between us, Chase strode away, his steps slow but with the same purpose he normally had, determined to escape the hospital. Exchanging a look with Aaron, I followed on with him behind.

Chapter Sixteen

Initially, I thought it was embarrassment that woke me up the next morning. The memories of the night before came flooding back – Chase with blood dripping down his forehead; having to take a roadside breath test to prove I wasn't under the influence to the amused police officers first on scene; the ambulance ride to the hospital, where Chase spent the whole journey telling the paramedics that I had tried to kill him; Aaron's reluctant expression as he dropped me off home.

But then I realised Poppy the cat was at the foot of the bed, trying to force her way under the covers to bite my toes.

And then I heard the knocking at the door.

Without much haste, I pulled myself up, feeling fresh aches of pain in my shoulders and neck. I stretched, telling myself I was lucky to get away with just some sore muscles. I wondered how Chase was doing.

The knocking on the door turned frantic, accompanied by a worried cry calling out my name.

There was no hurry to answer it, though. They had a key.

By the time I put on my dressing gown and wandered out of bed, my mum had forced her way into my flat, almost breaking the lock with her impatience. She paused when she saw me, walking stiffly and yawning, before throwing her arms around me and pulling me into a forceful hug.

"Mum, get off," I said, pushing her away. "I'm fine."

"Fine?" she replied shrilly. "Fine! You wrecked your car! And the first I find out about it is when Marie from down the road texts me to ask how you are!"

"How did Marie know?" I blinked away my tiredness.

"Jonathan told her," said Mum, as if I was meant to know who Jonathan was. My mum's friends and their network stretched far and wide. Sometimes this was useful, often giving me snippets of local gossip when needed. Sometimes, like this morning, it was less helpful.

"What happened?" Mum demanded.

I sidestepped her and made my way to the kitchen, flicking on the kettle. I needed a strong coffee before I could face her inquisition.

"Where's Dad?" I asked.

Right on cue, Dad came up the stairs and through the front door of the flat. He leaned on the door, breathing heavily.

"Susan," he snapped at Mum. "You could have waited for me!"

"I needed to know Anna was all right," she replied.

"And, as I said, I'm fine. No one was hurt," I assured her.

Making three cups of coffee – one with decaf since Mum was hyped up enough already – I settled onto the sofa and my parents followed suit. I watched my mother as she started to relax, shooting me pointed looks every so often as if she thought I was lying about my welfare. I knew I should have been grateful that they cared so much. Not everyone had parents like mine; occasionally intrusive, but with their hearts in the right place.

Once I had given them a watered-down version of the events last night, conveniently leaving out any mentions of Aaron or Chase to avoid them asking any awkward questions, Mum blew softly across the top of her mug before she spoke.

"You should have called us. Or the hospital should have. Why didn't the hospital call us? We're listed as your next of kin."

"It wasn't that bad," I said in my best reassuring voice. "I was able to sort it out myself."

"But we *are* listed as your next of kin?" she pressed. "Aren't we?"

Dad cut in, "You know we are, Susan. They called us when she got stabbed."

A faraway expression crossed Mum's face as she remembered that night. From the little I recalled, it had been traumatic for my parents. It was the one time I wasn't able to protect them from the dangers of my job and they saw first-hand just how vulnerable I was.

"Yeah, see," I replied, keen to push those thoughts away and move the topic along. "You get called when I'm too incapacitated to do it myself. Otherwise, I'm fine. The car was the most serious casualty."

For a brief moment, nothing more than a flicker, I wondered what would've happened if it had turned out worse. I didn't remember ever listing my parents as my next of kin but I'd been in so many scrapes and scuffles over the years, I must have put them down at some point.

Who did people call when they had no next of kin? Like Barney King. He had no one. What would he have done if he was ever too ill or injured that he couldn't look after himself?

I put a mental pin in that thought. Barney King had no one but there must have been help out there somewhere for people like him. I needed to get to the office to check that out.

Slurping down the last of my coffee, I stood up and smiled at my parents.

"Mum, Dad, I'm glad you came to check on me. I'm glad you're here," I said, with enough sincerity that it made Mum give a little awe and bite her lip.

"You can give me a lift to work," I finished. And I hurried off to get dressed.

* * *

When I arrived at the police station a short while later, marginally more ready to face the day ahead, I found Chris and Jay standing at the door to the office. They still had their coats on and a peek through the door showed me they hadn't even made it inside. Something had stopped them in their tracks.

"What is it?" I asked cautiously.

"Chase," came the simple answer from Jay.

Chris shushed him.

They nodded down the corridor, where the unmistakeable sound of Chase's self-righteous voice floated from Aaron's office. He sounded animated, excited. What he was saying wasn't clear, but he was saying it with conviction.

"What are they talking about?" I asked.

The three of us waited in the corridor, not making a move. I had half a mind to go down the hall myself and see what all the fuss was about but I knew I couldn't just go barging in without opening myself up to awkward questions. The volume rose a little more.

"Don't know." Chris shrugged his shoulders under his heavy coat. "He just came flying out of the office, saying he had an idea."

"About the case?"

"Your guess is as good as ours," said Jay, tilting his head sideways as if that would help him hear better. "Go down there and see if you can hear."

"Not a chance," I replied. "He thinks I tried to kill him yesterday. You go."

Chris and Jay looked me up and down, their lack of surprise telling me they had already heard on the grapevine about the car accident. Satisfied I was okay, they returned to the matter at hand.

There came a sudden bark from the office, a decisive "No!" that rattled along the corridor. That voice was Aaron and he sounded appalled.

"Bloody hell," said Jay. "We should probably step in."

Chris shook his head. "Nah, let the DCIs fight it out. None of us are paid enough to step in."

"What if they actually do fight it out?" Jay appeared genuinely worried about that prospect.

"Aaron's not a fighter," I said. I couldn't imagine anything more absurd than Aaron getting in a fist fight.

"He hasn't spent a prolonged amount of time with Chase yet," Jay pointed out. "Even the man's presence is annoying. Just listen to them."

It was true, the voices were growing tense and starting to sound clipped and pressured. A debate was underway, each side as gritted and determined as the other. Chase's muffled speech used a thousand words, whilst Aaron got his point across in just a handful.

With an unexpected creak, the door down the corridor flew open and Chase appeared. He spotted the team and pointed into the office, like a headteacher summoning a naughty student.

"McArthur, I need your help to make a point."

"Me?" I asked.

Chase bounced on the balls of his feet with barely contained energy and an expression that told me he knew he was right. There were little signs of his involvement in the crash the previous night except for the bandage on his head. He still looked as keen and animated as usual.

Chase clicked his fingers with impatience.

"That's an order, McArthur. Chop chop."

I relented and stepped towards him. I wasn't getting out of this until I played along with whatever he was doing. A knot of dread curled itself into a hard lump in my throat, rationing the air supply to my lungs.

Chris and Jay used the distraction to dive into the Serious Crimes office, safely out of the firing range. I walked into Aaron's office and Chase closed the door behind me. Aaron was sitting at his desk, pen in hand which he tapped on the wooden surface, the only sign of him being agitated. His face didn't react to me, not even offering a small smile as I sat down in one of the chairs opposite him.

"Morning, Anna."

"Morning," I replied, looking between him and Chase. "What's going on then?"

Chase didn't join us sitting down, but instead paced the room right in front of the wide windows that overlooked the car park. Today, patchy fog sat on the fields, hovering like ghosts trying to listen in on our conversation.

"So, last night, I was thinking," said Chase, drumming his fingers on his chin as he spoke. "We're running out of people who knew both Barney King and Clara Burns. Why would he confess to a crime if he didn't commit it? The only way we will find out what really happened is if we track down someone who knew them both."

I shot a quick look at Aaron. He watched Chase pace across the room, with a look in his eyes that made me wonder if he was secretly a fighter after all.

"But we have already spoken to DI Daley," I said. "He didn't know Clara."

"No, no, no." Chase waved his arms, but fell quiet, waiting for me to catch up. "There's only one person who could possibly remember such a time and still have the faculties to speak to us." Chase glared at Aaron.

"You can't," I said. "Aaron was only two when Clara disappeared."

"Wrong again," said Chase. "No, I mean Callum Burns."

I glanced at Aaron. He hadn't moved, his impassive glare resting on Chase.

"He was ten when his mother disappeared," Chase carried on, oblivious to the looks he was getting, "and he lived next to Barney King for several years afterwards. I want to call him in for an interview."

"And as I pointed out," Aaron said through gritted teeth, "he lives in Cornwall, almost four hundred miles away. Bringing him in at all is unacceptable."

"This isn't the sort of investigation that should be dealt with over the phone. I need to hear, first hand, what his impressions are after reopening the case." Chase spun on his heels and set his sights on me. "You notified him that we were reinvestigating his mother's disappearance, right? What did he say?"

"Well," I replied. "It was only a short conversation; he didn't really react to the news. He didn't ask to be kept informed; he didn't even ask how Barney King had died. Only said he understood and ended the call. I don't think bringing him here is a good idea."

"Nonsense. He'll want to help the investigation," said Chase.

"He will," Aaron agreed. "And I know, because of that, he'll feel obligated to come."

"Then I don't see what the problem is."

"The problem is you making him," said Aaron. He gripped the pen in his fist. "Callum has never recovered from losing her, and forcing him back here to relive it all won't help anyone. None of this helps anyone. It won't bring her back."

"Aaron," I said gently. His agitation was rising, aimed squarely at Chase, although the other man didn't appear to have noticed that Aaron's temper was on a knife edge.

"Don't you want this case solved?" Chase continued.

"Of course I do," snapped Aaron.

"I don't need your permission anyway. I was being courteous by letting you know."

"And since you asked my opinion, I'm telling you it's a shit idea. Focus on the old man's death. Dragging my brother up here won't help you find out what happened to our mother."

"You don't know that. This is what reopening a cold case does – it drags up the past, no matter how uncomfortable it is. Your brother could be the key to solving at least one death."

"I don't see how. He was just a child."

"You know, your objections could be seen as obstructive, DCI Burns."

"All right, enough!" I cut in, silencing them both. "This argument is getting us nowhere. We need a decision."

Over by the windows, Chase stopped pacing and crossed his arms.

"Do you really let your constables talk to you like that?" he asked Aaron incredulously.

"She's not wrong," he replied.

Chase turned to look out the window and gave an exaggerated huff. "Fine. Since it's my case, it's my decision. I'll call Callum Burns now."

But he made no move from where he watched Aaron and me out the corner of his eye. I wished I could tell what he was thinking, but as he observed us, a niggling thought struck me. What if Chase had done this on purpose? What if he'd started this argument to draw out a reaction from Aaron, and added me to the mix for extra drama?

Aaron must have reached the same conclusion as me, as he threw down his pen and turned away from me. "Fine. But don't come in here again until you have solved these cases."

A tentative agreement reached, I rose to my feet, knowing that it was the best outcome we were going to get. I couldn't shake the feeling that Chase was purposely trying to provoke this, but he maintained an innocent and authoritative stance, not moving an inch as I stepped towards him.

"Come on, then," I said. I motioned to the exit and he narrowed his gaze, searching for something in my expression.

With my back to Aaron, I met Chase's eye and allowed him to read me. I must have passed his little test as with a deep inhale, he spun on his heels and I followed him out the office, closing the door behind me as gently as I could.

Chapter Seventeen

In the time that it took me to explain to Chris and Jay what the argument was about, Chase managed to make his phone call to Callum Burns. He burst back into the Serious Crimes office, still bouncing with excess energy, but didn't move to sit down. Instead, he took a measured look around the room, taking his time to gauge our reactions to the decision he'd made about the case.

"He's agreed to come," he eventually said, not bothering to elaborate and rightly guessing that I'd told Chris and Jay everything.

Chris broke first, tutting under his breath. "Waste of time, if you ask me."

"Well, I didn't," Chase bit back. He took a steadying breath and strode over to the whiteboard of progress. As he gazed over it for a full minute, I shared a look with the guys. We waited and wondered what would come next.

"Let's review," Chase said, turning so he was facing us like a teacher at a blackboard. "Barney King. Post-mortem was inconclusive as to whether he killed himself or not. Circumstances are unusual and several things don't quite fit in place. There are no signs of obvious foul play, except…" He pointed to the photocopy of the suicide note, written in the jagged handwriting. "This odd note written in a handwriting style that doesn't look much like King's. Add into the mix the fact that King displayed no signs of poor mental health or suicidal tendencies, then we have reason to believe that perhaps all is not what it seems. And there are several outstanding matters with King. How far have we got with tracing his wife or her death certificate?"

"Not very far," said Chris. "The archivists at the records office are looking but they're council employees. We can't force them to go any faster."

"And the Hythes?"

"Well, you got their statements yesterday," said Jay. "It's all a bit too coincidental if you ask me. King found out about their extramarital affair and baby the day before he died. Suspicion is bound to fall on them."

Chase clicked his fingers. "Then we need to gather their alibis!"

"We've already done that," I replied. "The wife was at work in Fakenham the day of King's death. Garrett was working at the quarry and Luisa was looking after Harry. But without knowing exactly what time King died on Tuesday, we can't really rule any of them out."

"Fuck's sake," Chase whispered under his breath. "All right. A few loose ends to tie up with King's death. Let's move on to the other big unknown – the cold case." He pointed to a photo of Clara Burns. It was one used in the original investigation, a posed snap of her on her wedding day with her husband cropped out. She looked youthful, carefree and joyful enough to make my insides twist whenever I looked at it.

"We've made precisely no headway on this one, no more than DI Daley made forty years ago," said Chase, throwing not so subtle glares at Chris and Jay. "We can't speak to King's wife, so we have no idea why she left him before Clara Burns disappeared. We can't speak to Clara's husband either, he's dead. We have no new evidence in her disappearance other than a questionable suicide note. What we need is…"

He drifted off, turning back to the board and stroking his chin as he mulled over some deep thoughts. Chris, Jay and I waited for the temporary team leader to emerge from his daydream.

Chase mumbled under his breath. "What we need is…"

"What we need is a bloody break," Chris chimed in. "We've still got lines of inquiry to follow with King's death. You want to go forging into the cold case by pulling Callum Burns in when we've got a much better chance of finding out what happened to Barney King. Callum Burns isn't going to be able to give us any more information than what we've already got from the cold case files."

"And is dragging him here really the way forward?" Jay added. "We were told we needed to be sensitive with this case."

"It's not even really a case," said Chris. "Cold cases this old don't get solved. We'll spend all this time re-examining everything and will conclude that King probably killed himself and Clara Burns is still missing. It's all a waste of time."

"It's not a waste of time for Aaron," I pointed out, earning a glower from Chris across the top of our computer screens.

"He didn't even want the case reopened anyway!"

"What we need," Chase said loudly, as he spun back round on his heels. From the broad smile on his face, it was clear he hadn't been listening to a word anyone had said. He clapped his hands together and clicked his fingers. "Is a team-building exercise!"

* * *

Pepperwell Farm Cottages still looked like a scene from some sort of winter grotto – or perhaps one from an icy horror film. Freezing fog was struggling to lift over the land, leaving behind crunchy grass and solid cobwebs. Everything sparkled, but rather than look magical, it was daggered and deadly.

Chris and Jay stood in front of Barney King's cottage, jiggling up and down to keep warm. They were even too cold to mutter insults about Chase, who had just arrived after leaving us waiting in the cold for twenty minutes. His car was bumping carefully down the track towards us.

"What the fuck are we doing out here?" Jay asked, wholly unimpressed. "It's minus two degrees. I can't feel my nose."

"I told you to bring a hat," Chris said. His own was pulled down right over his ears and eyebrows.

"That's not going to help my fucking nose, is it?" Jay stamped his feet, as if crushing the crispy grass beneath might help warm him up. "This isn't bloody team building. Team building's a decent afternoon down the pub."

"That, we can agree on," I grumbled back. The prospect of being in a heated pub with plenty of wine to warm the blood was infinitely more appealing.

"The sooner Chase is gone, the better," Jay mumbled.

"It'll be nice for things to go back to normal," Chris agreed.

We fell silent as Chase made his way over, his footsteps crunching on the grass. He was still bounding around with enough energy to power a city, causing the off-white bandage on his forehead to peek out from under his black woolly hat. Perhaps we were starting to get used to his hyperactivity now; none of us batted an eyelid.

When he reached us, Chase looked out wistfully across the freezing landscape and held up a small silver object; a dog whistle.

"Right," he said, rubbing his gloved hands together. "We'll start over there." He pointed to the group of trees opposite the cottages. "Blow this enough and the dog should respond. Keep your eyes and ears open and hopefully we'll solve one mystery."

"We're going to look for King's dog?" I asked.

Chase responded with an enthusiastic nod.

"What makes you think the dog is even still around? King died over a week ago and no one has seen it since Tuesday." Jay reached out for the whistle but Chase snatched his hand away.

"Oh, ye of little faith. It's a gun dog; it'll be very loyal to its master. It'll be around here still." He glanced at me out the corner of his eye before handing a whistle over to Chris. "Who knows, the dog could be the key to solving this mystery."

"Oh yeah, I bet it's dying to tell us what happened to Barney King," Jay muttered back.

Chris snorted too. "Why are we wasting our time doing this?"

"Two reasons," Chase said smoothly. "One, we're running out of leads on unravelling Barney King's death. We can't even decide if it was a suicide. And two, we need a nice activity such as this to bond as a team. Put yourself in my shoes." Chase found another whistle from his pocket and waved it around. "I'm the new guy and you're all... close. Weirdly close, if you ask me. If we want to work effectively as a team, we need to work to tear down some of these barriers. So, last to find the dog buys the first round later. McArthur and I missed the last trip to the pub. If we can make some good progress today, we can get a few drinks in later."

And with that, he stomped off across the grass, leaving perfect footprints across the ground.

"Come on, let's go!" Chase called without looking back.

With little choice in the matter, and already losing the feeling in my fingers, I followed and Chris and Jay trudged after me. We fought our way into the undergrowth, trying to follow the natural paths between the vegetation laid out by animals. Before long, we were out of sight of the cottages and so deep into the woods surrounding Pepperwell Farm, I was worried we might fall into the quarry or fail to find our way back. In our haste, we'd forgotten to come up with some sort of Hansel and Gretel-style way to map our route.

Chase wasn't worried by this. "Blow the whistle harder," he ordered Chris.

"It's a dog whistle; how can you even hear it?" I asked.

He cocked his head to the side and offered me a frown. "You can't?"

Not in the mood to be dragged into his oddness, I ignored him and carried on. A few meters ahead, there was a clearing in the trees and we stumbled upon the sheered edge of a lake. It was a filled-in quarry pit, and I recognised the muddy expanse of shoreline on the opposite side; it was the same one that Barney King had drowned in. We had somehow travelled in a wide, arching circle.

Jay peered over my shoulder. "Where to now, boss? No dog here."

The lake was beautiful once again, no longer marred by the disturbance of death. The water barely rippled, touched only by a cloud of fog that hung over its surface. Not a breath of wind rustled the trees, or a single chirp of a bird. All was calm and peaceful. I pulled in a lungful of fresh air through my nose, bitingly cold but revitalising.

The beauty bypassed Chase and he handed me the dog whistle and ushered me back into the undergrowth. It was easy to see the path we'd forged already, so he picked another direction and pressed on.

"So, come on, all of you," he called over his shoulder. "We've still got lots of outstanding questions and not nearly enough answers. What do you think of the Hythe family? Do we think they're involved?"

I hummed back, feeling Jay's breath on the back of my neck as he clambered over the fallen trunk of a silver birch tree right behind me. "They're the only people who appear to have a motive right now. And their only alibis are each other."

"Yeah," Chris agreed, on the verge of grumpiness. "Strange family dynamics going on there. When King found out about the affair and pregnancy, he said Garrett Hythe would owe him a favour."

"Could the favour, whatever it was, be a reason for one of them to kill him?" asked Chase.

"We don't know someone did kill him. It could still be suicide," Jay pointed out.

"But a suicide doesn't explain the scribbled handwriting on the suicide note," said Chase and I could hear the smug grin in his words. I blew hard on the dog whistle, hoping it might burst his eardrums. No such luck. "Or the fact he had a bloody shotgun in his house and yet decided it was easier to drown himself… The truth is, we still don't know jack shit."

Ahead of us through the trees, I spied the sparkle of another quarry pit filled with water. Chase diverted right, following a thin trail left behind by some wild animal that morning.

"What do we think of Mags Bowen?"

"She said she hadn't seen her father in almost sixty years. I see no reason to disbelieve her," I replied.

Jay huffed as he tripped on a hidden tree root. "Just face it, we've got no tangible leads to follow. Lab reports are inconclusive, post-mortem couldn't confirm or deny foul play. This case will get sent to the coroner to rule on and closed."

"And with it, the case of Clara Burns will be closed too," said Chris.

"And we'll never be able to find out what happened to her," I finished. With my next breath, the cold air prickled down my throat, as if something was in its way. The thought of closing this case with no answers for Aaron made me feel like I'd somehow failed him. I didn't want all of our efforts, all of the distress caused, to be in vain.

"Has anyone ever told you you're all very pessimistic?" Chase said, just as something made him falter in his step. Standing on a slick patch of ice, I crashed into the back of him, but he didn't move. Jay caught me.

"We're realistic," Jay corrected him, an unusual harshness in his voice as I pulled myself upright. "And you said it yourself, we're a close-knit team over here. Which means we want to close these cases whilst protecting those involved. We don't want to drag this out any longer than we have to."

"Shh," said Chase, holding out his hand, but at the back of the group, Jay and Chris didn't hear him.

"There's reopening a cold case, and then there's prolonging the investigation into an old crime that should have been laid to rest years ago," added Chris.

"Shh!" Chase held out his hands, waiting until silence fell over the woods again.

Behind me, I heard the rattling breaths of Chris and Jay, but nothing else pierced the eerily quiet surroundings. Out here, we were too far away to hear the groaning of the machinery at the quarry. Out here, we were on our own.

"Do you hear that?" Chase whispered.

We all shook our heads.

"Blow the whistle again."

Popping the metal whistle between my cold lips, I blew hard. A bark responded. Short, distant and pained.

"What's the matter, Lassie?" Chase asked under his breath. "Little Timmy fell down the well again?"

I strained my ears as I blew the whistle again. It wasn't too far away, but the trees distorted the sound, bouncing it around. It had to be ahead of us, because there was nowhere else to hide in the frost-covered morning. Chase set off with urgency and we hurried to keep up.

We made it to a stack of undergrowth, weaved in amongst a group of pine and birch trees. Almost completely camouflaged against it were the remnants of an old shed, crumbling but still a solid structure, held up by thickets of brambles.

"There." I pointed to where the door must have once been.

The dog's barking was coming from inside, strained but persistent. At another blow of the whistle, the shed erupted with a pitiful whining. It was clearly housing a creature feeling very sorry for itself. It scratched to come out, like a monster locked in a cage.

"Poor thing must be stuck inside." I scouted around, careful of the brambles until I found the panel of wood that was once a door. It had now fallen off its hinges, covering the opening. It didn't take much force to pull the door off altogether with Jay's help, and an almighty cloud of foul, stale air whisked out into the open. It smelled like the inside of a compost bin.

A black shadow escaped out the opening, shooting straight past me to Chris, who stood a few feet away. The emaciated dog lay down by his feet, whining again, pleased to have found a man just like her old master.

He bent down to scratch its ear. "Good girl... or boy. Why were you hiding in there?"

Chase's body warmth seeped into mine as he joined me at the door frame to peer inside the rickety structure. I searched every corner, unsure what to expect, but there was nothing. The walls threatened to cave in from rot and the pressure of the bracken outside, and as sunlight streamed in around me and Chase, spiders scurried away to hide. Inside was empty bar a wilted bouquet of supermarket flowers laying on the mushy dirt floor. Remnants of dozens more bouquets littered the shed.

"What is—" I began to ask, but Chase cut me off.

"Don't go in," he said. When I looked at him, his expression was grim and shadowed by the darkness of the lair. "One of you call forensics. I think we've found a mausoleum."

Chapter Eighteen

When I left the site as the afternoon sun disappeared over the horizon, I felt a chill in my bones that I couldn't shift. It wasn't just the cold eating at me. I'd watched the day pass with a team of forensic investigators, who painstakingly stripped back the layers of dirt until they uncovered what we all hoped they wouldn't find.

Rags. Bones.

Human ones.

Chase insisted that Jay and I stayed to oversee the discovery, giving neither of us the chance to argue. Even with portable heaters scouring the area in an attempt to thaw the frozen ground, the ice inside of my body didn't relent. It didn't shift, not when the remains were first discovered, not when enough of the body confirmed it had likely lain there for decades.

It gripped me tight, holding the air in my lungs, the blood suspended in my veins. I knew it wouldn't let me go until official identification confirmed my worst fears; that it was Clara Burns buried in that shed.

We made it back to the police station as a starry evening took over the sky, thoughts of heading to the pub long gone from our minds. Most of the staff were knocking off for the weekend. I trudged up the stairs, each step harder than the last. Jay followed behind.

"Someone needs to tell him," I said.

Jay understood right away. "He's probably already heard." His voice was weighed heavily with despondency. It wasn't the same irritation as his bad mood. This time he just sounded worn down.

I paused near the top step. "No, I mean one of us has to tell him. I know Chase said we can't give him any information but we've just found a body in the woods. A body that could be his mother. We need to tell him."

"I know," said Jay with a sigh. "But if Chase—"

He was stopped abruptly as a door opened in the corridor at the top of the stairs.

Aaron appeared from one of the other offices. He smiled, although it dropped away as he read our expressions. He had his coat on, and closed the door to the Firearms office before putting his hands into his pockets.

"Long day?" he asked.

Jay and I nodded.

"Why were you in the Firearms office?" I asked, keen to change the subject. I checked the door but it was firmly shut. The Firearms team wasn't nearly as exciting as its name suggested; it comprised of three desk-bound coppers who were assigned to following up on cases involving suspected firearms and vetting the applications for licences. The Armed Unit – the ones who actually got the guns – were a tactical team based out of headquarters.

"You guys might not like this, but you're not the only team that sometimes need my expertise," Aaron replied. "Firearms are still having some problems with someone they denied a licence to."

Jay waved his hand. "They're always pissing people off."

"Still, we shouldn't take any threats lightly, they've got to be dealt with."

Aaron waited a moment, as if he expected us to say something. We didn't.

"Well," he said, sidling past us and taking a few steps down the stairs, "don't stay too late."

Aaron turned his back to us and something wrenched in my gut. I wanted to follow him. I didn't want to keep it all to myself anymore. Jay stirred next to me, sensing my reluctance. When I took a step after Aaron, Jay put his hand on my shoulder and stopped me before I went further.

"You know we can't," he murmured under his breath.

And by the time I shrugged his hand off, Aaron had already descended the stairs and was gone from sight.

I rounded on Jay. "I hate this. I hate not being able to talk to him or tell him anything."

"I know," he replied, despondently. "But you had the chance to excuse yourself and you didn't. You've got to see this one through, Anna."

* * *

I rubbed the bridge of my nose. It had taken hours for my extremities to thaw out, well into the evening. Chris had used the family card to get home at a reasonable time. Jay had tapped out an hour later. That left DCI Chase and me in the office.

Despite having two empty desks to choose from, Chase had still perched himself on the edge of mine, his laptop dangerously close to tipping off with each of his heavy-handed keystrokes.

"You can go home, you know," he said, not looking up from his screen. He wasn't being subtle in his attempts to get rid of me.

"The next bus isn't for another twenty minutes," I reminded him. "Although, if you want me out of here, I'll go wait downstairs."

He huffed, like I was an imposition. "No. You're fine here. It is your office, after all."

He rubbed a hand over his forehead, crinkling the bandage over his wound.

"How's your head?" I asked.

"Thumping," he replied. "But then, I suppose I got off lightly for a murder attempt."

"Stop saying that," I hissed. "Given our line of work, people might actually believe you." I rummaged through the drawer of my desk, finding a half-empty blister pack of paracetamol, and I threw them at him.

He smiled at me, took two tablets, then returned to his laptop screen.

"I had a thought earlier," I said, leaving the statement hanging in mid-air.

"Before or after you decided to kill me?" Chase flashed a smile again. "Sorry, sorry. Go on. Let's hear it."

"King had no one," I said. "He had no emergency contacts listed with the hospital, his GP surgery or his bank. We tracked down his daughter, but what if something happened to him and he needed care. Who would be contacted then?"

Chase considered this a moment, leaning back in his chair. "Well, I guess that's when adult social services would become involved. If someone becomes incapacitated or unable to look after themselves, they would step in and arrange care. Barney King never got to that point though."

"He might have been getting there though," I replied. "He certainly had a lot of medical appointments. The neurology department were running lots of tests. The fact he missed two appointments in a row was what triggered a welfare check in the first place. Could there have been any other agencies involved in his care?"

"It's possible," said Chase. "Looking through his medical records, his health was declining. It's worth asking the social care team." He checked his watch. "In the morning though. We won't get anywhere tonight."

"And when are you going to call it a day?"

"Any minute now," he said. "And then I will head back to my lonely hotel room, raid the minibar, and read any malicious communications my wife has sent me today."

"Are things that bad?" I asked. I knew I shouldn't intrude on his personal life but after my conversation with Izzy Chase the day before whilst at the hospital, I couldn't help myself.

"They're not good," admitted Chase. He pushed himself away from the desk and stretched his arms above his head. "Why? Are you after some gossip?"

"Gossip is rife around here," I replied.

"Oh, I know. I've only been here a few days and I've been hearing rumours."

"Like what?"

Chase didn't answer, but his eyes sparkled with intrigue. He slapped the lid of his laptop down and stood up.

"Night, McArthur. Be here bright and early in the morning. We've got Callum Burns to interview."

And with that, he put on his coat, winked in my general direction, and left.

* * *

"You know what a bad day calls for," Maddie declared, standing at my front door and holding up a bottle of red wine like a prize she had won. She raised an eyebrow at my disappointed expression. "Am I not who you were expecting?"

"No, I guess not," I replied but I stepped aside and let her into the flat. "But how do you know it's been a bad day?"

Maddie made herself comfortable on the sofa whilst I found two clean glasses. It had become a habit of ours to while away the evening together with several glasses after an unexpectedly bad or frustrating day.

"How do I know anything?" she replied. "I heard about it. You can't uncover remains buried in the woods without there being a little bit of chatter at the station."

I sighed as I joined her on the sofa, an uncomfortable realisation occurring to me. If Maddie had heard about the body, then Aaron must have known too.

"You're finding this case hard, aren't you?" Maddie pouted at me, just one degree off from giving a condescending tut. As much as I tried to hide my frustrations, it rarely worked with her. Maddie had a way of digging into people until she uncovered the truth. Usually, it involved alcohol.

"I'm just worried about him," I admitted. "Aaron's going through this all by himself."

"Aww." Maddie let out a little squeak, before taking a hearty gulp of wine. "I am sure that once everything is over and done with, things will go back to normal."

"That's unusually optimistic of you."

"I'm trying out a new positive-thinking thing," she replied. "It wasn't my idea, it was Cass. She says I'm too negative all the time. So, if I think positive, then it will be positive. DCI Chase will solve this case and bugger off back to HQ. Everyone will get the closure they are hoping for. Chief Constable Price will back off and let the Ali Burgess case lie, and will stop trying to ruin everyone's careers. Positive mental attitude." She overly pronounced the last three words and schooled her expression into one of serene calm.

"Really?" I watched her for a moment. "You're full of shit."

A knowing smile crossed Maddie's face. "I know, but please don't tell my girlfriend that. She thinks it's working."

I silenced the TV, which had been droning on with the depressing weather forecast for the weekend. Cold, rain, and a bit more cold and rain. At least no more freezing fog for now.

"Would you rather I told you the truth?" Maddie asked. When I nodded, she took a deep breath, preparing herself. "Well then. The chances are that this cold case might never get closed, Aaron will remain distant and aloof, and DCI Chase will continue to feed back information about the team to the chief constable."

I gulped down some wine. "Thanks. I knew I could rely on you to wallow in negativity with me."

"I do have some news for you, though," she said. "DCI Chase is definitely here to spy."

"I could've told you that," I replied. "Chase has told me as much."

Undeterred, Maddie continued, "People are divided when it comes to him. Most say he's good police, great track record, but tends to rub people up the wrong way. But he's not just that, he's also part of Price's inner circle. One of his top men."

I considered this a moment. "Are you sure?" I asked.

Chase wasn't as sycophantic towards Chief Constable Price as I expected one of his trusted advisors to be.

"I am," said Maddie, biting her lip. "It gets worse. He's not just one of Price's lackeys; he's also his son-in-law. He's married to Price's eldest daughter."

"Izzy?"

So, Izzy Chase was actually Izzy Price. That was what she meant when she said 'as soon as my dad finds out what he's done, he's finished'. It wasn't just a threat against Chase, it was a threat against his career. The Price family had Chase over a barrel.

Maddie nodded. "Yep. She's some legal advisor for the Crown courts and just as formidable as her father, apparently."

"Oh yes, I know that," I said, thinking back to the brief conversation with Izzy after the car accident. "And she also kicked Chase out recently."

"Really?" Maddie's eyes widened. She was like a dog caught on a scent, and whilst she respected my boundaries and didn't use me for her gossiping much, Chase was clearly fair game.

"Yeah. Things aren't very cordial between them at the moment."

She rubbed her hands together with glee. "See, gossiping is fun. You always sneer at me for finding out these juicy details but you never know when they may come in handy. Without me, none of you would know about Chase being married to Price's daughter."

"What else do you know then?"

"Nothing," replied Maddie. "Unless you want to know which of the probation officers are shagging each other."

"Nah," I said. I took a moment to finish off the last of the wine in my glass, before pouring another full one. "Although, do you know what's wrong with Jay?"

Maddie tutted. "Is he still being a miserable bastard?"

"Yes."

"It's stress," she said simply. "I've seen him like this before. Although..." She absently traced her fingertip around the rim of her glass. "I wonder if he's starting to fade."

"Fade?"

"You know. Lose the love of the job. Because, let's face it, we only do this job for love. We risk our lives, deal with the worst of society, and get paid a pittance for it. Sometimes an officer just loses their spark and it can be hard to get it back again."

"Do you really think that's happening to Jay?"

Maddie took a moment to think this over, as if weighing up the evidence in her head.

"I hope not," she decided. "But I think it happens to all of us eventually."

Chapter Nineteen

Detective Chief Inspector Chase was conspicuously absent from the Serious Crimes office when I arrived the next morning. Chris was there, deep in conversation with someone on the phone. Jay was adjusting some of the information on the whiteboard, adding details about our gruesome discovery from the day before.

"Have you heard the news?" he asked, nodding at Chris.

"What news?" I shrugged off my coat, just as Chris's voice rose, his annoyance becoming clear.

"We can't test Clara Burns' DNA against the remains we found yesterday," said Jay. He pursed his lips, as if trying his best to not say any more.

"Why not?"

"They have lost the comparison samples."

Chris set his phone back into its receiver with a forceful clang, making the device beep in disagreement. He grumbled some swear words under his breath.

"Ah," said Jay, holding his hand out. "Remember to use toddler-friendly words."

"Fine," Chris snapped, although for a moment it looked as though he was going to swear back with every possible word in his vocabulary. "The silly colleagues at the archives cannot find any DNA samples for Clara Burns from the files. They've either been lost or disposed of, but they're not sure which. That means the lab don't have anything to test the remains against. Silly… twats."

"Well done," replied Jay, turning back to the board. "Then we'll just have to go to Plan B, I guess. As much as we don't want to."

"What's Plan B?" I asked. Their reluctance told me it wasn't the preferred option.

"A familial match," Chris said. "We could ask one of Clara Burns' living relatives for a sample to see if it matches the remains. If it does, we know we've found her."

"We can't do that," I replied. "That means we have to ask Aaron or his brother. We can't ask them to do that."

"It's our only choice," said Chris flatly.

"It might be best to ask the brother," Jay suggested. "He doesn't know us; it won't be so awkward."

Chris nodded at the idea. And then, as if in sync with one another, they both turned on me.

"What?" I asked. "You want me to be the one to ask Callum Burns for a DNA sample?"

"You are the kindest one," Chris pointed out. "You get on with people better. You're good at breaking bad news."

"And you're just buttering me up so I'll do it," I replied.

"Maybe." He shrugged. "And if it doesn't work, there's still the old-fashioned way. Pulling rank. Go on, Detective Constable."

"Can't we get DCI Chase to do it?"

"He's not here yet," said Chris. "But Callum Burns is. He's in Aaron's office."

This wasn't an argument I was going to win against them. I growled under my breath, until I managed to settle on an appropriate insult.

"You're both… twats," I said, before I stormed from the office.

Down the corridor, I found Aaron's office door had been propped open. Both men inside stood at the windows, discussing something in low voices. Although I'd seen a picture of Callum before inside Aaron's house, I was surprised yet again by how alike the brothers were. Callum's fair hair was much greyer and he wore a pair of half-rimmed glasses, slightly tinted in the dim light. However, they both stood with their arms folded, had a similar stature, and wore the same unimpressed expression.

I knocked lightly on the door.

"Good morning," I greeted them. They both turned from the window. Apart from their positioning, nothing else of the brothers' stances changed.

"Callum," said Aaron. "This is Detective Constable Anna McArthur. She's on the team dealing with the... case."

Callum raked his gaze over me, his frown turning upwards very slightly.

"The famous Anna," he said, smirking a little at his brother's awkward introduction. He held out a hand to shake. "Pleasure to meet you. I've still heard nothing about you."

"Same here," I lied, taking his hand. "Thank you for coming all this way."

Callum looked around, giving the office a sour look. "So where is this DCI Chase who's forced me here?"

"I'm sure he'll be along soon. In the meantime, let's get you through for processing." Breezily done and spoken with confidence, I hoped neither of them would second-guess my words and would assume this was all part of the plan.

"Hold up." Aaron stuck his arm out, stopping me in my tracks. Of course, it didn't work on him. "Processing for what? Is Callum under suspicion?"

"Of course not," I said and bit my lip. "Please, Aaron, you know I can't go through this with you. Just trust me."

The look on his face, a quick flash of guilt followed by magnitudes of disapproval, was enough to make my own guilt simmer inside. I hated every inch of this situation.

Aaron didn't give much of a reaction, but eventually he muttered, "Right."

I released the breath I was holding.

"And where is Chase?" he demanded.

"I'm sure he'll be along any minute," I replied, assuredly. "We can wait for him, if you wanted to talk to him first. You know, DCI to DCI."

Aaron bristled and gave me an indignant scowl. "Why would I do that?"

"I didn't think so," I said back with a smile.

Next to me, Callum huffed. "Come on then, let's get this done. Whatever it is we're doing."

Leaving Aaron behind, I led Callum downstairs and to an unoccupied side room. Usually used to taking fingerprints and DNA samples, it was the perfect place to take a few moments and try to explain myself.

"What exactly am I doing here?" Callum asked the second the door to the room closed behind us.

"Well," I said, the words weighing me down, "DCI Chase wanted to ask you some questions about your mother's disappearance."

"I know that."

"And we had a development in the investigation yesterday that we could use your help with."

Callum raised an eyebrow. His expressions were more animated than his brother's; Aaron was quite skilled in schooling his face so little emotion showed. Callum was much more adept at looking disapproving.

"What development?" he pressed.

I took a deep breath. However, Callum must have guessed what I would say before the words left my mouth; his face crumpled by the second word.

"We found remains yesterday in the woods surrounding Pepperwell Farm Cottages. We need a DNA sample from you to confirm a familial match."

"A familial match," he repeated, testing the words. They tasted foul. He glanced back at the door, as if he could see the whole station beyond.

"Where?" he demanded.

"Buried. Not far from the cottages, just beyond the first pit. In an old shed."

Callum rubbed his hands over his face and scrubbed his eyes. He paced the small room, growing agitated at the containment. "I know where you mean. We grew up there, played hide-and-seek. We knew every inch of those woods. Are you telling me she was there the whole time?"

"We haven't confirmed anything yet," I said hastily. "This is why I need your help. We need to work out the identity of the remains before jumping to any conclusions."

"Well, who else are they going to be?"

I didn't have a reply. Callum's reaction cut me, stinging far deeper than I expected. It was an unwelcome reminder that this wasn't just another case; not just an investigation. Two children lost their mother. The effects of that were still evident, even forty years later.

"Fine," Callum said, sounding exactly like Aaron and even throwing his arms up in the same exasperated way. "Fine, I'll give the sample. Whatever will end this fastest."

"My boss will still want to talk to you," I said. I found the necessary paperwork and DNA evidence kit in the storage cupboards of the room and started filling them in before Callum could change his mind.

"What for? What information can he want that he doesn't already have? Other than to drag up forty years of buried trauma."

Once again, I didn't have a reply. When Callum realised that I wasn't able to answer him, he sat down in the spare chair across the room from me, crossed his arms and huffed. He glowered not just at me, but at the entire room, right down to the badly laminated signs reminding us to lock the cupboard and turn the lights off.

"Do I need a solicitor?" he asked.

I shook my head. "No, no need for a solicitor. DCI Chase just wants some insight from someone who might remember the original investigation."

"That's not what my brother said."

"Oh?" I said, meeting Callum's gaze. His face was fiery, ready to cut me down at a moment's notice.

Callum fixed me with a harsh, unyielding stare. "He said he's playing a game. That this Chase seems to find it amusing to sow discord. That he might try to dig for some dirt. I hope you don't expect me to lie for you."

It wasn't a question so I avoided giving an answer and instead pushed over a form and pen for him to sign. I felt his glare pressing into me as I pulled on a pair of rubber gloves and prepared the swab kit.

"Because I'm not lying for you," Callum continued. "For Aaron, maybe, if needed, but not you. I don't know you, Anna."

"Hopefully you won't need to." Drips of dread rolled down my neck like cool raindrops.

"Can you be sure?"

No, I couldn't. Truth was, I didn't know what Chase was planning now that he had Callum Burns in the building. He hadn't divulged anything to me and I got the impression his interview strategy was more speak-before-thinking rather than an actual technique.

Just as Callum opened his mouth at my indication, allowing me to swab the inside of his cheek, the handle of the door rattled. It swung inwards and Chase appeared in the frame, his face lighting up at his find.

"Callum Burns." In two swift strides, Chase reached across to shake Callum's hand. "I'm DCI Matthew Chase, thank you for coming in. I appreciate how hard this is. I take it DC McArthur has informed you of our findings from yesterday."

Callum rose to his feet. "Yes. Let's get this over with, please. I have clients to get back to."

"Then follow me." And Chase swept from the room, heading for the interview suite and expecting us to follow.

I hastened to finish up and package the swab kit, whilst Callum rose to his feet. At the doorway, he faltered.

"You shouldn't be on this investigation," he said as he gritted his teeth.

My mouth ran dry but I stood up and strode for the door, channelling the same confidence I had used earlier. "I'm doing this for Aaron."

"You're playing with fire, Anna, and sooner or later, someone will get burnt," he replied.

Chase reached the interview room and held the door open. He noticed we were lagging behind. Time was up.

Callum strode ahead, his head held high, and I had no choice but to follow on and ignore the apprehension building inside with each step.

* * *

"So," said Callum Burns, wasting no time as he sat down opposite Chase in the interview room, "I consent to the DNA sample being used, but I want to know why you believe the remains you've found in the woods belong to my mother."

I took the seat next to Chase, avoiding Callum's gaze. If Chase noticed my jittery hands fiddling with my pen and notebook, he made no indication of it. His attention flickered to Callum, a little taken aback by his hostility, but he settled on the case file he had brought with him. He thumbed through the papers slowly.

"First things first," replied Chase. "Can you tell us your whereabouts on Tuesday of last week?"

Callum's expression sullened into a further frown.

"What time?"

"All day," Chase answered, not missing a beat.

"I was at home. Then I went to work. And then home again."

"Is that it?" Chase pressed. "No hobbies? No trips to the pub or the shops." He still had his attention fixed on the case file, and his lack of eye contact only seemed to irritate Callum even more.

"No," replied Callum. For a moment, I thought that might be the only reply he would give but after taking a second to measure the man opposite, he continued. "And before you ask your next question, yes, I have a dozen colleagues and my wife who can vouch for me. I'd be happy to provide you with their details."

Chase looked up across the table and grinned. He produced a piece of paper from the file and turned it for Callum to see. It was the preliminary post-mortem report.

"Well, in that case," said Chase, "the remains we found near Pepperwell Farm Cottages are definitely that of a female, age mid to late thirties. The body structure suggests someone who has had at least one child. The remains have been in the ground a few decades, although more testing and a full post-mortem will solidify those details. You have to admit that it's a close match so far, found so close to where your mother was last seen."

"Close, but not conclusive," said Callum.

"Which is why we need your DNA," replied Chase.

"Why mine? Why not my brother? After all, he is right here, working in the same police station as you."

Chase did a double take, as if noticing my presence for the first time. "A case like this requires the utmost sensitivity, especially when it involves someone close. We've done everything we can to keep DCI Burns out of this. Isn't that right, McArthur?"

I didn't expect the question thrown my way but I nodded hastily. Callum's eyes met mine, just for a moment, and I hoped he took my empathy as genuine.

"Well…" Callum stretched his neck, looking older with each passing second. "I guess I can only thank you for that. You can't imagine what my brother and I have been through. To reopen the case after all these years came as a surprise."

"I wouldn't want to cause any further distress," said Chase, slightly missing the mark if he was aiming for sympathy, "but now could be the last chance for us to find out what happened to your mother. I've read all the statements, interviews and such from the old case file, but yours was lacking, shall we say."

Callum scoffed. "Lacking? What did you expect? I was only ten."

"Old enough to know what was going on."

"I did know what was going on. I was traumatised."

"Well, you've had forty years to come to terms with it," replied Chase. "What can you tell me about your mother and Barney King?"

Callum wrinkled his nose, the same way that Aaron did. "That old man. He was a miserable bastard; he never spoke another word to us after she disappeared. Of course, Dad was convinced he'd done something to her. He'd get drunk at every chance, harass Barney until he'd give in and punch his lights out. It was only a few more years before we moved from that godforsaken cottage and I never saw the old man again."

"And what about before your mother disappeared? How much did they interact with each other?"

"She was friendly," Callum said with the hint of a sad smile. "She was lovely to everyone. Kill them with kindness, that was my mum. Everyone loved her. She'd give King the extra meat whenever we had Sunday roast, get his washing in if it was raining. She'd even let me go poaching with him… As far as I can remember, there was nothing untoward."

"Just friendly neighbours?"

Callum nodded. "To my ten-year-old eyes, yes. If you're asking me if there was anything more going on, I don't know. I never thought so. But I was a child; what would I know?"

"I think you know more than you realise." Chase sat up in his seat, a smirk tugging on his lips.

"Like what?"

"Like what happened just before she disappeared. Things like this rarely happen out of the blue. Most times, people who choose to disappear leave some clues behind – a change in personality, odd behaviour like changing plans at the last minute or an unwillingness to commit. Anything like that with your mum?"

Callum shook his head. "Not that I remember."

"Then that leads me to my prevailing theory – that something happened to her out of her control. Think back, Callum. Did anything noteworthy happen in the lead-up to her disappearance? An argument with King, perhaps?"

"I don't think so... She argued with my father, but that wasn't something new. He liked to drink more than anything else; when he'd been to the pub, he'd pick a fight over anything. There was one argument a few weeks before she... Anyway, he was getting jealous of how nice she was to other men. Not just Barney, but Harry at the farmhouse, and Ray, one of the lorry drivers."

"Did he suspect something was going on between her and any of these other men?"

"No," said Callum. "Well, he might have, but as I said, he'd pick a fight over anything. Mum promised not to talk to any of them anymore. The walls were so thin on those houses that Barney probably heard the whole thing, but he never said anything, even if he did."

"What if he did hear?" Chase asked. "What if he didn't like the fact that your mother promised not to interact with him anymore? He was on his own at this point, wasn't he? His wife and daughter had left him."

Callum shrugged his shoulders. "He never said anything about having a wife or daughter and I don't remember them, if he did have them. He might not have liked it, but as I said, he never said anything. He was respectful to my mother; she was too nice for anyone to be anything but."

Once again, Callum stretched his neck, rolling his head from side to side. He sighed as though a weight had been lifted but his face didn't match the sentiment. If anything, he looked just as haunted as he did when we first began.

"How long will it take?" he asked, filling the silence Chase left open. The latter was staring at the case file in his hands, deep in thought

"Huh?"

"The DNA results," said Callum. "How long will it take to come back?"

Chase tutted. "Depends. Results can be back within seventy-two hours. With a cold case like this, it tends to get pushed to the back of the queue – what's another couple of days on a forty-year-old case? But with the surname Burns attached, I expect results will be quick. Your brother's reputation will pull some strings."

"Will you tell him when you have the results?" Callum asked. He aimed the question at me.

Chase didn't notice. "We'll contact both of you when we have a result."

"Tell him," said Callum. "Don't keep him in the dark any longer." He aimed his words at me, as though this whole situation was my doing.

"He asked to be kept in the dark," I pointed out. I wasn't keeping anything from Aaron through misguided intentions.

But Callum frowned. "You should know by now that he doesn't always know what's best for himself. He likes burying his head in the sand. Don't let him."

Chapter Twenty

"What did you make of him?"

Chase and I stood outside the station, watching Callum Burns drive away in his sleek Mercedes C-Class estate. The air was as bitter as the day before and the brooding grey clouds promised more foul weather was incoming.

"Huh?" I asked, too lost in my own thoughts to register Chase was speaking to me.

He rolled his eyes as he repeated, much slower, every word I'd just missed. "I said, nice car, we must be in the wrong business. Then I asked what did you make of him, Callum Burns?"

I folded my arms across my chest as I shivered.

"He seemed genuine. It's hard to judge when we're relying so heavily on the testimony of someone who was a child when all these events happened."

"True," said Chase with a nod. He reached up with a trembling hand and touched the sterile gauze on his forehead, covering the sutures where he'd hit the windscreen. He was doing a remarkable job at covering up how much of a headache he must have had, but for a very brief moment, he slipped.

"Right, two jobs now," he said, shaking away whatever pain still bothered him. "Get that DNA sample to the lab ASAP, and update the others on what we've learnt. And find some painkillers. And I suppose we should tell DCI Burns about our discovery in the woods yesterday. We shouldn't be relying on gossip keeping him in the loop."

"That's four jobs."

"Yes, I can count, McArthur." Chase rolled his eyes.

"I'll get right on it," I replied.

As we were speaking, a beat-up old Land Rover pulled into the car park, its driver with a face like thunder. I pitied the officer on duty at the front desk today.

"And I'll give Goodwin an update on our progress," Chase replied with an exaggerated groan. "I can't wait for this bloody case to be resolved. I want to get back to civilisation and decent internet connection. Somewhere a half-mile drive doesn't take twenty minutes because of a damn tractor on the road."

"It's not so bad round here," I said.

He scoffed at me, but a smile broke out on his face nonetheless.

"I guess so," he said quietly. "Right, fine. Let's get to it. I can't avoid Goodwin forever."

"Why are you avoiding her?" I asked innocently.

Chase chewed his lip. "You're not stupid, Anna. You know I was sent over here to keep an eye on some things."

"What things?"

"Well, you and your escapades. The working dynamics of the team. The progress with the Ali Burgess case."

"And what have you told them so far?"

A car door slammed somewhere around us, but I dare not look away. Chase avoided my gaze and exhaled, the cold stealing his breath in cloudy wisps. He thrust his hands in his pockets and strode back towards the station, its automatic doors already open, as though waiting for us.

"Nothing incriminating."

I hurried to catch up with him and the warmth of the station hit us like walking into a sauna. "What is that supposed to mean?"

Chase stopped abruptly a few steps inside the threshold. He turned to me and lowered his voice.

"You sound worried, Detective McArthur. Is there something you're hiding?"

I felt a prickle on the back of my neck and glanced around the foyer, teeming with people. There was someone in a large overcoat exchanging hushed, tense words at the front desk with the officer on duty. A fretting young woman being consoled by her mother over in the corner. A teenager paced back and forth, as a disembodied voice scolded him from his mobile phone. Several officers came and went, barely looking twice at what was an ordinary day for us; a collection of chaos that needed to be handled – would be handled – as it was every day.

And then there was Aaron, making his way from upstairs and through the secure access doors. He spotted Chase and me, and at the last minute, diverted his course to approach us.

"Here comes one task," said Chase, barely moving his lips. "Time we told him about the body in the woods, don't you think?"

"Let me do it," I cut in. "Without you. This will be a difficult enough conversation."

I saw the flicker of a scowl on Aaron's face as he read my expression. There was concern in his eyes, masked by the time he reached us.

"How did it go with Callum?" he asked.

"Interesting," Chase replied, and in an instant, he was back to his usual conceited self. "In fact, McArthur was just on her way to speak to you." His face was still flushed from our time outside, but he didn't appear to be as uncomfortable as I felt. The room was boiling. I didn't remember it being this hot before I stepped outside.

"What about–"

Aaron's words were cut off by the deafening sound of a gunshot, rebounding off the station walls.

* * *

Flakes of plaster rained down from the ceiling, like sleet showering from the sky. The shot shook the building, leaving my vision wavering and my ears ringing like I was inside a bell. It blocked out the muffled gasps and screams around me but it only took a moment before it all returned. The shock and confusion rushed back like a tidal wave in the wake of the gunshot.

I remained crouched on the floor, Chase and Aaron by my side. Cautiously, the three of us raised our heads to survey the room. By the front desk, the disgruntled gun-wielder stood tall, overcoat flapping open and double-barrelled shotgun facing the crumbling ceiling tiles. She was aged and haggard, but a gruff expression only confirmed that she was not to be messed with. By the mud on her boots, the worn tweed of her jacket, I guessed she was a farmer. And a pissed-off one at that.

"Who's in charge here?" the woman demanded, her face twisted like a gargoyle.

Beside me, Aaron stirred. I spied the front desk officer, one of the panicked newbies, searching for his radio. He felt for the emergency button, but the black holes of the shotgun found him and trapped him in their sight. He froze, mouth opening and closing uselessly. There was a screen between them, but judging by the fragments of ceiling tiles scattering the floor, it wouldn't be much protection.

The woman wasn't perturbed by the shock she'd caused; behind her, the young woman and mother were cowering behind their seats, and the teenager lay on the floor with his hands covering his ears. The handful of officers caught in the mayhem were also stuck in place, stunned by the danger so close to sanctuary. Helplessly assessing, searching for a way to end this.

Aaron steadily rose to his feet. He gulped hard and I realised what he was about to do just a fraction too late to stop him.

"That would be me."

"No," I gasped.

"I'm in charge," he said as he took a step forward, catching the attention of the woman.

With his free hand, he pushed me back as I grasped at him, desperate to pull him back down. Chase caught my arm and held on tightly, straightening himself upright.

"Aaron, don't," I begged him. There was a panic in my voice I had never heard before, along with a pinching pain in my chest with every step forward he took.

He glanced back at me, his calm, focused gaze cracking slightly, but Chase gripped onto my forearms, holding me in place. I didn't know what they expected me to do but my feet were inching forward.

Aaron stopped as he approached the gunwoman.

"Violet Tointon, I presume," he said carefully. He held his hands up as he made his way forwards, moving slowly as though approaching a spooked horse. The woman turned her murderous glare on him, but the gun remained pointed at the officer behind the front desk.

"How do you know?" she demanded. "Who are you?"

"Detective Chief Inspector Aaron Burns. I know all about your problems with the Firearms team. Your licence being revoked."

"Ridiculous!" the woman spat at him. "I've had a shotgun licence for the last thirty years. How am I meant to defend my farm without one?"

"Those are the rules." Aaron inhaled deeply, his hands held out in peace, vulnerability. "We don't make them but we have to enforce them. And the rules state you can't have a firearm."

"A pointless, bureaucratic rule that makes no sense!" she screeched back.

"Maybe," said Aaron. "But rules are there for a reason, to keep people safe. So, hand over the gun, Violet. I don't want anyone here hurt."

Still aimed at the desk officer, the gun shook violently in Tointon's hands. Her fingers trembled so much that I wondered how she was still able to aim.

"I wouldn't hurt anyone!" she exclaimed. "I never have!"

"I believe you," said Aaron. "But with a diagnosis like yours, things are only going to get worse. Put the gun down, Violet. We can talk about it but not like this, not with all these people here."

Somewhere in the station, a silent alarm had been raised. I spied action out the corner of my eye; a handful of riot-gear-clad officers inched into view outside and the odd head raised above the parapet took a peek through the glass of the secure access door. I knew we were ill-equipped for a situation like this here. It'd take a proper negotiator to defuse things, and even if we had someone trained in the station, they'd still have to wrangle their way into the stand-off. Something told me we didn't have that much time. A new urgency rose within me, the urge to act.

"We have to stop her," I hissed at Chase, my sights stuck on the gunwoman. I could feel him by my side; one hand still gripped my forearm as though he expected me to bolt.

"How?" he whispered back before giving a slight shake of his head. "Let Burns handle it; he's doing well so far."

I tugged on him to let me go and nodded to the gun. "She's not in control. Look at her. She's shaking so badly she could accidently pull the trigger."

"Then what do you suggest? She's got a gun!"

I didn't know. All I knew was the rising panic within. It was going to be hard to contain it for much longer, especially with Aaron at centre stage. Tointon's wild eyes were focussed on him, her mouth spitting out hateful words and streams of curses. He remained calm throughout, hands held up, as he accepted the barrage of insults.

"I can't change the situation," said Aaron.

"Of course you can. You're in charge!"

"Only of this station," he said. "Of these officers, who you're currently pointing a gun at. Their safety is my greatest concern. Just put the gun down, Violet."

She swung the barrel round on him.

"Aaron!" My cry made him glance back at me.

He glared, as though he could tell what I was thinking. 'Stay back' his pointed look told me.

"Oi, eyes on me!" Tointon growled at him. She strode forwards until the barrel of the gun pressed into the material of Aaron's white shirt. Her fingers danced over the trigger, doing an animated jive as she decided what to do.

"Chase," I begged. She'll kill him. One accidental touch of the trigger and he'll be dead.

"I know," Chase replied through gritted teeth.

"We have to stop her."

She could kill him. One touch.

"Anna, it's crazy."

"She's got one shot," I said. "She won't be able to reload. You tackle her, I'll take the gun."

"That's—"

Whatever he was about to say — crazy, idiotic, impossible — didn't matter as I took a cautious step forward. To my relief, I felt him on my tail. He had my back.

I saw Aaron inhale a deep breath, expecting the worst. He was pinned under the aim of the shotgun. It was now or never.

Like lightning, I sprung forwards, knocking into Aaron's shoulder as I reached for the barrel of the shotgun. Chase was a blur beside me, his arms outstretched. He tackled Violet Tointon at the same time I took grasp of the gun.

The resounding shot pierced my ear drums and shattered my world.

Chapter Twenty-One

Now there were two holes in the ceiling. The second had destroyed a smoke detector, and the whole police station was filled with the ear-splitting wails of the fire alarm. Even from outside, the noise was disorientating.

I sat on the bonnet of Jay's car in the station car park, his coat around my shoulders. Around us, well-organised efforts were being made to pick up the pieces after the stand-off. Officers were consoling the poor civilians caught in the action. Violet had been taken to a cell. Her gun still lay on the floor of the foyer and I could just see it through the automatic front doors every time they opened as another person crossed from the crime scene within to the makeshift sanctuary outside.

Chase wasn't far away, telling an animated tale to the armed officers who had arrived only minutes after our actions. They didn't look as impressed with his heroics, or his waving arms, as he did.

Jay leaned on the car next to me. No sign of Aaron or Chris.

"Have you stopped shaking now?" Jay asked me gently.

When I nodded, showing him my steady hands, he handed over a warm mug of coffee.

"Thanks," I said as I took a welcome sip.

He watched the scene around us. The whole station had been evacuated but now people were being allowed back in. The wailing alarm fell silent. Still no sign of Aaron.

"You know what you did was…" Jay didn't need to finish that sentence. I knew what he was going to say; stupid.

"She had a gun pointed at Aaron," I said. "What was I meant to do?"

"He could have talked her down."

"And what if he couldn't?" I bit back. "Did anyone really expect me to just stand there and watch as he…" The words died off as the reality of the situation lay obvious before us.

Jay took a long draught of his own coffee. "Good point, I suppose," he said. "Out of all people, you're not the one who can sit by and wait something out. You have to act." He jumped to his feet, shivering dramatically. "Come on, let's get inside."

"What about Aaron?"

"He's fine, he's with the Firearms team upstairs," he replied. "From what I heard, that woman had been causing trouble for them for weeks since they revoked her shotgun licence. I bet they're all feeling a little sheepish now, for underestimating her and him nearly getting… you know."

He mimed holding a shotgun.

An uncomfortable nausea tickled at the back of my throat as I followed Jay inside and back to our office. Chris was there, his eyes following me round the room and he opened his mouth as I landed in the chair.

"Don't say it," I warned him.

"Crazy McArthur strikes again."

"I said, don't say it."

"Relax," said Jay. "It's over now. No harm done."

"Pure luck," Chris mumbled under his breath. "That crazy old bat could have killed you."

I huddled down deeper inside Jay's coat; the station suddenly felt freezing cold compared to my boiling blood. The reality of what I'd done was beginning to dawn on me, just how close I'd come to watching Aaron die or facing the gun myself. I pushed it as far out of my mind as I could and focused on my colleagues sitting before me.

"She wasn't your typical gunslinger," Jay was saying, as he tucked himself in at his desk.

"I asked one of the Firearms team about her while you were out," Chris said. "She's a local farmer, out Feltwell way. She's lived on her own since her husband passed away a few years ago. She's had a shotgun licence for years, for pest control and such, she claimed. Anyway, a couple of months ago she was diagnosed with Parkinson's disease and that's an automatic disqualification for a licence. She didn't take the news very well."

"Why is it an automatic disqualification?" I asked.

"It's a degenerative disease and affects the motor skills. The patient will lose the ability to move and it only gets worse over time. For some the process takes months or years, for others it can take decades."

"If she's been threatening the Firearms team for a while, why didn't they do anything about her?" Jay asked.

"Hindsight is a wonderful thing." Chris shrugged his shoulders. "A few threats are a bit different to aiming a gun at the DCI, though. Is he okay?"

Jay glanced at Chris. "Aaron? We haven't seen him."

I sat up in my chair and turned on Jay. "You said he was fine."

"He is," Chris said quickly, keen to calm me. "He'll be fine, he was just a bit quiet. I didn't know if you'd checked on him."

"I'll go do it now." The nausea finally relented as I rose to my feet and strode from the office before either of them could stop me. I needed to see him for myself. Everything after the second gunshot was still a bit hazy, the ringing in my ears and blurs of activity all merging in my memories.

Just as Chase had tackled Violet Tointon to the ground, I had reached the gun and aimed it above our heads. It triggered with a noise that shook deep in my bones. The barrel burned in my hand. At the same moment, a dozen officers burst into the room from every angle; I tore the handle of the gun from Tointon's loose grip and tossed it to the floor. Chase pinned the woman on the ground. And Aaron stood, gobsmacked, but all in one piece.

I reached his office and listened to the closed door. His voice floated through from the other side, talking with flat efficiency and a lack of emotion. He could project the image of being fine to everyone; surely, I knew him well enough by now to know whether that was true or not.

I knocked lightly and let myself in. On my entrance, Aaron put down the phone on his desk. He wasn't sitting, and I got the impression he had been pacing as far as the spiralled phone cord would allow.

"Are you okay?" he asked urgently, making his way to me in three strides. In an uncharacteristic show of affection, he took me into his arms, folding me into a light hug.

"I'm fine, I'm fine," I assured him quickly.

Aaron exhaled, his breath rasping unevenly. "Good… because I could kill you."

"What? Why?"

I untangled myself from his grip, only to be met with an expression of anger. He looked fine, seemingly all held together, but there was something else there. A wavering under the surface that was only barely being contained.

"What the hell were you thinking?"

"She was pointing the gun at you!"

"I know that!" He gritted his teeth together. "And I was trying to talk some sense into her because that way she was focused on me, and not you or any other innocent person in the room. You and Chase were close enough to the door, you were close enough to get out."

"Was I really supposed to just leave you there?" I shot back. "Why didn't you tell me that a gun-wielding old woman was threatening you?"

"It was none of your concern."

"Of course it is!" I exclaimed. "You *are* my concern. But you still insist on doing everything on your own."

"I don't."

"You do," I said. I felt guilty at the torrent but now unleashed, the tide wouldn't be easy to stop. I had a week of frustrations pent-up inside. "I'm sorry for the way this case has got between us, but you can still talk to me. You don't have to push me away. I keep telling you; you don't have to deal with everything on your own."

"That isn't the point, Anna," he snapped back. "This isn't about me. How can you expect me to open up to you when you throw yourself into any situation without a thought?"

"I don't."

"You tackled someone with a gun! You had no regard for your own safety. Just like always; you dived in with no thought, no common sense, no plan."

A realisation hit him and he took a step back, as though I'd physically pushed him. Blinking slowly, he rounded towards his desk and leaned heavily against the top. I could do nothing but wait until he spoke again.

"Why do we keep doing this?" he eventually said, barely more than a whisper. "We have the same old argument, time after time, even before we started seeing each other. You do something reckless and I get angry with you for making me worry."

"Only because you care," I pointed out.

He shook his head. "We can't carry on like this."

"What do you mean?" I asked, my voice just a husk. Those pent-up emotions had fizzled out quickly and they left behind a deep well, sucking all my energy and thoughts into it.

Aaron took a deep breath. "I can't keep doing this, Anna. I can't keep worrying about you all the time."

"Why not?" I inched closer. I knew the answer. This was Aaron's fear talking – his phobia of commitment, his brush with death only moments before. This wasn't what he really wanted.

Was it?

He sighed, the breath quivering on its way out. He wasn't fine, as Jay and Chris had assured me. He was far from it. These past few days were taking their toll on him, and me and my thoughtless actions had only made it worse.

"You should go," Aaron said. He swallowed hard, able to push back whatever feelings were on the brink of coming out.

"I'm not—"

"Anna, that was Chief Constable Price on the phone. He's on his way over with his team. There's going to have to be a press release. There's a station full of people that just witnessed what happened and he could walk in on us any second. We can't discuss this now. We have to get back to work."

"Then promise me, we'll talk about this later," I said.

Aaron gave a shrug, unable to meet my gaze. "There's nothing to talk about. You won't change. And neither will I."

His words punctured like a dagger. And the worst part was that I couldn't disagree.

The sound of urgent footsteps filled my ears as someone approached the office. There came a knock at the door, urgent. Aaron finally raised his head.

"I'm busy," he called out. His voice had a dangerous edge to it, on the brink of telling the interrupter where to go.

"Actually, I want DC McArthur," came Chase's voice from the other side of the door. "I've had a thought about the case."

Chapter Twenty-Two

Back in the Serious Crimes office, DCI Chase threw a case file at me like a frisbee. The surge of adrenalin from the events still had a tight grip on him, and he paced the short length of the room, kicking Jay's chair as he went.

"What now?" Jay asked, his fingers poised above his keyboard.

"Look up Barney King's last shotgun licence application," Chase commanded. "I don't know when it was, but the records will be on there somewhere."

"But he had a shotgun," Chris pointed out. "What does having a licence matter? He didn't use it to kill himself."

"He *used to* have a licence," replied Chase. "And then for some reason, stopped renewing it. I want to know why."

After a moment of typing, Jay hummed with interest. "Here it is. His licence expired about two months ago. King failed to respond to any of the reminders to apply for a renewal."

Chase clicked his fingers at me. "Find those hospital letters. Which hospital clinics had he been seen by recently?"

Now knowing why the case file had been aimed at my head, I leafed through the letters from the local hospital we'd taken from King's house. "In the last six months, King was seen by the audiology team, the diabetic nutrition team, ENT—"

"No, no, no." Chase threw his hands in the air. "None of those fit. Keep going."

"Cardiology?"

Chris turned round in his seat, watching Chase. "What exactly are we looking for?"

Chase shook his head and motioned to me to carry on.

"Neurology," I said. "It's the only other department he was seen by. His last two appointments were there."

"And he went there the day before he died," Jay pointed out.

Chase drummed his fingers on his chin. "He was an ill man. Did he know just how ill he was though…" He clicked his fingers and pointed to Chris. "Medical records. He was having lots of tests done. What was the neurology consultant testing for?"

Chris tapped onto his computer. He must have been slightly intrigued by where Chase was going by this because he didn't mutter any insults under his breath.

"All sorts," came the answer. "Age-related degeneration, dementia, something called PSP and Parkinson's."

Chase strode over and leaned over Chris's shoulder to read the screen.

"I knew it. Of course."

"What?" I asked. "I don't get it."

Chase stood up straight, as if to make an announcement.

"King was experiencing memory problems, stiffness and problems controlling his movements. It was probably early-stage Parkinson's. Just like our gun-toting farmer downstairs."

"Wouldn't that have been picked up by the post-mortem?" Jay asked, cutting Chase's moment short.

"They weren't looking for brain diseases," Chase replied. "They were looking for a cause of death. Drowning. With the aggravating factor of intoxication."

"It doesn't mean much," Chris piped up. "King's licence didn't get revoked; he failed to renew it. And we all know he still kept a shotgun. It was in his bloody kitchen. Whether he was suffering from a brain disease means nothing."

"No, don't you see? It means everything," said Chase. "He'd said to the Hythe family he wanted a favour, something he wanted from them in the future. He could have meant his care. It explains the handwriting on the note, how different it was from his usual writing. It would explain the unexpected suicide, the confession now after all these years. The chemical changes in the brain caused depression. It all makes sense. The old man was deteriorating and he didn't know what to do."

"So, he decided to kill himself?" Jay asked. "I thought we were leaning away from suicide."

"He didn't use the easiest method available to him," added Chris.

"And he didn't display any signs of poor mental health or making plans for his death," I said.

Our arguments appeared to go right over Chase's head. "King had been alone for sixty years," he continued. "Losing your independence like that must have been hard to deal with."

Chris sat back in his chair and sneered, making no attempt to hide it. "And what about the shotgun? If he wanted to kill himself, why not use that?"

"Maybe he couldn't," said Chase as he held his hands up, mimicking the trigger of a gun. "Maybe he was struggling to grip things."

"He managed to hold a pen if he wrote that suicide note," Jay pointed out.

"All right, fine, that bit is still open to debate." Chase waved his hands as though a fly was buzzing around his head. "But the reason he would have wanted to kill himself is starting to make sense."

"No, it's not," said Chris. "In fact, your mental gymnastics are undoing all the progress we've made this week."

Jay leaned across the desk towards me. "Are you sure they said it was just a *mild* concussion?"

"Right," said Chase. He clapped his hands together and strode to the back of the room. He stood in front of the small window. "It's entirely possible. Anything in this case is possible because we know so little for certain. So, rather than arguing with me, head over to the Hythe house. Speak to Dr Paula Hythe. King wanted a favour from her cheating husband and she should have had the medical knowledge to see his deterioration." He waited a second, then clicked his fingers again. "Hamill, Fitzgerald. Get a move on."

Chris didn't budge, not looking thrilled at the prospect of heading out on inquiries, but another snap from Chase made him roll his eyes and climb to his feet. Jay followed suit, pulling his coat from where I'd left it on the back of my chair.

"And speak to the mistress too," Chase called after them. "She was a nurse. She should have recognised the signs of Parkinson's."

With some mild grumbling which Chase ignored, Chris and Jay departed the office. As the door closed behind them, Chase sank down in Jay's empty chair. His jitteriness dissipated until it was nothing more than an irritating jerk of his knee, up and down, up and down.

"Don't you want to get out there and speak to the Hythes?" I asked him. From what I'd seen of him so far, Chase much preferred to be involved, especially if that meant questioning people. He was not the type of senior officer who preferred to stay behind in the office.

But he shook his head. "I think me and you need a few minutes' peace and a strong coffee."

I couldn't argue with that; in fact, it was the best suggestion he had ever made.

"Did you tell Burns about the body found in the woods yet?" Chase asked.

A cold shiver ran over me. In all the commotion, I'd forgotten what I was meant to tell Aaron. I pulled a grimace and shook my head lightly.

"Do you want me to do it?" he asked, no hints of anything other than concern in his voice.

"Maybe not right now," I said, thinking back to Aaron in his office. "Maybe later."

"Suit yourself," said Chase and he rubbed his forehead. "But you're making the coffee, Detective Constable."

"Yes, sir," I replied with a deflated sigh and I rose to my feet. The quiet of the office felt like a cocoon and I was reluctant to step out of it.

"Do you think I'm right about King's condition?" Chase asked before I reached the door. He cocked his head to the side like a curious puppy as he waited for my answer.

"I think it's plausible," I replied. "But at the minute, it's just a theory. It doesn't help us with what happened to King or Clara Burns."

"No, it doesn't," Chase agreed. "I guess we'll have to wait and see. If I'm right, then that's Clara's body we found in the woods. And it's game over. The old man killed her all those years ago, then got so ill he couldn't live with himself anymore. A tragedy, I guess."

He flicked his gaze away from me, the last drops of adrenalin fading away and leaving him hollow and defeated.

"And case closed," he finished.

* * *

The station didn't fully relax for the rest of the day. It was hard to describe how, but the building itself was somehow on edge after the events of that morning, as if it was holding its breath and waiting to see what disaster might come next. The air felt fragile and wounded. Everyone walked around not on tiptoes, but with the same sort of apprehension and slight twitchiness, no matter how hard they tried to hide it.

Our sanctuary, our police station, had been victim to an attack. The building and its occupants were used to unhappy customers, but the hold-up with the shotgun, although very brief, was a new danger no one had ever expected.

Aaron avoided me. Or maybe I was avoiding him. Either way, we didn't cross paths again as the afternoon waned. Chase was called to go downstairs after we'd sat in silence and drank our strong coffees, recovering. Although he gave no explanation, I knew he was summoned to meet with the chief constable, and I assumed I would be next, hauled before him to explain my reckless actions. But it didn't happen. I remained alone in the office until Jay and Chris returned from the Hythe household. They flopped down at their desks, downtrodden.

175

I asked them how they had got on.

"About as well as you would expect," Jay replied. "The wife, Dr Paula Hythe, says she recognised some of the signs of something being wrong with Barney King. She said it could have been Parkinson's but he was a private man so she never spoke to him about it. And Luisa denied noticing anything, but she did admit that she avoided King whenever she could."

"You could cut the tension in that house with a knife," said Chris. He turned the heater up by his desk. "I think we turned up in the middle of an argument."

"Well, our investigation did uncover their affair and secret pregnancy two days ago," replied Jay. "To be honest, I expected them to be more hostile to us."

"Two days," I said, fighting off a yawn. "Has it only been two days since then?"

Jay took pity on me and declared he was going to make a round of tea before he disappeared off to the break room. Chris waited for me to stop yawning before he leaned over the desk to catch my eye.

"So, what have you been doing?"

"I contacted social services," I said. I hadn't been as productive as I normally was, but I was hoping he wouldn't chastise me for that. I had stopped a gun-wielding farmer earlier in the day.

I handed him a form from my desk.

"They received a referral from the hospital, two weeks before King died. It was put in by the neurology team, asking for care and safety assessments for King. There had been an assessment, but nothing else put in place yet."

"Oh," mumbled Chris as he leafed through the referral form. Most of it was medical jargon we didn't quite understand the meaning of, but the gist was that King's doctor wanted carers to check in on King at home, once a day.

"Oh?" I asked, mimicking his noise.

"Well," Chris said thoughtfully. "This supports everything Chase was babbling about earlier. Whether it was Parkinson's or something else, King was deteriorating. He needed care. He could have had a guilty conscience too and confessed to the murder before killing himself."

Chris wrinkled his nose and I could guess his next words before he even said them.

"Don't tell Chase, but he might be right."

"But where does that leave us?" I asked. "Does that mean King's death will be ruled a suicide?"

"Maybe," said Chris. "But we've looked into all other angles. All signs that point towards murder can be explained by this. I think this might be the end of the road."

Chapter Twenty-Three

I was hoping for miracles. I was hoping, despite the next day being a Sunday, that the DNA report for the remains in the woods might be back, with the world record for the speediest turnaround. With little else to do with my weekend, I dragged myself to work via the local bus network and happily whiled a few hours away alone in the office, until someone interrupted me.

They opened the office door. Stopped. Blinked.

"What are you doing here?" Chase asked. Before I could answer, he continued. "Don't tell me you're one of those workaholics. No social life. Spends every free hour at the office, stressing about cases and tormenting yourself. You're a bit too young to be a hard-drinking, twice-divorced, trench-coat-wearing detective, you know."

I knew I should have been offended by his words, but I didn't have the energy to engage in one of Chase's strange conversations.

"What are *you* doing here?" I asked him.

He strode over to the desk and sat down with a flourish. "Oh, I am one of those workaholics," he said with a smile. "Not divorced yet, though, but give it time. Anything to report?"

"Nothing," I replied. Any miracles I was waiting on were yet to appear. No matter how hard I stared at the team inbox, no reports had pinged into existence yet.

"Shame." Chase leaned back but he quickly stood up again and made his way to the whiteboard of progress. His gaze flitted over the information.

"We should retrace their last steps," he muttered, stroking his chin.

"We already did," I reminded him. "We retraced Barney King's last steps the day before he died. We went to the storage locker, the hospital."

"No, no," said Chase. "Not him. I mean Clara."

"You want to retrace Clara Burns' last steps? How?" I asked. "She disappeared forty years ago. We can't figure out forty years later where she went."

"Oh, ye of little faith," he scolded. He gestured to the office door. "Sure, we can. Come on."

I remained clueless of his intentions all the way from the police station to the village of Wormegay and along the bumpy track at Pepperwell Farm. Chase stopped his car at the duo of cottages, one held up by the bushes of ivy, and the other looking forlorn and forgotten. It wasn't quite as icy today as it had been, but the grass still had a small crunch to it as we walked across towards the cottages.

"What do we know about Clara Burns' last day so far?" Chase asked using his long legs to stride ahead.

If he was hoping to go inside of the dilapidated cottage, he was going to be disappointed. The brambles and ivy were so thick around the bottom of the cottage walls, I doubted there was any chance of getting inside.

"We know she put her children to bed," I said. "Her husband was at the local pub in the village. He staggered home later that night and found the children in bed alone, but no Clara."

"And Callum said something about there being an argument," said Chase. He continued walking, heading around the back of the cottage. "Between his parents. But it's possible Barney King heard it. When was it that Clara went missing? Winter, summer?"

"Summer," I confirmed. "Early September."

"Still warm then," said Chase. "They probably still had their windows and doors open."

He arrived around the back of the cottage and surveyed the black holes of the windows. Each cottage had a small, walled garden, although the wall to the derelict cottage had fallen down over the years. Moss covered every exposed inch, slick and shiny with frost. Each wall had a break in it, where once a garden gate probably stood, but had long since rotted away. Now they opened up directly into the surrounding woodland. The lake where King's body was found wasn't far away through the trees.

"Imagine," said Chase. He drew in a deep breath through his nose and closed his eyes. "You're Clara, arguing with your husband. He's jealous."

He looked at the cottage next door.

"You think your neighbour has heard, so what do you do? Go over there to apologise?"

"I guess so," I said, although I had no idea where he was going with this.

Chase made off into the garden and surveyed the wall.

"Look," he said, pointing to a gap in the brickwork. It looked like over the years, the cement had worn away and the stones had fallen to leave a little gap, just narrow enough to squeeze from one garden to the other. "A little neighbourly gateway," said Chase.

"That might not have been there forty years ago."

He shushed me. "So, you've argued with your husband and to keep him happy, you've promised not to talk to the man next door anymore. But once he's out at the pub, you pop over to explain yourself, maybe hoping to remain civil, or friends. Or maybe more." Chase sucked in a deep breath before sliding through the gap in the wall, into King's small yard. He continued talking from the other side. "Don't forget, Barney King was forty years younger. He might not have been that bad-looking back then. Maybe him and Clara had a thing going on."

"Callum said they didn't," I pointed out.

"Callum Burns was a child. He probably wouldn't have noticed. Especially if his mother was sneaking out after he'd gone to bed."

"You're making a lot of assumptions here," I said.

Chase fell silent from the other side.

"The thing with assumptions," he finally said, "is that if you make enough of them, eventually you will be right. If we explore every possibility, we will find out what happened to Clara Burns."

"So, what are the possibilities?" I asked.

Given that Chase hadn't come back through the gap, I guessed he intended to remain on that side, so I squeezed through myself. The stones of the wall scraped across the back of my coat, no doubt leaving a nice mossy trail across my bum.

"Two," Chase answered. He held two fingers up to me. "It's like we said before; she either made herself disappear, or someone else did it for her."

He spun on his heels and started off out of the yard.

"If someone killed her," said Chase, calling back to me, "then they had to have done it here. Can you imagine trying to abduct her with her children sleeping in the house? They would have heard a commotion and woken up." He turned but continued walking, now going backwards so he could watch me hurry to catch up with him. "But then, if she was murdered here, where is the body? Well, it must be nearby because her family is right next door, so trying to drag it far or out to the car is going to get you noticed. Dragging it out the back, though" – he motioned to the walled gardens – "is an easier option."

"The remains were found in the woods," I reminded him. I pointed in the vague general direction I expected the old shed to be in. It was out there somewhere, not easy to find however. We'd only found it accidentally.

"Still quite a distance to drag a body, but not impossible," said Chase. "But there's something closer. Some easier way to dispose of a body right on the doorstep."

He turned back, facing forwards again, and thrust out his hands. Through the frost-tipped bracken and leafless trees, I could just spy the still waters of the lake where King's body had been found.

"If I was King and I had just murdered Clara Burns, I would put her body in here," Chase said quietly. He lowered his arms. "Wouldn't you?"

From somewhere unseen, a bird called out, as if warning its friends of our presence. Something flapped and ripples spread across the water. They crashed into the muddy shore and vanished from existence.

"I guess so," I said. "Bodies float though."

"Not if they're weighed down," he replied. "And these waters are deep."

He set off to fight his way through the undergrowth. I followed close behind until we emerged by the expanse of water. The disturbance was caused by a black bird bobbing on the surface, with a white on its beak and tuft of white on top of its head. Its beady eye watched us with caution.

"Coot," Chase mumbled under his breath.

"Excuse me?" I asked.

He rolled his eyes at me. "The bird. It's a coot."

"How do you know that?"

He shrugged. "Not everything about the countryside is bad. Birds are cool."

He glanced at me and did a double take when he realised that I was staring at him, confusion taking my attention.

"You are full of surprises."

He ignored me. "That shed we found in the woods. That was the work of someone who regretted the death of that person. Whoever it was we found buried, she was loved, cherished, and the person who put her there wanted to keep her nearby."

"Well, given that we found King's dog in there, I suppose it's safe to assume it was Barney King who kept the remains there. His dog must have known about the place somehow."

Chase nodded. "I think you're right. Which means he was sentimental towards her. He left her flowers. He loved her."

He spun on his heels and faced me, dropping his voice low. "If you love someone, you want to give them a decent burial. As gruesome as that shed was, that's what it was meant to be, a burial. If you murder someone and dump their body, you don't create a shrine for them like that."

"So, King loved Clara?" I asked and he nodded again. "He regretted whatever happened and wanted to keep her close."

"Bingo," said Chase. "Whatever transpired between them, King must have felt some form of affection to keep her close for so long."

"But not enough affection to tell her family what happened to her," I replied. "He left them wondering for all these years."

"Yeah," Chase said with a hum. "That's the part I still don't quite understand."

* * *

Miracles could happen, but only on weekdays it seemed. Chase burst into the office halfway through the next day, slightly more than forty-eight hours after Callum

Burns' DNA sample was sent to the lab for comparison and the gun-wielding farmer had held up the station.

"DNA results are back," he declared.

His words tore a silence into the room, a void sucking the life from the world around us. Jay and Chris froze in place, both glancing at me. An overwhelming sense of foreboding fell over my head, shrouding me in a cover of dark thoughts and nausea. Even Chase wore an expression of gravity, which for him was an unusual sight, as he fiddled with his mobile phone, turning it over and over in his hand.

This was the end of the road. The mystery of Clara Burns could be finally put to rest.

"Already?" Chris asked, sounding dubious. "That's quick."

"I have a friend who works at the lab," said Chase. "She rushed the results through for me. But it's as I suspected… the body we found wasn't Clara Burns."

My ears began to ring. Sober air filled the office as we all felt the weight of Chase's words.

"It wasn't?" Jay asked.

"You suspected?" questioned Chris as he raised his eyebrows. "Care to share with the rest of us?"

"Yeah, that wasn't what you said yesterday," I pointed out.

Chase shrugged his shoulders as he sat down next to me, hustling me along to the end of the desk. He didn't meet my gaze, and I realised that not once had he looked at me since his arrival.

"The DNA taken from the buried remains was not a match to Callum Burns," he confirmed.

"Then who is it?" I asked. I couldn't deny the relief that swept over me at hearing the DNA wasn't a match, but that was only because it meant there was no need to give Aaron the bad news. There was still a set of unknown bones in the morgue that needed identifying somehow.

"Think about it," Chase said. "Who else is missing from Barney King's life? Who haven't we been able to track down, dead or alive?"

Chris nodded, catching his drift. "His wife."

"Bingo," said Chase. "The DNA from the remains was flagged up as a familial match – a parent – to someone already in the system. Margaret Bowen. Mags."

"Why is her DNA on file?" Jay asked.

"Her record is long and varied," Chase replied. "Mostly breach of the peace, public nuisance from her younger days, a few domestic charges. No custodial sentences though."

He didn't give any of us a chance to digest this information before he clicked his fingers at each of us and started issuing orders.

"Fitzgerald, get on the phone. I want to know the cause of death for Mary King. Hamill, we need a diving team out to Pepperwell Farm and a search of the water for any signs of Clara Burns. Get them to use sonar, or radar, or whatever the hell it is. McArthur, with me."

"Where are we going?" I asked.

Chase pulled his lips together into a tight grimace. "We're going to pay another visit to Mags Bowen. We need to know why she lied to us about her mother."

Chapter Twenty-Four

We arrived in Wisbech as the lunchtime rush waned, making good time, which Chase didn't appreciate, not being local. He hadn't spoken a word the whole drive over.

The moment we arrived at the tightly packed estate where Mags Bowen lived and exited the car, I could hear the screaming.

"Lucy Bowen, you little turd. Get your arse back to that school! Lunch finished an hour ago."

"I'm not fucking going! You can't make me!"

"Sounds like a normal day in the Bowen household," Chase mumbled as he strode for the front door of the loudest property on the street. It did indeed sound like the same conversation we'd overheard on our first visit; Mags cursing her granddaughter and the youngster giving back as good as she got.

Chase hammered his fist on the front door, but it didn't make a dent in the stream of swear words coming from the house. With a tut, he rolled his eyes, glanced over at me and nodded his head to the back gate. I led the way round the back of the property where once again, the back door was wide open, despite the elements. The frost had come back with a vengeance, bringing with it a blisteringly cold wind from the north.

"Knock, knock," Chase said, using his fist on the kitchen window as we approached.

The shouting stopped instantly and we were met at the doorway by both Mags and her granddaughter. They looked surprised by our arrival, and just as quickly, infuriated by our presence.

"What the fuck do you want?" Lucy asked, puffing out her chest. Her shoulders were almost as broad as the door frame and cast a dark shadow into the house.

"Steady on," said Chase, hiding a smile at the girl's defiant stance. "We're here to talk to your grandmother. Shouldn't you be in school?"

"It's a day off," Lucy grumbled, although the school uniform she was wearing begged to differ.

The girl looked to her nan for confirmation and Mags nodded, patting her on the shoulder. She steered the teen back into the kitchen, like a guard dog being called to heel. I got the impression that any moment, she could be set to attack again. The girl was a tightly wound coil.

"What now?" Mags asked, still hanging off the door frame, reluctant to move.

Chase rubbed his hands together. "Mind if we talk inside? It's freezing out here."

Mags ran her eyes over us, full of suspicion and wariness. I found her reaction odd, given that she'd met us before. She knew we weren't a threat.

"Please," Chase added.

After a moment, she stepped aside and Chase and I piled into the tiny kitchen.

"I already told you," Mags said, leaving the back door wide open. "I'll have nothing to do with him. Give him a pauper's funeral, chuck him in the furnace and be done with it. I'm not paying for anything for that old man."

"We're not here about the funeral, Mags," Chase said. "We're here about your mother."

Mags scuffed her feet as she hobbled over to where her granddaughter sat at the dining table, a look of disgust on her face. She settled a hand on Lucy's shoulder and the girl tensed up. Side by side, I could see there was a strong family resemblance.

"What about her?"

"We found her," said Chase.

For a moment, Mags didn't react, her expression not changing a millimetre. However, I saw the whitening of her knuckles as she dug her fingertips into Lucy's shoulder. The girl didn't even flinch.

Chase continued, giving no sign that he'd noticed their stiffness. "You told us she died of cancer a few years back. But that wasn't true, was it? At least, not really, because if she did die of cancer, there would be a death certificate. Medical records and hospital logs at the very least. No. Your mother didn't have any of these because she died long before then, probably fifty-five, sixty years ago. And she was buried in the woods behind your father's house."

Mags's bottom lip roiled as she frantically chewed it from the inside. Her gaze grew wilder, fixed on Chase as though she had welcomed the very devil into her house.

Underneath her unrelenting grip, her granddaughter glowered also and her fists balled in her lap.

"Was she?" Mags managed to say, but a crack of emotion gave her away.

"Yeah," said Chase, not missing a beat. "So why did you lie to us?"

Lucy shuddered like an electric current had run through her. "Watch your tone. Or I'll give you a reminder of whose house you're in," she said.

Chase squinted at the girl. "It won't matter whose house we're in when we arrest your nan for obstructing a police investigation."

"She didn't obstruct anything!"

"She lied to us," said Chase and he turned his gaze on Mags. The woman stood in place, like a statue of a witch, hunched over her granddaughter's chair. She blinked slowly at Chase. "You lied to us, Mags. Why? What were you trying to hide?"

She shook her head and I could almost hear her joints and tendons creaking in her neck.

"Nothing."

Chase sucked air between his teeth. "I don't believe that."

"Well, it's the truth," she snapped back.

Under her hand, Lucy leered, as if readying to pounce.

I leant forward in my seat, catching Mags's eye. She seethed at Chase but her expression softened at me, just a little, remembering the kindness I showed her before. Chase's heavy-handed approach worked well sometimes but others it was more of a hindrance.

"It can't be the truth," I said softly. "Why invent a death for her if you didn't already know what had happened to her? What really happened to your mother, Mags?"

Like the creaking of a tap steadily releasing pressure, Mags released her grip on Lucy's shoulder. Under my patient gaze, her stoicism faltered.

"All right, fine," she surrendered, falling into the chair next to Lucy.

The teen sat up so quickly, she almost launched herself out of her seat. "Nan! No."

"It's all right," Mags said as she waved a hand feebly in the air. "In fact, I can deal with this. Get yourself to school."

"I ain't leaving you!"

"This isn't for you to hear," she replied fiercely. "Just old family secrets best left buried. Go on, get out of here."

Lucy, with a face like a petulant child, folded her arms and wiggled back firmly in her seat. "I'm staying."

"Suit yourself," Mags hissed back before turning to us. "I want nothing coming back on me. I was only a child. One who'd already seen far too much."

I glanced at Chase and he grimaced back.

"Whatever it is, you can tell us. We just want the truth," he said.

Mags sighed, the noise halfway between a growl and a cry, and her body almost folded itself in two as the ageing lady crumpled before our eyes.

"I knew he'd done something bad. One night they were rowing, like they always did. My dad had no patience and Mum was stubborn as hell. He'd been drinking too, which turned him nasty. I hid in my room upstairs but even there I could hear them shouting, hear him hit her and her crying. When I got up the next morning, she was nowhere to be seen. He took me over to Wisbech, to my aunt Anne's, and told me I was living here from now on. He told Anne that Mum had left us and that he couldn't cope with me on his own."

"And that night was the last time you ever saw your mum?" I asked.

Mags bit her lip and nodded. "Last time. My old mum."

"Didn't your aunt raise the alarm?" Chase asked. "Didn't she try to find your mum at any point?"

"Nah, she liked the attention she got from taking me in, all the pity people gave her for having to raise me as well as all her own kids. A bit narcissistic, my old aunt."

"Why didn't you report it?" pressed Chase. "Didn't you wonder what happened to her?"

Mags sucked in a breath through her teeth. "Of course I did. But I was a child," she said again. "Up until a few weeks ago, I didn't even remember where we lived back then. But I always knew he'd killed her. I've always known it…"

For a moment, silence descended on the room, as startling as the cold air blowing in from outside. Lucy was speechless, mouth floundering like a fish as she stared at her nan, her rock, who was now nothing more than a wrinkled old lady, desperate to stay upright. Mags had aged twenty years in the last two minutes, even her spiky hair losing its edge and flopping down by her temples. Her head remained down; the checked pattern of the tablecloth reflected in her dewy eyes.

Chase cleared his throat. "Thank you, Ms Bowen. I know that must have been hard to relive."

She nodded, saying nothing more.

"We're awaiting a full post-mortem examination on the remains we found. Hopefully we'll have some more answers for you then. And we'll need you to come down to the station to give a statement."

Lucy bristled at this. "Like fuck she is. She's not going anywhere she doesn't have to," she said. The idea of going to the police station had set her on edge again, but her nan sniffed loudly, taking the wind from her sails.

"It's all right, Luce," Mags said. "I've kept this secret for long enough. It's about time I shared it."

The chair scraped on the floor tiles as Chase rose to his feet. "Thank you. We'll let you have some time to yourself. Come on, McArthur."

* * *

Back in Chase's car, he turned the engine on, set the heater to full, and placed his forehead against the top of the steering wheel. He let out a long, frustrated, overdramatic sigh.

As soon as his sigh was over, he sat up straight again.

"Do you believe her?" he asked forcefully, as though my answer would determine our next moves.

I took a moment, but Chase gave an irritated huff when I didn't reply fast enough.

"I don't know," I replied. "We believed her last time and it turns out she's a convincing liar. She could be lying now."

If it was the truth, then it answered a lot of questions and fit into the version of events as we knew them. King, deteriorating due to a possible illness such as Parkinson's disease, found his guilty conscience and admitted to murdering his wife before killing himself.

But the picture wasn't complete. Something was missing. Before I could grab and pull on the thin thread of a thought as it dangled temptingly in my mind, my phone rang in my pocket. It was Jay and I put the call on speaker so Chase could hear too.

"Some interesting results," he said, his voice sounding tinny down the line. "Although it's hard to be sure given the age of the remains, Pete and the pathologist are both fairly certain that Mary King was strangled."

Chase cocked his head to the side. "How do they know that?"

"There's a small bone in the neck," Jay replied. "The hyoid, or something like that. When force is applied around the windpipe, most of the time the hyoid breaks. Usually, when we see a victim who was strangled to death, we have their whole body and the other signs like bruising make it more obvious what's happened, but Mary King's hyoid bone was snapped in two."

"And that is the cause of death?" Chase asked.

"That is looking most likely at the moment," said Jay. "It was the only sign of significant trauma on her. A few old fractures of the fingers and wrists, consistent with someone holding their hands up to defend themselves."

"Fuck…" Chase mumbled back. "How's Hamill getting on?"

"The search of the water has just started. It's deep though. They said a thorough search could take a few days."

We ended the call and Chase mulled over the new information. He blinked hard, as if the excess thinking was hurting his head.

"What do you think?" he asked. "You look confused."

Slowly, I shook my head. "Something doesn't add up."

The thread was there, ready, willing to be pulled. I could feel it, the answer to all these questions, the end to the long and emotional case, but I still couldn't get to it.

"What doesn't?" asked Chase.

"Well, if Mags Bowen is to be believed, then King killed her mother and we have her body, so that adds up. But where is Clara Burns? She doesn't fit into this version of events. A woman, a mother, like her doesn't just disappear for forty years – something happened to her. She disappeared in nearly identical circumstances to Mary King almost twenty years after. It can't be a coincidence."

"No," Chase agreed. "It most likely isn't. King probably had a hand in her death too."

"Then why was his suicide note wrong?"

Chase watched me with wary eyes, his expression flickering as he thought. "How do you mean?"

"It said, 'I did it. I killed her.' King admitted to one murder. But if he had a hand in Clara's disappearance, or knew anything about it, then surely, he would have confessed to that too?"

Chase thought this over, chewing on his bottom lip. It occupied his mind for a few minutes but eventually he let it go. Like me, the inconsistency bothered him, but without knowing the fate of Clara Burns, it would lead us nowhere.

"Do you know what confuses me?" he asked rhetorically, continuing before I could answer. "Mags said she didn't remember where her father lived. Not until a few weeks ago. What changed a few weeks ago for her to remember Pepperwell Farm?"

"I... didn't even pick that up," I admitted.

He smiled. "That's why they pay me the big bucks, McArthur."

"We could go and ask her?" I suggested, but he shook his head.

"She's lied to us before. There's nothing stopping her from lying again. No, we can't speak to her again just yet, we need something more substantial than a slip of the tongue. But how would she have found out where her father lived..." He tapped the wedding band on his finger on the steering wheel, as if drumming along to a tune only he could hear.

He stopped and turned to me.

"Can you find that referral? The one to social care."

I nodded; it had been sent via email and I pulled up it on my phone. The document was hard to read on the small screen but I splayed my fingers out until it zoomed in.

Chase snatched the phone from my hand.

"Barney King... Barney King..." he muttered as he read. And he stopped.

He grinned.

"Look who the care assessor was. The person sent to old Barney's house to assess his needs."

He turned the screen to me.

Kelly Bowen, Assistant Adult Social Care Assessor.

"Mags said her daughter – Lucy's mum – was a carer," said Chase. "Her daughter named Kelly. What's the betting that she told her mum about the man she visited a few weeks ago for an assessment?"

"And Mags didn't just suddenly remember where he lived," I concluded. "She found out from her daughter."

Chase threw open the car door, the heat escaping in a violent whoosh. His exhaled breath floated away in a cloud but he made no move to get out. He glanced back at the house, where a net curtain twitched downstairs. Someone was watching us.

"After sixty years, Mags found out her father was still alive and was elderly and frail," he said. "Maybe she saw her chance to punish him for what he did to her mother all those years ago."

I followed his gaze to the run-down uncared-for semi, with weeds sprouting from the drains and curtains still drawn around the mouldy windows. I felt eyes on me, watching, obscured by the dirty curtains. I was certain Mags Bowen and her granddaughter Lucy were there.

The curtain twitched again. Chase watched the house vigilantly, as though the very building would swipe out at us any second.

"She's an old woman," I said, picturing Mags as she crumpled at the kitchen table. "Could she have drowned her father?"

Chase hummed back. "Maybe not. But her granddaughter could."

He glanced at me, catching my eye. In it I saw a spark, a determination that resonated with me deep down. It was the same spark of action that I felt when I knew I needed to act.

"I think we'd better go and talk to them again." He jumped from the car, a surge of energy propelling him forwards.

The twitching curtains fell still.

Chapter Twenty-Five

Things had fallen oddly silent in the Bowen household in the short time Chase and I were outside. As we made our way to the back door again, I felt something watching us and our tentative footsteps across the frost-dusted path. The whole neighbourhood was subdued, not even the bark of a dog to disturb the chilled air. The hairs on the back of my neck stood on end. Just the cold, I told myself.

Chase took the lead and approached the back door, still wide open. No movements could be heard inside. If Mags and Lucy were there, they were holding their breath.

"Where have they–" Chase asked as he crossed the threshold.

His sentence was cut off as he was propelled backwards, knocking into me and sending us both to the ground. The man was solid, winding me for a moment as he struggled to get his bearings and realise that I had cushioned his landing. I scrabbled out from under him the same moment he sat up, and I saw blood pouring from his nose.

"What the fuck?" he exclaimed.

In the doorway stood Lucy Bowen, frying pan in hand and held at head height. I could see the shadow of Mags behind her, hovering like a guardian angel.

"No fucking way," Lucy said, spit flying from her mouth. "You're not taking my nan. No way!"

"We're not taking her anywhere!" Chase said as he climbed to his feet. "At least, not yet. You're under arrest, though, for assaulting an officer."

Lucy steeled herself, adopting the stance of a rugby player. Mags scrambled behind her and disappeared into the shadows of the house.

"Don't be an idiot," Chase warned. He held out a hand to help me up but his eyes didn't leave Lucy.

The girl snarled back at him. "I'm not stupid," she said, bouncing on the balls of her feet. "I know what you want with us. But you're not taking her. You're not taking my nan. The old bastard deserved everything he got!"

I inched forwards, holding out my hand in surrender. "Lucy, put it down," I said gently, indicating to the frying pan. "We can talk about this. Whatever you and your nan have done, it'll be much better if we're all calm and talk it through sensibly."

From the shadows of the house, a hand appeared, holding out a large carving knife in front of Lucy. The teen stared at it for a second, before releasing her grip on the frying pan. It clattered to the floor. She took the knife from her nan and held it out with a worrying amount of confidence. Not the first time she'd threatened someone with a blade, evidently

"Lucy," Chase warned.

The girl made no move. Not until Mags appeared again and leant close to her ear and whispered, "Get 'em."

Lucy sprang forwards, but Chase was ready and caught the girl's flailing arms before the knife came close. I aimed a kick to her knee and Lucy fell down, only to jump right back up again. Adrenalin made every inch of her body shake and she rabidly slashed through the winter air.

Out the corner of my eye, I spied Mags disappear into the house. I heard the click of the front door opening.

"Go get her!" Chase roared as Lucy made another lunge at him. He was a little dazed by the frying pan to the face, a bit too slow to dodge Lucy, but he managed to grab the girl's wrist before the knife got too close to his stomach.

I paused. Ordinarily, Chase probably would have had an unfair advantage in a fight with someone like Lucy, a fully grown man against a teenage girl, but he was still mildly concussed at best. Together we could put Lucy down in seconds, but Mags could vanish into the estate. We could lose her in the alleyways and tightly packed houses. The bustling town centre was only streets away.

Chase dodged another lunge, this one glancing off his arm and slicing through the material of his coat.

"Anna, go!"

I sprinted through the house, straight through the open front door and out into the deserted street. All was solemn and still. I pulled out my mobile phone, dialling the control room as I scanned the surroundings. She couldn't have gone far. She was old, unfit. She was still nearby.

Just as the call connected, a movement from behind a parked car two houses along caught my eye. A streak of red hair crossed the street at a hobbling run.

Ignoring the control room operator on the line, I ran for Mags, her back to me. I tackled her to the ground, the old lady landing hard on the slippery pavement. It didn't stop her though, as in an instant she twisted round and I felt a sharp, hot scratch across my jawbone. She held another kitchen knife, glistening with blood.

"Get off me!" she screamed at the top of her lungs, swinging the knife back and forth.

I retreated back, skidding over the icy ground and losing my grip on my phone.

"Mags, stop it," I tried. It fell on deaf ears. The knife swiped side to side, forcing me back.

My phone was lying a few inches away, its bright screen showing the call was still connected.

"DC McArthur requesting urgent assistance! Southwell Road, Wisbech," I shouted, hoping the operator could hear me, but Mags slashed at me when I tried to edge closer to the device. Once again, the knife came down, aiming for any exposed skin.

"Mags! Stop!" I cried, dodging each lunge until I was on the back foot, forced to back away out of her reach. "It's over! Put it down."

"No!" she screamed, loud enough to wake the dead. "You know nothing! You've no proof it was me!"

"Mags!"

It was no use; the woman was rabid. She lunged with every step, like a fencer, hoping I'd parry the blows away with my arms.

Her screams drew out the neighbours from the closest house to us, a middle-aged couple in their pyjamas hanging out their front door. They scowled at the scene.

"Mags?" they asked, bewildered and concerned. They gathered at the sidelines as though watching a spectator sport.

"Stay back! Police!" I told them. The last thing I needed was some unhelpful neighbour deciding Mags needed a hand.

Over the road, a howling cry rattled through the cold. It was either Chase or Lucy.

Mags dived for me, aiming for my neck. I reeled back. I kicked out at her, making contact with her knee and she stumbled hard. The knife slipped from her grasp and landed a couple of feet away. Mags wailed in agony, as though I'd amputated her limb rather than just a glancing kick.

"Police brutality!" she cried to her neighbours. "You saw that, she kicked me!"

"Shut up," I said. Out the corner of my eye, I saw the neighbours approach us across the grass, uncertain.

"Stay back!" I warned them again, but that was the distraction Mags wanted. She spun on her heels and legged it, disappearing quickly behind a parked Transit van, glistening with thick ice.

Ignoring the burning scratch on my chin and the warm blood trickling down my neck, I started after her. I rounded the van and was surprised to see nothing but an empty alleyway. She'd vanished.

Although Mags knew these streets well, I was faster. I could catch her up.

Pounding my feet hard enough that the slippery ground didn't get a chance to trip me up, I made it to the end of the alleyway. She was still gone from sight but a helpful trail of footprints on the shiny pavement gave away her route. I followed them to the end of the road, where the housing estate became an industrial one.

It was busier here and icy paths were forged from the tyre tracks on the tarmac. I looked left and right, and my heart skipped a beat as I spotted the familiar red hair over the other side of the road. A horn blared at me as I ran across the street, a flat-bed van made an emergency stop just a dozen feet from me. I faltered but ignored the angry shouts of the driver and the colourful language coming out of his open window. I made after Mags and caught up with her as she reached the end of the road.

The road opened out into a single-track carriageway, with large industrial units on one side and a waist-high concrete wall the other. I didn't need to look over the wall to know what was on the other side. The bobbing masts of a few boats gave it away.

Mags had one leg over the wall.

"Get down," I snapped, sounding far more like an unimpressed parent that I intended. She paid me no attention, heaving herself up until she was balanced on the wall and looking down at the muddy brown water of the River Nene below.

"Mags," I warned her as I approached.

Whatever she intended to do, it wasn't going to be an escape. Getting back out of the river wouldn't be easy, and I highly doubted she had a getaway jet ski on the other side of the wall.

She waited until I was close enough to reach out before she moved.

Her tight grip latched onto my forearms and she pulled. Her body slid off the wall, over the other side, and her weight pulled me with her. I tumbled head first over the concrete, my feet slipping before I could get any purchase to stop myself.

And we fell, rolling ungracefully down the small, muddy embankment until we hit the water with a muffled splash.

The cold struck me first. The water reached into every gap, hugging every inch of skin and paralysing me. It sucked the air from my lungs and squeezed them to stop any more from getting in. The roar of the water blocked my ears. Mags's tight grip on my arms relented and I felt something almost solid beneath my feet. I kicked at it and it pushed me upwards.

As I broke the surface of the opaque river, my eyes stung and my hair clung around my face. The icy water wasn't done with me, gripping onto my arms and legs and making them hard to register. My body was telling them to move but I had no idea if the message was reaching my limbs; however, I guessed it was by the fact I didn't immediately sink straight back under the surface.

Bubbles and splashes rose next to me. I tossed the hair from my eyes as a ghostly hand reached up and clawed at me. It found my shoulders and pushed me down, forcing my head back under at the same time as Mags's appeared and gasped for air.

"Can't… swim…" I heard her cry as she spat out mouthfuls of brown river water.

When the pressure on my shoulder relented, she disappeared back under. I pushed back up and escaped the water. I gulped down a lungful of fresh air, blissfully pleased that my tight throat allowed it in. Circling my arms around me, I was unsure if they had even responded until I bumped into something under the water. It grabbed for me again, the ghostly hands finding my upper arm.

A floating platform bobbed on the water up ahead. Before Mags had a chance to pull me back under, I pushed myself forwards, dragging her with me. The current helped me along to the floating boards of the jetty.

The cold finally released its grip on me as I pulled my body up, forcing the structure to dip below the surface of the water. I grabbed and dragged until Mags got the message, able to pull herself up too. The cold had also taken its toll on her, unkind in its treatment; her skin had turned a ghastly grey colour, her limp hair was plastered down her forehead. Whatever she'd been thinking about the impromptu swim, it hadn't turned into the great idea that she'd hoped.

"Margaret Bowen," I said, barely able to push the words through my chattering teeth. "You're under arrest…"

"Ah, sh-sh-shove your fucking arrest," she stammered back, before collapsing into a heap on the jetty.

* * *

Around the back of the Bowen household, blood peppered the shiny path. I could hear a whimpering cry and I hoped deep down it wasn't Chase. Not far from the path, the carving knife lay glistening in the frosted-white grass.

Blood dripped through the garden like a breadcrumb trail. The first person I saw was laying on the floor, writhing in pain. Then I saw Chase standing over them, with his foot on Lucy's arm and a thoroughly pissed-off look on his face.

"Ah good, about time," he said as he spotted me, looking me up and down. "Been for a swim?"

"Are you okay?" I asked him.

Blood dripped down his arm. He gave me a withering look and wiped a hand over his face where a black eye was starting to form.

"I will be when this bloody case is over with."

Chapter Twenty-Six

It was no surprise to me that Chase was still pumped with adrenalin when we arrived back at the police station. I let him to get on with issuing orders to a bewildered Chris and Jay whilst I showered and sourced a towel and a dry set of clothes. I'd learnt from many mishaps over the years to keep a spare set in the back of my car, but of course, I didn't have my beloved old vehicle anymore. Thankfully, I knew Maddie also kept a spare set in her locker. After a bit of bribery and the promise of tantalising gossip later, I had her clothes and was able to dress myself in a pair of police-issue trousers and a slightly baggy T-shirt. I scrounged a fleece from the station's lost property and was all set.

In the Serious Crimes office, I found Chase collapsed in his desk chair, alone.

"Fitzgerald is booking Mags and Lucy Bowen in," he said, answering the question before I even asked it. "And Hamill has gone to supervise the water search. I've told both of them not to bother coming back until they have something good to tell us."

I settled down next to him, in my own chair. The perpetually grey sky outside was starting to darken as the afternoon set in. I placed a first aid kit on the desk between us, which Chase eyed warily, as if it was some sort of trick. I had already stuck a plaster over the slight nick on my chin. Chase held a makeshift bandage around his forearm, made from a tea towel he'd nabbed from Mags's kitchen whilst we waited for a police van to arrive. He didn't put up a fight as I took his arm and unwound the tea towel to take a look.

It was a clean cut, perhaps a bit deeper than I was able to deal with. However, I set to work with butterfly stitches and proper bandages whilst Chase sat back and closed his eyes. He looked like he might fall asleep.

"What's the betting neither of them cop to it?" he asked as I was finishing.

"To what?"

"Murdering Barney King. Mags has done well so far to maintain she didn't even know him, she had me fooled. If she's smart, she'll stick to that story."

"She's not that smart though," I replied. "I mean, she jumped in the River Nene. She's emotional. That's why she reacted the way she did. There's a lot of anger and resentment inside that woman. I bet if we push the right buttons, we could get the full story out of her. What about her daughter?"

"Jay will go pick her up once he's booked in the other two," Chase mumbled.

He rested his chin on his fist and indicated to his face. The bandage on his head was dirty and loose and his black eye was swelling nicely.

"I'm not your nurse," I said.

He smiled. "No, but someone needs to take care of me. And you got me into this mess."

"Don't say you weren't warned," I said with a hollow laugh. "You'd heard of Crazy McArthur. This is the sort of stuff that happens with me around."

I prized off the bandage and started to dab clean his head wound. Now a few days old, it was still raw and red.

"I think I've learnt that the hard way," he grumbled back, but the words drifted off with a nervous laugh.

He was watching me, his big eyes taking me in as his breathing quickened at my touch. I smiled back, feeling warmth for the first time that day. It had been a hard case, an emotional roller coaster for everyone involved. The end was in sight now, but that also meant the end of working with Chase.

"Anna…" he said, something on the tip of his tongue. He stopped as the sound of clanking footsteps on metal rattled up the stairs outside the office door. Seconds later, someone burst in.

"Aaron," I said, almost jumping at his appearance. I hadn't realised just how close to Chase I was, hardly a few inches separating our faces. Aaron's expression didn't change at all as he surveyed us, taking the longest on me. I could almost read his thoughts as he looked me up and down, looking for bruises and cuts and whatever else I usually ended up with.

"Hospital," he said, flat and unimpressed. "Now."

"We're fine," I assured him but a flicker of annoyance told me now was not a good time to be arguing back.

"You might be," he said and then he pointed to Chase, "but he isn't. Ever heard of second impact syndrome? Get him to the hospital, now."

And with that, he closed the door. Aaron's footsteps faded away.

After a moment, Chase exhaled deeply. "Is he always so…"

"So what?" I said as I packed away the medical supplies. "Bossy? Officious?"

"Insufferable."

I gave Chase a small smile. "He's right, though. We should get you checked out. You did take a frying pan to the face."

Chase growled under his breath but pushed himself to his feet. "Fine. But you can drive this time… No, wait. Never mind." He touched his forehead. "I'll drive."

* * *

It was early evening by the time Chase was released from hospital with a clean bill of health. It seemed his long wait in the A & E department had given him time to recuperate and he was back to his normal, energetic self, only with a few new bandages replacing my first-aid efforts.

"Any news?" he asked as we drove back to the station. Traffic was building and a fine rain had settled over the surroundings, making the street lights sparkle through the windscreen.

"Jay has brought in Kelly Bowen," I replied. "And the water search has ended for the night. They'll pick it back up again tomorrow."

"Ah brilliant," said Chase. He flexed his fingers and rolled his shoulders. "I fancy a round in the interview room before the day is out."

Once inside the station, his energy maintained momentum and he headed for the interview rooms. Kelly Bowen was already set up in one. She still wore her carer's uniform, a pale-lilac tunic with white piping. Along with this, she wore her dyed black hair in a messy ponytail and a sour look on her face. Jay was already inside, talking her through the formalities when Chase entered and took the other empty seat.

Relegated to the sidelines, I watched on from the viewing room.

"Miss Bowen," said Chase, offering up a conceited smile. "Thanks for coming in."

"Well, you didn't exactly give me a choice," she replied, her voice on the edge of turning into a shriek. "Where's my daughter? I want to see her. She's a minor."

"And we can assure you she's being looked after to the highest standard. We will take you to see her right after we've had a chat," said Chase. He took a manilla folder from Jay's grasp and leafed through the contents. With a triumphant "Ah ha!" he flourished a piece of paper in the air. He laid it down on the table between the three occupants.

"Miss Bowen, can you tell me what this is?"

Kelly Bowen glanced at the paper, her lips wrinkling as her sneer grew. "It's a form."

"We know that," Chase replied. "Believe us, we in the police are not averse to a good form. What sort of form is it?"

"It's a care assessment referral," Kelly answered bluntly. "We get them through from the social care team at the council."

"And who is this form for?"

Kelly looked at Jay, hoping he might intervene and put a stop to the blindingly obvious questions from Chase. Jay only gave a little shrug back.

"It says right there," she replied, pointing out the name at the top of the paper. "Barney King."

"And who is Barney King?"

"What is this?" Kelly demanded. "Are you even a copper? What's with all the stupid questions?" She indicated to his bandages and bruises. "Have you had some sort of conk on the head and forgot how to read?"

"Yes," Chase replied instantly. "In fact, it was your lovely daughter who did it. With a frying pan. But we're not talking about that yet. Who is Barney King?"

"Some old bloke," Kelly spat back. "I did an assessment on him a few weeks ago. He lives on his own, struggling with care. Nothing bloody new to me, I spend all day with old codgers like him."

"Did anyone accompany you to the assessment?" Chase asked.

Kelly snorted. "You think we have the staff to go in pairs? Yeah, right. No, I went alone."

"Then how did your mother know about you visiting Barney King?"

Chase's forthright question made Kelly Bowen falter. She licked her lips, taking a moment to size Chase up. Her hand disappeared under the table. From the rhythmic circling movements of her arm, I could tell she was stroking her abdomen.

"I don't know," she mumbled back.

"I doubt that," Chase started.

Kelly Bowen snapped her gaze up to him. "Well, what a bloody surprise. The police don't believe me. That's the whole bloody reason I'm in this mess and living back home with my mum. Because you lot never listen to me. Not when that useless fucking ex of mine nearly knocked our door down last month, or put all that stuff online about me. You lot did fuck all then."

"We're not here to discuss your dysfunctional relationship, Miss Bowen," said Chase.

"Then why the fuck have you dragged me here?" Kelly retorted.

For the time first since Chase had barrelled into the room, Jay made himself known. He shuffled in his seat and cleared his throat.

"We're here to help, Miss Bowen," he said kindly. "You may not believe it, but we are. Right now, your mother and daughter are in quite a bit of trouble. We want to make sure we get to the bottom of it."

I smiled to myself. It was exactly what I would have said in that situation. Sometimes I was ridiculed for being too soft, but a little compassion and sympathy had the desired effect. Kelly Bowen relaxed, her taut expression lessening.

"Sometimes, I bring my paperwork home," she said quietly. "We don't have an office, so I have to work out of my car. But with this thing" – she pointed to her pregnant stomach – "it hurts my back, so I've been doing my paperwork at the kitchen table. Sometimes I leave it there."

"Out in the open?" Chase asked.

"Yes, out in the bloody open," snapped Kelly. "I know, I've breached confidentiality and GDPR and whatever fucking else."

"What sort of information is available?" asked Jay, his tone calmer.

"Whatever you see on that form," said Kelly, waving a hand at the paper between them. "Name, address, diagnosis, symptoms. All contact info."

She shuffled in her seat, arching her back a little. As she sat up, I saw the bulge in her tunic top, not quite fitting comfortably over her rounded stomach. Chase and Jay noticed too. They waited in silence until she was settled again.

"I don't understand," said Kelly, looking between the two detectives. "What has any of this got to do with my mum? Or my daughter? What's happened?"

She absently stroked her hand over her baby bump and waited for an answer. Her sour expression gave way to one of worry, of confusion.

"What have they done?" she asked. And her voice cracked on the last word.

Chapter Twenty-Seven

"No," said Chris. Short, simple, annoyed. His usual tone when speaking to me, accompanied by his standard trademark withering look, although this was aimed more at Chase.

It was Chase who had arrived at the station first the next morning, as cheerful as the early sun. I could feel his energy like static in the air. One full week after the discovery of Barney King's body and today we were close enough to finally get some answers. We congregated as a team outside the interview rooms, where Mags Bowen was already waiting inside.

"Why not?" I asked.

"Don't you at least want to hear her arguments?" Chase chipped in. He was thoroughly amused by the exchange, almost egging me on.

"I arrested her," I said. "I've met Mags before. I should be the one to interview her."

"Ooh, let's do rock, paper, scissors for it!" Chase declared and he held out his fist.

Chris ignored him and turned his impatient glare back on me. "You can't interview her," he said. "Neither of you can. Not if we want the assault charge to stick."

"Yeah," said Jay. "If we want to get her for murder as well, you need to let us take the lead. We can't risk her getting off on a technicality because you two can't keep your noses out."

Although unable to hide my disappointment – it was never fun being on the sidelines – I reluctantly let the argument go. With a gesture, Chase followed me to the viewing room. Over the few months of being on the Serious Crimes team and watching my colleagues interview, I had grown used to observing through the two-way mirror. I had set up a perfect little area to sit and watch, with an old, discarded blanket for a cushion on top of an unused table. I perched myself in my place and shuffled along to allow enough space for Chase to sit next to me.

He sat down and crossed his legs, ready to watch the show.

"I still think we'd do a better job at getting her to crack," I grumbled under my breath.

Chase laughed, but didn't reply.

A night in the cells had not done the murderous glare on Mags Bowen's face any favours. She sat on the opposite side of the table in the interview room, her dour face barely hiding a seething expression. Even the duty solicitor next to her looked a little scared of the old lady.

Jay started the recording and did the necessaries, whilst Mags glared at him, her face turning sulky.

"Where's Lucy?" she demanded, cutting off Jay's last words as he introduced himself and Chris for the tape.

"In a custody cell down the hall," Chris replied, pointing his thumb to his left.

"She's fifteen."

"She's still under arrest," he replied simply. "You both attacked our colleagues."

"That wasn't her fault," said Mags, the words sticking to her teeth.

"Then whose was it?" asked Chris. "Whose idea was it to attack DCI Chase and DC McArthur? And whose idea was it to kill your father, Barney King?"

Cold dread flashed up my neck as Mags turned her glare away from the two detectives in front of her and to the mirrored glass on the wall. I remembered her wild eyes, the glint of the knife as she slashed at me, the cold water paralysing my lungs. She was still on the edge, barely containing her anger and her worry for her granddaughter.

"No comment," she said.

Chris leaned back in his seat and tapped the tabletop with a finger. "Was it your idea or Lucy's idea?"

"Leave her out of this," she snapped back. "She didn't do anything."

"So, you're saying it was you?" Chris pushed.

Mags fell silent, her glowering enough to heat the room into a sauna. Chase had been right; Mags was an impressive liar. She'd been smart enough to convince us on our first meeting that she hadn't had contact with her father since she was a child. I had no doubt she'd be smart enough to convince a jury of that, capable enough to lie her way out of a prosecution. We needed more in order to prove Mags was involved in her father's death, because if she continued to deny it, then we were back to being one step behind her.

Her next words came out like she was under torture. "No comment."

Chase glanced my way, his eyes tracing over me. His patience was paper thin and now I was a little relieved that Chris and Jay had dissuaded us from interviewing. After the roller coaster of the last week, I doubted he had it in him to wait for Mags Bowen to crack.

Jay cleared his throat. "Okay, you don't need to talk, Ms Bowen. Just listen to us. We have you bang to rights on the obvious crime of assaulting a police officer and causing bodily harm. We could even push to attempted murder if we wanted to. But what we're really interested in is what happened to Barney King."

Mags clamped her lips together.

"You found him, didn't you?" Jay continued. "Your daughter had left her work on the kitchen table and there you saw it, your father's details. You must have thought you'd won the lottery. His name, address, details of his ill health, all right at your fingertips."

"No comment."

Beside me, Chase shuffled in his seat, his energy levels rising with his excitement.

"So, what did you do?" asked Jay. "Did you take Lucy with you for a bit of backup? Just in case the old man still had a fight in him? He didn't though, he was eighty-five. He might have tried but it must have been easy to kill him and then write a note in scrawling handwriting to make it look like a confession."

At this point, Mags shared a look with her solicitor. A smug grin tugged at the corners of her mouth.

"Do you enjoy making up stories, officer?" she asked.

Chase shuffled once again, brushing against my arm. It must have been taking all his self-control not to burst into the interview room.

"If we were in the business of making up stories, we wouldn't be here with you," replied Chris, seamlessly picking up the thread. "What we know for certain is that you were one of the only people still alive who had a reasonable suspicion that Barney King had killed his wife. You told our colleagues that yourself."

Out the corner of his eye, the duty solicitor surveyed Mags.

"No… comment," she said through gritted teeth.

"It shouldn't be too hard for us to prove our theory," Chris continued. "And if you won't talk to us, we're sure Lucy will. So it's probably best for you to speak now. Saying 'no comment' won't help you or Lucy when you're in court."

"And you want to help Lucy, don't you?" continued Jay. "She's only a child."

"That's enough," the solicitor cut in. "You're trying to emotionally blackmail my client. It won't work."

Chris and Jay exchanged a knowing look with one another.

"We wouldn't do such a thing," Jay assured the man across the table, before focusing back on Mags. "We're simply telling Mags what would happen if she continues to be uncooperative. Which would be prison for her until she's too old to get out of bed. And Youth Offenders Institution for her granddaughter until any chance of an actual job and life and successful future are down the drain."

"You're trying to coerce a confession from Ms Bowen."

"We're trying to get anything other than 'no comment' out of Ms Bowen," said Chris sharply. "This is your client's chance to tell her side of the story. I suggest you tell her to take it."

"Ms Bowen is well aware of her rights and requirements during interview," replied the solicitor.

"What evidence do you have?" Mags asked, suddenly sitting forwards. She stared at Chris, then at Jay, but she wasn't hiding her contempt for them very well. Her lips curled into a sneer as she spoke. "Do you have DNA or fingerprints, or whatever? Do you have a confession from Lucy or witnesses?"

She waited a beat, measuring the silence. Then she let out a low, harsh laugh.

"You've got nothing," she hissed at them. "You got nothing on me and you know it. You can't prove I visited the old bastard. You can't prove I killed him. Everything you've said is just made up."

Just as she opened her mouth again, the impatient beep of a mobile phone filled the tense air. Chris pulled his from his pocket, as did Jay, and a movement from Chase beside me told me he'd also got the same message. He turned the screen to show me.

Diving team have found something in the lake

"Margaret Bowen," Chris said as he rose to his feet. Jay stood too and his fingers hovered over the recording device, waiting to turn it off. "This interview is suspended pending new information."

* * *

Once more, my feet crunched on the crispy grass outside the front of Pepperwell Farm Cottages. Coordinated efforts were underway on the other side of the trees, the specialist diving team leading the charge and the backup listening on. A body bag lay on the cold ground. Empty, but hopefully not for long.

I moved away, not keen on seeing whatever they were about to pull out of the water just yet. Chase wasn't in a hurry either. Instead, he busied himself chatting away to Pres and PC Falini, who were guarding the scene and monitoring the activity.

I headed for the cottage, where I found a handful of forensic investigators combing over the inside of King's house once again. From the lack of little evidence markers around the place and the fact that most of them were milling around not doing much, I guessed they had found everything they possibly could in the premises.

"Anything?" I asked one.

Their white paper suits crinkled as they turned to face me. They shook their head, which didn't appear to move much underneath their elasticated hood.

"Nothing really," one of them said. "We found some hairs in the kitchen. We'll send them off to be analysed but they look like dog hair. We found plenty of that the first time around."

"No signs of anyone else being in the property?" I asked. I motioned to the front door. "Inside or out."

"No. The elements had taken care of anything outside. And we pulled fingerprints from surfaces earlier last week. If other people had been in the property, there's no evidence of it."

"All right. Thanks." I left them to it, before my face displayed just how disappointed I was by this.

Heading back across the grass towards the potholed track, Chase glanced my way as I approached. Pres and Falini took their chance with him momentarily distracted and edged away. Chase didn't notice. Using his long legs, he met me halfway and looked over my head towards the hive of activity going on near the water.

"I take it they haven't found anything inside," he said. "I mean, judging by your expression. No miracle DNA sample or *I murdered Barney King* written on the bathroom mirror."

"No luck," I replied.

"Eh, it was a long shot anyway," he said. "If King had been found sooner, we might have been able to get some evidence from his body but time is against us on this one. Too much of it had passed before we got involved."

"Forty years," I agreed.

"Well, technically sixty if you count Mary King," said Chase. "But that's not to say anything would have turned out any differently, even if we had been around to investigate King all those years ago. Sometimes, despite giving it your all, cases just don't go the way you want them to."

I sighed, and my frustration escaped as a cloud of breath into the icy air. Chase smiled to himself and began a slow walk towards the lake, motioning for me to follow.

"Have you ever watched *Star Trek*, Anna?" he asked.

"Not really," I replied. "What's that got to do with anything?"

"There's a great episode; I can't remember what it's called. Or what it's about. But it's a good one. Anyway, at the end Captain Picard says sometimes you can do everything right and still not win."

"That's not what he says," I replied. "He says it's possible to commit no mistakes and still lose."

"So, you have watched it!"

I gave a little shrug and ignored his look of triumph.

"I don't get all my inspirational leadership quotes from TV," Chase continued. "But that one is a good one to trot out every so often. We haven't made any mistakes with this investigation. We've just been too late to the game."

"And what about Mags and Lucy Bowen?" I asked.

We were nearing the edge of the lake now. There was a small orange dinghy, with two divers aboard. It looked like a third was already in the water. There was lots of arm gestures and pointing going on.

Chase gave a thoughtful hum back. "Well, given this development," he said, nodding his head to the water, "we can apply to keep them in custody for a few hours longer. Probably until tomorrow. And then we'll decide if we've got enough to get them for murder."

The two team members in the boat stood and leaned over the side of the vessel. The third diver bobbed, before producing something black and flexible from the water. He lifted it into the hands of his teammates who pulled it over into the boat. Water escaped from the black bag as it was held up. The two divers in the boat laid it down with extreme care.

Then, with expertise, they hoisted their fellow diver from the water and piloted the dinghy back to the shoreline.

"And what if we don't have enough to charge them?" I asked.

Chase smiled at me. "That's a problem for tomorrow."

Chapter Twenty-Eight

I was submerged in water again, blood coursing through my ears and making the conversation hard to follow. My limbs were weighed down by an invisible force as I gazed at the pile of rags, bones and other unidentifiable matter on the steel table. I didn't listen too hard; I couldn't. Something in my brain was blocking it all out, protecting me maybe, and I had to force myself to pay attention.

I stared at the early morning sun streaming through the frosted window and let it leave spots in my eyes so I didn't have to focus too much on the sight in front of me.

"There's a number of factors at play here," said Pete, the pathologist assistant, looking pleased with himself as he took the lead, until he spotted the unimpressed expressions of Jay, Chris and I. "Sorry. I don't mean it to sound clinical, but it is what it is. You all right for me to carry on?"

"Do it," said Chase, the only one willing, even eager, to break the heavy silence hanging over the room. "Go on. I don't know why this lot are acting like they've never seen a dead body before."

"All right then," Pete said, taking a deep breath. "The most obvious factor is the condition of the body. Cold water delays decomposition, quite considerably in some cases, and as most of us locals know, those quarry pits are cold. That's why we're still seeing evidence of liquidation, even after forty years. However, the most notable thing I wanted you guys to see was this."

He pointed to a small area, under what was once a chin.

"The hyoid bone is fractured. That means it's very likely our victim was strangled before she entered the water."

"Any idea who by?" Chris asked.

"No," said Pete. "It's been far too long for any DNA left on her by her killer to survive. To break a bone, you need a bit of strength, so I'm thinking an adult, probably male."

"Barney King." Jay sighed, echoing what we were all thinking.

Pete gave a solemn nod. "It is the same method we saw on the last victim, Mary King. Similar force used. These victims met their fates in a similar way."

"God..." Jay turned away from the contents and wiped his hands over his eyes.

Chris looked at Chase but the latter strode from the room, dusting his hands as he went.

"Well, that settles that," said Chase. "Case closed. All three murders explained."

The door closed softly behind him, not nearly as dramatic as he wanted. The uncomfortable silence settled over the morgue like a cloud, smothering out the light, the warmth. It seemed to take the very air from the room.

"Of course, DNA will prove her identity," Pete said. His face was a picture of concern, not used to such an audience, or such a subdued one at that. "The results should be back by tomorrow. But from what the pathologist and I can gather, the remains are a good match for the missing woman and have been in the water for the last few decades at least."

"Thanks, Pete," Chris grumbled, clapping Jay on the shoulder to pull him from his daydream.

"Yeah," said Jay. "Sorry we're all a bit quiet. It's not every day you wrap up a case like this one."

Pete grimaced, giving each of us a sympathetic smile. "I get it. At least now she can be laid to rest."

That wasn't the end of it though. Someone still needed to tell Aaron and Callum.

As we stared at the crumbling corpse pulled out of the lake, the forensics lab was combing through the last pieces of evidence, looking for any signs that placed Mags or Lucy Bowen at the scene. I knew they wouldn't find anything. It'd be a miracle if they did.

Back at the police station, there was no sign of Chase in the Serious Crimes office although his car was in the car park, so he wasn't far away. Chris, Jay and I sat down with the heaviness of the task ahead weighing on us. None of us made a move, and after several minutes of the only sound being the impossibly loud ticking of the clock, Chris cleared his throat.

"Right," he said, not an ounce of energy in his voice. "We need to do the obvious. It'd be better coming from us."

"All of us?" Jay asked, hiding a groan. "I hate this part of the job."

"We take the good with the bad," replied Chris. "It's been a difficult week and Aaron's taken the brunt of it alone. We owe him closure. Isn't that right, Anna?"

Eyes on me, I nodded. This was what we'd wanted after all. Closure for Aaron. It felt like a million years ago since we'd first learned about this case, and now we'd found the terrible truth, none of us had the heart to tell him.

I pushed myself to my feet. My limbs felt like blocks of lead.

With equal reluctance, Chris and Jay followed me down the corridor to Aaron's office, where the sound of stilted chatter mumbled through the door. I knocked and the room fell to silence, before Aaron's voice called out.

"Come in."

I led the way, my bravery waning with every heavy step, only to stop a few feet inside the door when I spotted who Aaron was talking to. Chase sat on the other side of his desk.

"Took you guys long enough," he said, merely throwing a glance our way before turning back to Aaron. "As I said, I knew it'd take them a while to build up their courage."

"Well, thanks," said Aaron and to my surprise, I think he meant it. "I guess you saved them all one horrible task." He offered a fond smile at Chris, Jay and me, before it faded away like the tide washing away the sand.

"What are you talking about?" Chris asked.

Chase rose to his feet. He gave Aaron a tight grimacing expression, one of sympathy maybe, before heading for the door. "I was just filling in DCI Burns on our findings. Including the likelihood that we've found his mother's remains. I knew you'd all find this a hard conversation, so I took the liberty." He leaned in close to Chris, whose face had settled in a disapproving frown. "I know what you're thinking; it wasn't my place to tell him. And actually, it was; this is my case. So, now that I've done the cold and clinical part, you're all free to do the supportive, friendship part. We'll wrap up everything else later."

And with that, he left the room. His footsteps echoed down the stairs until they blended into the hubbub of the station. Jay closed the door behind him and we tentatively made our way further into the room.

Sunlight was trying to break around the edges of the thick, monotonous clouds, acting like a blind. So far, it had been enough to clear up all the frost on the ground, but not enough to take the glumness away from the world. Not enough to cheer everything up. Out of the windows, I saw a patrol car leave the station, its blue lights flicking on and its speed building. The world was carrying on, but in here, it had all stopped.

Chris sat down in the seat Chase had just vacated. "He told you? Sorry. It should've been us."

"It's all right," Aaron said. "I get his intentions. He said you were all a bit stunned at the morgue this morning when Pete confirmed your findings. DNA will be back tomorrow but I think we all know what it's going to say. That body recovered from the lake was her…"

"We're sorry, Aaron," said Jay.

"It's okay," he replied, almost with a nervous laugh. "You've done something a whole team of police couldn't do in the last forty years. You found her. We all suspected this would be the outcome, didn't we?"

Chris shrugged his shoulders, running his hand over his mouth as he glanced between everyone in the room. "Still. It's not the outcome anyone wanted."

"No," Aaron agreed. "But it was the one I expected. And I've been expecting it a long time. I didn't get into this job because I live in fantasies. I know reality is harsh and unfair, sometimes to the most innocent. I didn't want the case reopened because I didn't want to face that reality, but now that it's here… it's not as bad as I feared. A part of me has always known she didn't survive."

"What about Callum?" I asked.

Aaron grimaced. "I'm not telling him. One of you guys will have to bite the bullet for me."

"Yeah, we can do that," said Chris. He leaned forwards. "Anything else you need; you know where to find us."

"Yeah, exactly," said Jay. "News like this might take a while to sink in. We're here for you."

"Thanks."

With that, Chris stood up, groaning like an old man as he clapped Jay on the shoulder and spun him around to leave the office. Aaron's gaze returned to his computer, careful not to look at us but not really focusing on the screen either. I followed the two of them right out of the door, until a voice called after me.

"Anna?"

I turned back to Aaron from the doorway. "Yeah?"

He only glanced at me. "Aren't you going to stay a few minutes?"

I paused and waited, expecting more; an explanation, an apology, anything. It wasn't going to come, I knew that, and I was fine with it. This was just the way he was.

I closed the door quietly behind me, shutting out the rest of the station, the cold draft and the work I needed to deal with. There was a mountain of paperwork still to do; Mags and Lucy Bowen were still sitting in the cells. If only wrapping up a case was so simple.

But – I supposed as I sat down in the seat opposite Aaron's desk and he finally met my gaze – it could wait. Everything could wait.

* * *

On my return, a dark pressure of melancholy hung over the Serious Crimes office. The clock was ticking, and I was promptly dispatched to fetch lunch for the team. When I arrived back, I found Chase alone.

"They're speaking to Mags Bowen one last time," he explained, motioning Chris and Jay's empty desks. "Fitzgerld seems to have found his stride with interviewing – this is the happiest I've seen him. But I don't think it'll be enough to break Mags."

Then he held his hands in the air, ready to catch the bacon butty I had for him. When I threw it, he fumbled, but ultimately saved the foil-wrapped sandwich from becoming a mess on his laptop in front of him.

I left Jay and Chris their sandwiches on their respective desks and sat down next to Chase to eat in a moody silence. I was finished before he had even made it halfway through his soggy, overfilled mass of butter and brown sauce.

"DCI Burns all right?" he asked through a mouthful.

I gave a small nod. "He will be. What are we going to do now?"

"You're not very good at being patient, are you?" Chase remarked. Still feeling the effects from the beating he'd taken from Lucy Bowen, he sat back and rubbed his temple.

"No," I answered simply. I tapped my fingers on my desk, hoping they'd find something to do.

"We need to speak to Mags Bowen again," I suggested.

"You know we can't," said Chase, through a mouthful.

"She's lying," I replied. "She can't 'no comment' her way into getting away with this. I'm sure we can get the truth out of her if she had to face me and you, rather than Chris and Jay."

"Oh, I didn't know you were a human lie detector."

"Chase," I said. The word came out a little more pleading than I intended, but I put that down to the emotional start to the day and hoped Chase hadn't noticed it. "Mags and Lucy Bowen had something to do with Barney King's death. Are we really just going to let them get away with it?"

I could feel a deep fire in the pit of my stomach, flamed by the injustice. We'd been through all that, through the roller coaster that this case had turned into, and it was all for nothing. No one was going to be held responsible for the murder of Barney King. No one was going to pay for taking a life.

"It happened forty years ago," Chase pointed out unhelpfully. "DI Daley was sure Barney King had had a hand in Clara's disappearance but he couldn't prove it. The old man went free and unpunished."

"But that was forty years ago," I replied. "We have better technology now, better techniques. We can't let this case get pushed aside just because they aren't admitting it."

Chase tutted to himself. "We're not pushing it aside. Gut feelings are great and all, but they're not admissible in court, Anna. We need evidence. And at the moment, apart from a theory, we don't have the evidence to put them in front of a jury for murder. We just don't."

"But we do have evidence," I replied. "The social care referral, the fact they attacked us—"

"It's not enough," said Chase. "Take it from someone older, wiser and with a great deal more experience. We don't have enough to charge Mags and Lucy Bowen for murder. One day we might. Who knows, maybe forty years down the line, our successors will be reviewing this old case and will find something new, but right here, right now… we don't."

And with his defeated words, the fire of rage at the injustice puttered out into nothing more than a pitiful spit. It was ready to flare again but Chase's discontent weighed me down and dampened it all with new waves of frustration.

"What did you want from this case?" Chase asked me. Sandwich finished, he abandoned his laptop and spun round to face me. "Back when you met with Chief Superintendent Goodwin, what was the outcome you wanted? What did you hope to achieve by working this investigation?"

"I wanted to get answers," I admitted. "Somebody wrote that note and admitted to a murder. I wanted justice to be served."

An idea tickled me. I glanced at Chase. He gave a lopsided grin back; a rather boyish look for someone trying to act the expert mentor.

"There will be a next time, Anna."

"Next time?"

He nodded. "Next time. We'll get them next time. We'll work harder on the next case; we'll be smarter the next time we approach a suspect. Next time, we'll make sure justice is served to those who deserve it."

"And which TV programme is that advice from?" I asked with a disparaging look.

"No TV programme," Chase replied. "This one is purely from experience."

He leaned forwards in his chair, grunting with the effort. I wondered what he was thinking but as ever, it was fast, too many thoughts and emotions flickering across his face. His eyes searched mine. His hand reached out. His fingers lightly danced on top of mine.

"Trust me. There's always a next time, Anna," he said.

With a sudden groan, he fell back into his chair and the moment was gone. He stretched his neck and nursed his aching joints, cursing under his breath.

"Next time, I won't be beaten up by a bloody fifteen-year-old girl."

I managed a smile back at his indignation. At least now I wasn't angry. Instead, I felt it; the same thing Chase did by the expression on his face. Defeat. Finality. Despair. The end of an adventure and the return to the mundane.

But the flicker of an idea was still there. It was a flame that refused to go out.

A phone began to ring, somehow its usual ringtone sounding urgent, demanding attention right away. Chase grumbled under his breath as he pulled it out from his pocket. He groaned as he glanced at the screen.

"Goodwin," he said. "I need to update her on our progress."

With a heave, he climbed to his feet, swaying ever so slightly. He gave me an apologetic smile before he exited the office.

Left on my own, I willed the faint idea in the back of my mind into a full existence. I didn't know where it would lead me, but I already had the feeling it would be the answer to my problems. The end to my frustrations.

I picked up my phone and started to dial a number.

Chapter Twenty-Nine

Although Kelly Bowen looked more comfortable in her own oversized clothes, no longer restricted by her ill-fitting work tunic, she didn't look any less on edge than when I'd seen her the evening before. She greeted me in the station foyer; it appeared she had been waiting there all morning for some news. Her hands were tied together in a knot of anxiety and the first words out of her mouth were the ones I expected to hear.

"What's happening with Lucy?"

It was obvious she was far more concerned about her daughter than she was her mother.

"We're still investigating, I'm afraid," I replied. I glanced around, careful not to look too conspicuous. Chase hadn't returned from his phone call with Chief Superintendent Goodwin, but he could well turn up at any moment.

With a gesture, Kelly Bowen followed my lead and we headed for the interview rooms.

"When can she come home?" Kelly demanded. "You've had her here for hours."

"I'm sure there will be some news for you soon," I replied calmly. "You've seen Lucy, yes?"

"Yeah," replied Kelly. "They said she needed an adult with her to be questioned, so I was there. But I don't know what else I can do to help. I don't know anything. I can't make Lucy say anything; I can't even make her go to bloody school. I can't make her tell you what really happened to that old man."

I gave Kelly Bowen a sympathetic smile and indicated the way with a wave of my hand. "Just down here. End of the corridor."

She hadn't asked me what I wanted her for yet. And truthfully, I didn't know what bullshit reason to give her if she did. My plan wasn't to interview her. It wasn't even to get her in the room.

I knew Chris and Jay would be finishing up their conversation with Mags Bowen – there was only so long either of them could put up with a 'no comment' interview. The only part of the plan that I had thought through hinged on perfect timing.

Up ahead, a door opened in the corridor. Jay filed out first, looking back rather than forward. Then came the solicitor, Mags Bowen, and Chris.

The group paused as they came face to face with us.

"Mum!" Kelly Bowen exclaimed. Her hands dropped to her sides.

"Kel," replied Mags.

Behind her, Chris peered over the older woman's head to scowl at me.

"Detective McArthur," he said through gritted teeth. "What are you doing here?"

"DCI Chase asked me to speak to Miss Bowen again," I replied innocently. A total lie. If he followed it up with Chase, I'd be easily found out.

"You shouldn't–" Chris began but he was cut off by the two women before us.

"Mum," said Kelly, urgently. "What have you got Lucy into?"

"Nothing," Mags snapped back. She threw a dirty glare at Jay to her side and the solicitor beside him. "It's all nothing, Kel. Me and Lucy will be back home soon."

"No, you won't!" Kelly replied. "Lucy is still in custody. She won't say a word to these people. Just like you taught her, I fucking bet. What did you make her do?"

"Nothing!"

"Mum! Don't fucking lie to me!" A dangerous flare blazed in Kelly's eyes, but one of her hands found its way to her bump. It cradled the unborn baby, as if trying to shield it. "Just tell them the truth so I can get Lucy out of here."

"Oh, don't act like you're fucking mother of the year, all of a sudden, Kelly," Mags hissed back at her daughter. "I've looked after Lucy more than you ever have. First you were always off getting pissed with your mates and nowadays you're too busy working."

"Well, I didn't exactly have the best role model, did I?" replied Kelly. She looked her mother up and down. "And at least I'm trying to make things right now. I'm trying to make things better for when this baby comes."

"Bit too fucking late for Lucy."

Kelly lowered her voice. "She's still my daughter. Mum, I don't know what you told her, I don't know what you made Lucy do. But don't ruin my family. Don't fuck it up like you did with me, like your parents did with you. Lucy is just a child. She needs her mum."

Mags opened her mouth, but nothing came out. Something changed in her expression. Her staunch defiance waned. Kelly had hit a nerve.

Chris took advantage of the lull to place a hand on Mags' shoulder and attempt to steer the woman in the opposite direction. She almost let him lead her away until I took a step forwards, catching her attention.

"Mags, you weren't the only one to lose your mother because of Barney King," I said quietly. "But you have the chance to make things right. Tell the truth."

"Anna," Chris warned. He was verging on furious, about to snap and put a stop to the whole charade.

But Mags shrugged off his hand. She turned to face her daughter. Her lips were pressed tightly together, the effort to control herself making her face scrunch up and redden.

She took a long look at Kelly, lingering on her desperate expression, her pregnant stomach, her trembling hands. She said nothing, and even if she had tried, I doubted the words would have come. Her chest heaved unevenly, as if sobs were gripping her from the inside and she was determined not to let them out.

After a moment, Chris once again placed his hand on her shoulder, firmer this time, and she allowed herself to be lead away from the confrontation. The group headed away, down the corridor, without a look back.

Next to me, Kelly Bowen let out a single, devastated cry, before remembering herself and falling silent.

Chapter Thirty

By late afternoon, the sun had retired, fed up of straining all day long to get through foggy clouds. Darkness set in over the station, along with an unwelcome gale, willing the day-shift workers to go home. Even the remnants of the sparkling frost trapped in the shadows had lost its shine now, as if someone had come along and turned the brightness down on the whole world.

Aaron found me hovering by the front desk, waiting for him. I couldn't go home without knowing he was okay. I couldn't come right out and ask him in the middle of the station, however, but I hoped there would be at least some subtle suggestion on his face that he would be fine eventually.

He already had his coat on, ready to face the outside world, where a howling wind was whipping up into a disgruntled frenzy.

"Going home?" he asked. He certainly didn't look like someone who had learned of his mother's brutal murder that morning, but as was always the case with Aaron, it was hard to tell anything from his expression alone.

I nodded, rubbing my hands together. I'd forgotten my gloves.

"And you?" I asked innocently.

"Yeah."

But that was it. He gave nothing else, except for a tight purse of his lips and a look of regret.

I dropped my voice. Plenty of our co-workers were filing by, creating a dull thrum but not enough to completely hide our words. "Do you... want to talk?"

"No," he said, keeping his voice low.

He watched me carefully, as if he expected some sort of reaction to the words, but I kept my disappointment firmly under wraps.

"Of course," I whispered back.

"What did you do earlier?" he asked, quick to change the subject. "Chris was furious with you and I caught him and Jay discussing how they were going to keep what you did from Chase."

"Oh," I said, with a slight smile to myself. "It was nothing. Just a bit of bad timing on my behalf. But I think it managed to work in our favour."

I heard footsteps from behind me, coming down the stairs; another worker heading out for the day. They slowed as they approached us, finally coming to a stop.

I spun on my heels to see Chase standing a few feet away, bundled in his coat and with a backpack slung on the shoulder of his good arm. His eyes glided over me before settling on Aaron.

"I've got good news," he announced. "After many, many hours of interviewing by DS Fitzgerald and DI Hamill, Mags Bowen has admitted to killing her father. She's quite adamant that her granddaughter wasn't involved in any way, which I don't believe for a moment, but we should take the win. We've finally got to the bottom of this messy case."

"Good work," Aaron replied.

Chase held out his hand. "Thank you for accommodating me in your station, Detective Chief Inspector Burns. Sorry we couldn't have met under better circumstances."

Aaron took his hand and the pair shook once before quickly letting go. Aaron opened his mouth, a nicety on the tip of the tongue, but then he decided against it and settled for a curt nod instead. Chase looked at me again.

"McArthur," he said stiffly. He gave me a rigid nod and turned for the exit.

"Wait," I objected.

Chase looked back with a huff of irritation.

"You're leaving?" I asked.

"We've got a confession. Any other paperwork can be completed in Norwich," Chase replied and gave a shrug.

"Just like that? Not even a proper goodbye?"

Chase cocked his head to the side. "A proper goodbye?"

"You know." I felt my face flush hot as both Chase and Aaron waited for me to elaborate. "Nice working with you, we make a good team… Something like that. You can't just leave after a case like this one."

Aaron bristled next to me, although he didn't make a sound. He was likely hoping Chase would move on without a fuss.

Chase mulled this over for a moment.

"Anna, did you have anything to do with Mags Bowen's sudden change of heart?"

"Me?" I replied as innocently as I could. "Of course not."

Chase smiled, amused by my answer, and he held out his hand to me. I shook it.

"It was nice working with you, we make a good team," he said, chuckling as he copied my words. "You live up to your reputation."

"Crazy McArthur," Aaron muttered under his breath.

Chase nodded. "Yeah, sums it up well."

"And is that what you told Price and Goodwin?" I asked. "That I'm crazy, I disregard orders? That the rumours are all true?"

Chase's face fell, as though he'd hoped to get away without having this conversation. I couldn't let him leave without knowing, though, exactly what he had fed back.

"What do you think I told them?" he asked me with a hint of a conceited smile.

"Please tell me you didn't..." I started. Too many people were around us for me to say it outright. "Whatever you've found out or whatever you've heard—"

Aaron murmured my name, a warning to remind me where we were and who we were with. Chase's smile faded away.

"I didn't," he said after a moment, offering me a tight grimace, as though the words pained him to say. "I didn't tell them anything. As far as they know, things over this side of the county run as smoothly as anywhere else. The Serious Crimes team are hard-working and compassionate. I didn't find anything untoward other than a DC with a penchant for trouble and a team keen to keep her in line."

And with that, he took another step back.

"As I said, Anna. Until next time."

My frustration dissipated as I watched Chase leave, merging into the crowd of colleagues heading home for the day. A nippy wind blew in from the open doors, whisking cold air around my neck and sending a shiver down my spine. Within moments, Chase was gone from sight, just another dark shadow heading across the poorly lit car park.

"What's wrong?" asked Aaron, pulling me back to reality.

"Nothing," I replied carefully. "At least now things can return to normal. I just... I still don't know if we can trust him."

Aaron looked to the darkness outside, the unwelcoming howls of the wind and the inky sky attempting to smother any light.

"We don't have much of a choice."

With a sigh, I nodded in agreement. I had to trust Chase. If he truly had wanted to tell Price or report back on his findings whilst working on the Serious Crimes team, then he'd had plenty of opportunities to do so. Chase had been a team player in the end, and I hoped that he would keep his word.

"At least now things can return to normal," I repeated under my breath.

When I looked back, Aaron's gaze had turned to the ceiling a few feet away from us. Two gaping holes in the tiles had been left after the confrontation with the gun-toting farmer. If we were lucky then they might get replaced quickly, but for now they were just another hole to add to the many scuffs, scrapes, dents and cracks the station was gaining as time went on.

"Anna?"

"Yeah."

"Will you be all right?" he asked, looking anywhere but at me.

I scoffed back. "Of course, I'll be okay. Why wouldn't I be?"

It took him a minute, but finally Aaron managed to meet my gaze.

"Because this is going to take a while," he replied sadly.

And then I could see it – the hurt in his eyes that today had brought. It wasn't evident on his face at all; to the rest of the station, today was a day just like any other for DCI Burns. But it was still there and probably would be forever more. As much as he pretended to be fine, this case had created a pain that might never go away.

Things might never go back to normal.

"I'll wait," I said simply. Aaron frowned and opened his mouth, but I jumped in. "I'll wait, even if months down the line, you decide you don't want to fix this. Even if you decide I'm too reckless or careless, and that I'm only going to end up hurting you somehow through my own stupid, crazy actions. I'm going to wait until you're ready."

"You shouldn't."

But I smiled. I wanted nothing more than to reach up and kiss him, to wrap my arms around his neck and pull him closer. But I couldn't, certainly not in the middle of the station. Rumours swirled around us already. If Aaron needed more time and space, then I would honour that, no matter how much he tried to push me away for good.

"Yes, well," I said with a grin, "you know me. I'm not very good at doing as I'm told."

Chapter Thirty-One

A churchyard on a grey, grizzled Saturday in December was about as grim as could be imagined. It wasn't a big churchyard, and the fact that it was still used at all came as a surprise to me. The church of St Michael lay half a mile down a single-lane track outside the village of Wormegay. In an effort to distract myself during a particularly lonely evening, I had read up on the history of the village. It dated back to the time of the Domesday Book and even had a castle, although only a mound of earth stood there now. Like in many villages in Norfolk, the church was rarely used for worship, and only parishioners could be buried in the churchyard. From the age of the headstones around us, it didn't look like anyone had been buried here in a long time.

A fine hazy rain pelted the mourners and the vicar who stood next to the fresh grave, where a shiny new headstone bore an epitaph no one really wanted to read.

Here lies Clara Burns. Beloved mother. Friend to all.

I huddled close to Aaron, feeling the relentless rain soak through the black suede coat I'd borrowed from my mother. I didn't own anything smart enough for such an important funeral. Chris and Jay were next to me and Maddie was at the end of the row.

Across the grave from us stood the other half of the Burns family. Callum stood a foot from his sniffling wife and daughter, oddly alone, staring at the gravestone with glazed eyes. According to Aaron, it had taken a lot of convincing for him to attend at all and it was only really because of his daughter Abigail that he'd agreed to come along. She wanted a chance to say goodbye to the grandmother she never knew. Apparently, Callum wasn't very good at saying no to his only child.

Next to me, Aaron stiffened as the vicar mumbled 'Amen', copying the words. He'd had the forethought to bring an umbrella but had surrendered it to his niece Abigail almost as soon as he arrived, so now he shivered as the rain dripped down his expressionless face. It felt like we'd been outside forever, the cold curling its fingers around my insides and trapping each organ in an icy grip, but actually it had barely been twenty minutes and the vicar was hurrying, keen to get finished.

Once the formalities were finished, Callum was the first to leave, stalking across the wet churchyard for his car without a second look back at anyone. His wife Valerie pulled Abigail closer to share the umbrella, kissing the top of her daughter's fair hair, and the two shot a sympathetic look at Aaron and I, one I returned. We didn't say anything – there was nothing to say. This wasn't the time for introductions or small talk. This was an event no one had wanted to happen. But now the necessary ceremony was done, Clara Burns could rest, and so could Aaron and Callum… somehow.

I bid goodbye to the vicar as Callum accelerated his car from the church, throwing up gravel in his haste to get away. Silence still weighed heavy on us as Aaron walked away, leaving Chris, Jay, Maddie and I out in the rain. We paused before following, sensing the need to allow a little space.

"Is he okay?" Maddie asked. She'd only just finished a night shift and the heavy bags under her eyes made her look more upset than the rest of us.

"He will be," I replied.

Maddie's gaze shifted between us; she knew something was off. Despite her eagerness to know the juicy details, she nodded with understanding.

The rain grew harder, turning into fatter drops which pattered onto the gravel. It wasn't going to relent today. I said goodbye to my colleagues and by the time I reached Downham Market, great puddles splashed up from the side of the road and the rain lashed at the windows.

I didn't feel as much relief as I expected to at the long-awaited event. I knew the final committal of Clara Burns would come but now I was left feeling hollow and lacklustre. My heart ached, but like the rain, it was here to stay for now.

I pulled up outside my flat to find there was already a car in my parking space. And despite the persistent drizzle, the driver was waiting for me by the back of the vehicle. Rain dripped down Aaron's nose and he gave me a fleeting smile as I got out of my car. It wasn't enough to convince me.

I hadn't seen him outside of work since the start of the investigation. In the station he seemed okay, his normal self. Now, standing in front of me, he clearly wasn't.

I dashed from the car to the front door, fumbling with the keys. Aaron was close behind me, pressing me to get inside. We both fell in, wiping water from our eyes.

Then, like a man heading for execution, Aaron plodded up the stairs without a word. I followed him.

I didn't know what to say to him. The small memorial had been planned with speed, and although we were not explicitly invited, Aaron had told Maddie the details, probably knowing she'd tell the rest of us and we'd all turn up. What was appropriate to say in such circumstances? Nothing came to mind.

Trudging up two flights of stairs, I heard Aaron pause as he reached the top of the building, and the door to my flat. Just below us, my neighbour Zola had some friends round, the posse now only just waking up after their revelry the night before. They shuffled underfoot like zombies, banging on the door and shouting at us to keep the noise down.

Aaron waited for me to unlock the flat and he followed me in. I shrugged off my wet coat and hung it on the radiator. After a moment, he did the same.

"That wasn't how I wanted you to meet my family," he eventually said, staying by the door as if he wasn't sure he was welcome inside.

I offered a soft smile, still weighed down by the sombreness of the morning.

"What are you doing here?" I asked. It came out more accusing in tone than I intended, as though I suspected he had an ulterior motive.

Aaron shrugged his shoulders and scowled. "I don't know. I wasn't thinking and just drove here. I wanted a distraction and, well, we both know how good you are at those."

I waved my hands at the flat. "Well, I was just intending to have a quiet rest of the day, but you're free to join me."

He thought about it and then nodded back. "I'd like that."

We settled on the sofa together and picked a film, playing it safe with an action comedy that was sure not to evoke any prominent emotions. The type with over-the-top villains and guns that never seem to run out of bullets. The type of film that usually we'd laugh at the absurdity of.

But the opening credits had only just rolled when Aaron's phone started to ring.

He shot a glare my way.

"That's your fault. You used the Q-word again."

I listened as he answered and replied with curt grunts of affirmation to the details given. Suspicious death, King's Lynn. Body recovered from the water at the port.

"All right, I'll send Serious Crimes to have a look," he said, finishing the call. Without missing a beat, he turned to me. "Who's on call this weekend?"

"Take a wild guess," I replied, pointing to myself.

With a half-hearted sigh, we both rose to our feet and I paused the film. Aaron strode over to the radiator on the wall, pulled his coat on and found his cars keys in his pocket, then held out my coat for me.

"Come on then," he said. "Let's go."

The End

If you enjoyed this book, please let others know by leaving a quick review on Amazon. Also, if you spot anything untoward in the paperback, get in touch. We strive for the best quality and appreciate reader feedback.

feedback@joffebooks.com

www.thebookfolks.com

Also by Sadie Norman

Detective Anna McArthur
Book 1: MURDER IN NORFOLK
Book 2: MURDER IN A COTTAGE

DISCOVER MORE BOOKS BY SADIE NORMAN

MURDER IN NORFOLK

Book 1 of the Detective Anna McArthur series

Detective Constable Anna McArthur is off duty – and barely holding it together. Ten months after a near-fatal knife attack, she's still haunted by the job that almost ended her career. But when she stumbles across a body beneath the medieval chapel in King's Lynn's historic park, instincts override fear. The victim is young, female, anonymous. The word *catfish* is scratched into her skin. There's no ID. No witnesses. No one has reported her missing. Drawn back into the Serious Crimes team before she's officially fit for duty, Anna must navigate the hostile suspicion of her colleagues and the looming shadow of her past. But as another body surfaces with the same mutilation, Anna realises the killer is only getting started.

Out now on Amazon!

MURDER IN A COTTAGE

Book 2 of the Detective Anna McArthur series

When church volunteer Yvonne Garrington is found dead in her cottage kitchen, her throat slashed and the scene awash with blood, DC Anna McArthur is called in to investigate. Still rebuilding her career after injury and scandal, Anna knows this is a chance to prove herself. But the deeper she digs into Yvonne's quiet life, the more contradictions she uncovers. As secrets surface and loyalties fracture, Anna must push past gossip, grief, and her own doubts to catch a killer who won't hesitate to silence anyone who gets in their way.

Out now on Amazon!

THE
BOOK
FOLKS

Thank you for choosing this book.
Join our mailing list and get FREE Kindle books
from our bestselling authors every week!

www.joffebooks.com/freebooks

www.ingramcontent.com/pod-product-compliance
Ingram Content Group UK Ltd.
Pitfield, Milton Keynes, MK11 3LW, UK
UKHW041832300725
461377UK00002B/82